D1013783

PRAISE FOR SIMON WOOD

"He writes like a dark demented angel."
— Ken Bruen, author of *Priest*

"Simon Wood packs his books with suspense, surprises, and superb storytelling."
— Ed Gorman, author of *Sleeping Dogs*

"Simon Wood offers a literary roller coaster ride that thrills and terrifies on every page."
— Sean Chercover, author of *Trigger City*

ACCIDENTS WAITING TO HAPPEN

"One of the most riveting first chapters I have read in some time. The pacing is spectacular and gets progressively faster as the reader nears the finale. An unqualified recommendation."
— *Deadly Pleasures Mystery Magazine*

"An impressive debut."
— *Mystery Scene Magazine*

"Simon Wood . . . delivers a suspenseful, brisk tale in his debut."
— *South Florida Sun Sentinel*

PAYING THE PIPER

"Wood keeps the pages flying, even as his plot gets more and more complex, accelerating nicely toward an elegant climax."
— *Publishers Weekly*

APR

"Revenge fuels Wood's fast-paced thriller and the good guys deliver a winning finale."
— *Oakland Tribune*

"An action-packed thriller that never slows down."
— *Midwest Book Review*

DID NOT FINISH

"Wood kicks off this new series with a streamlined narrative, a spot of believable romance and some deftly introduced tidbits about the British racing circuit. Think of Dick Francis' early thrillers, especially *Nerve*, but with a lot more horsepower."
— *Kirkus*

"A breathtaking finale will linger long in readers' minds."
— *Library Journal*

"Wood convincingly portrays Aidy's awkward efforts at amateur detection as well as his gentle, tentative romance with the dead man's fiancee, while entertainingly imparting information about the perils and exhilaration of single-seat Formula Ford racing. Dick Francis fans will find a lot to like."
— *Publishers Weekly*

NO SHOW

"Ambition, revenge, jealous colleagues, and lovesick reporters all stoke the plot of this dark, meaty whodunit."
— *Publishers Weekly*

"This is a suspenseful page turner . . ."
— *Spinetingler Magazine*

WE ALL FALL DOWN

"Action packed and intelligent, *We All Fall Down* is Simon Wood's best book yet. This is what they mean when they say a book is a thriller."
— *Crimespree Magazine*

"Simon Wood has talent to spare, and in *We All Fall Down*, he's crafted an entertaining and suspenseful novel that once opened simply won't close until the last nail-biting page. A terrific premise executed to perfection by a supremely gifted writer."
— Jason Pinter, author of *The Mark*

THE ONE
THAT
GOT
AWAY

ALSO BY SIMON WOOD

No Show
Hot Seat
Did Not Finish
Terminated
We All Fall Down
Paying the Piper
Accidents Waiting to Happen
The Fall Guy
Working Stiffs
Asking for Trouble
Lowlifes
Dragged into Darkness

WRITING AS SIMON JANUS

Road Rash
The Scrubs

THE ONE THAT GOT AWAY

SIMON WOOD

f THOMAS & MERCER

Text copyright © 2015 Simon Wood
All rights reserved.

Published by Thomas & Mercer, Seattle

www.apub.com

Amazon, the Amazon logo, and Thomas & Mercer are trademarks of Amazon.com, Inc., or its affiliates.

ISBN-13: 9781612184081
ISBN-10: 1612184081

Cover design by *theBookDesigners* and Jason Blackburn

Library of Congress Control Number: 2014951452

Printed in the United States of America

To all the people who fought back.

CHAPTER ONE

Zoë recoiled from the nightmare only to find it still existed in the waking world. She was lying naked on the floor of an oppressively hot shed with dust and dirt clinging to the sweat coating her body. Thick cable ties bound her wrists in front of her, as well as her ankles. They'd been cinched so tight her hands and feet tingled at the slightest move.

How had this happened? She tried to piece events together, but everything was a fog. When she tried to focus on a single thought, the fog draped itself, wet and heavy, over her brain.

A scream from outside split the night.

Holli! Her friend's name cut through her mental haze.

A picture formed. They'd been together for a long weekend in Vegas. In true *Thelma & Louise* style, too broke to fly, they'd driven from the Bay Area. They'd thought a road trip would be kitschy but discovered what a monotonous thing it was, driving hundreds of miles across state lines. Once they got to Vegas, they threw off the grad-student respectability and gambled, drank, and partied. It was just the shot in the arm they needed. They'd waited until dark before driving home—less traffic, less heat. That was where things turned vague. She remembered stopping for food and gas at some town that was just a pinprick on a map. Another hazy memory of eating at some restaurant or bar followed. The clink of glasses sounded in her brain, along with laughter. Then ... then ... nothing. What had happened after receded back into the murk.

Another scream. Zoë felt it vibrate in her bones. It was more than a cry for help. It was the cry of someone in pain, and it shocked Zoë into life. Whoever had Holli would come for her next. He couldn't find her here when he did. She had to escape for her sake and Holli's.

Moonlight shone through the window, cutting through the room at an angle. There wasn't enough to see the whole place, but it was sufficient for seeing what she had to work with. Her prison was cheaply constructed. Corrugated metal formed the walls and ceiling. The plywood floor sagged under her weight. Boxes, containers, and toolboxes were spread across it and climbed the walls, forming a canyon of junk. Did her captor see her in those terms— just trash to be dumped out of sight and mind until he came to dispose of it?

She didn't let the thought distract her. Escaping was all that mattered, and the room's contents held her shot at freedom. Toolboxes meant tools. Tools meant a crack at getting her hands and feet free.

"Please let there be a knife," she murmured to herself.

Another scream was followed by sobbing and faint pleas. Zoë had dumbly believed she was in the worst situation of her life, but it surely paled against Holli's plight. She couldn't imagine what Holli was going through.

"I'm coming, Holli," she murmured.

Her captor had made a mistake. Binding her hands in front of her gave her maneuverability. He obviously didn't expect much of a struggle from her.

She rolled from her side onto all fours. With her slight frame, it was easy to achieve, but her body screamed, forcing her onto elbows and knees. She tried to put her weight back on her feet, but toppled back onto her side.

She tried again. Determination trumped pain, and she forced herself upright. This time, she bent forward to keep her balance, then pushed down through her legs to stand. Giddiness greeted her on the way up. It met the fog layer clogging her brain and robbed her of her balance. She didn't realize she was falling until she crashed back onto the floor.

Whatever drug she'd been given had robbed her of her dexterity.

"You think you can stop me, you son of a bitch?" she murmured. "Not a chance."

She clung to her bravado. Misplaced or unrealistic, it didn't matter. It kept fear at arm's length.

She rolled back onto all fours and inched along wormlike on her knees and forearms while she listened to Holli's moans and whimpers filtering through the walls.

Poor Holli. She had the unfortunate bad luck of being chosen first. Things easily could have gone the other way. The thought forced a shiver out of Zoë, despite the hot and muggy atmosphere inside the shed. The sound of her friend's pain drove her on. She crept forward more quickly, but she couldn't stop the tears.

"Enjoy your fun while it lasts, you sick son of a bitch," she murmured as tears streaked her face.

She reached the closest toolbox and hauled herself up onto her knees, then leaned against the nearby crates. She had to be quiet; no more loud noises. If she could hear Holli's cries, then they could hear her. Using both hands, she turned the box to face her. It was heavy. She took that as a good sign. A heavy toolbox was a well-equipped toolbox.

She lifted the lid. Screwdrivers, wrenches, and a couple of pliers filled the top tray. She lifted the tray out and found her prize—a box cutter. She snatched it up and clutched it to her chest. "Thank you, God."

She dropped onto her butt and pulled her legs up to her chin. A sting of pain burned her left hip where the tops of her thighs touched her lower belly. She uncurled herself to find a wound. It was a knife cut. Blood still seeped from the incision. As she examined it, she realized it wasn't a random injury, but a marking. Two letters had been sliced into her—*I* and *V*. The son of a bitch had branded her. The thought brought bile to the back of her throat.

She pulled her legs back up to her chin to hide the mutilation, and parted her knees to give herself easier access to her ankles. Her feet tingled from the movement. She extended the box cutter's blade and worked it across the thick plastic of the cable tie. The blade was dull and the plastic tough. Progress was slow, but steel was gradually winning. Each fast, efficient stroke ate into her restraints.

An intense shriek from Holli jolted Zoë, and the box cutter sliced deep into her anklebone. The pain was sudden and intense. She bit back the flood of agony to keep in a cry.

She ignored the thick bead of crimson trickling down her ankle and kept sawing away. Finally, the cable tie broke. The rapid flood of blood to her feet was both painful and fantastic. She closed her eyes for a moment to take in the exquisite relief.

Her feet might have been free, but she wasn't halfway home. Trying to cut the other restraint while it was still around her wrists was a much bigger proposition.

She turned the box cutter on herself and tried to work the blade back and forth with her hands. She managed to get a sawing rhythm going, but her movements were so small that she'd be there forever at the rate she was going. She needed something else.

She ransacked the toolbox for anything that might help. She tried the pair of pliers, but her hands were so confined she couldn't work them.

She spotted a rusted old saw with a wooden handle, hanging on the wall. The serrated blade was at least eighteen inches long. A real carpenter's tool. And a real escape tool for her. She grabbed it and dropped to the floor with it. She turned the saw blade-side up, braced the handle against her groin, and clamped the other end between her feet.

Instead of working the blade across the cable tie as she had with the one around her feet, this time she worked her bound wrists along the blade. The large, serrated teeth made cutting through the plastic difficult. The cable tie bounced across the wide gap between the teeth, but each tooth snagged and chewed the restraint. After a few minutes of progress, the bond finally snapped.

She grinned as she massaged her wrists. She was free.

Her smile disappeared. No, not free. She had one more thing to do first.

She picked up the box cutter. The tool was now her weapon.

She pushed open the shed's door and peered out. Another shed was directly across from her, silent and dark, and a weather-beaten workshop sat off to her right. Beyond that, nothing. Desert stretched into the darkness, and mountains turned the horizon into a jagged tear between the ground and sky. There were no streetlights or house-lights to be seen. She was in the middle of nowhere. No wonder the bastard didn't seem worried about the noise.

Escape was a tough proposition. When she ran, where was she going to go? A dirt road running up to the workshop disappeared into the darkness. It had to be the only way in and out of this nightmare.

At least she wouldn't have to do it on foot. Her VW Beetle sat off to the left. She didn't see a second car, so he must have brought them here in hers. If she got away in that, he couldn't chase after her. For the first time, she felt real hope.

But she was getting ahead of herself. Driving away was the final part of the escape. Rescuing Holli was the first part.

Holli. Her heart fluttered at the thought of her friend's name. It took her a moment to recognize the source of her new and sudden fear. The screams had stopped. She strained to hear even a whimper, but she heard nothing. Not even the sound of his movement.

Please don't be dead, she thought.

She had to know the truth—know how bad it had gotten.

Light spilled from the workshop's small-paned, dirt-covered windows. It forced back the night and flickered as someone moved inside.

Holli was in there. So was he. She felt her courage waver.

There was movement but not sound. It had been several minutes since she'd heard Holli scream. Was she dead? There was only one way of knowing.

She slipped outside, with the box cutter in hand. The shed had been a sweatbox. Now, in the dry desert heat, her body dried in an instant, baking the dirt to her skin. If someone caught a glimpse of her now, they'd swear they'd witnessed a creature from the world's Neolithic past.

Staying low, she darted toward the workshop. A wave of light-headedness overwhelmed her, and she pitched forward onto her knees, dropping her weapon. The drug in her system still had its grip on her.

"Slow and steady," she told herself.

She retrieved the knife and edged over to the workshop, then dropped down underneath one of the windows. She listened for sounds but heard no voices, just movement. Her hand tightened around the box cutter's plastic handle.

"Don't be seen. Don't be seen," she said and slid up the side of the building to peer inside.

Her breath caught in her throat at the sight. She clamped a hand over her mouth to keep the scream rising in her chest from escaping.

Holli hung from a hook in the ceiling, like a side of beef. Like Zoë, she was naked, but leather cuffs bound her wrists instead of cable ties. Zoë saw no obvious signs of mutilation, but blood and dirt streaked Holli's body from head to toe. Her head hung down, her long brown hair obscuring her face. She was so very still. The total absence of movement frightened Zoë more than anything else.

The man who'd inflicted this abomination on her friend, on them both, busied himself with his work. He stood with his back to Zoë as he picked over a workbench. He was blond, tall, and broad shouldered. Beyond that, she couldn't tell what he looked like. The dirty windows and the drug dulling her system reduced him to a smudge when he moved. He picked up something small from the table and crossed the room to Holli.

He held the object up to Holli's nose, then snapped it. Holli recoiled from it, causing her to swing back and forth. He held her hips to steady her.

Holli was alive. Fresh tears rolled down Zoë's face.

"No, no, please, not again." He backhanded her. The strike was so intense that Zoë flinched from the slap as much as Holli did. The blow had its desired effect on Holli—it silenced her.

"Are you sorry for what you did, Holli?" he asked her.

"Yes." She spat out the word before he had a chance to finish asking his question.

"I'm not sure I believe you."

"Yes, yes, yes, I'm sorry. Please let me go. I won't tell anyone," Holli said before she broke into a sob.

Zoë felt her friend's despair. It was all so hopeless. So unfair. She didn't deserve this. Neither of them did.

Zoë palmed away a tear. She couldn't let Holli's despair infect her. She couldn't save them if she didn't believe she could do this.

She watched their abductor. She looked for a vulnerability that she could exploit. He seemed relaxed. No one was about to drop by or overhear, which wasn't surprising, considering the location. He wasn't working against a clock. He had the air of someone with all the time in the world. He thought he was invincible. He had left her in an unlocked shed with tools, after all. That made him either dumb or arrogant. *Two sides of the same coin*, she thought.

Her plan was simple—surprise. He wasn't expecting an attack. She could rush in, stab him, and leave him to bleed out on the floor while she got Holli down.

All her bravado disappeared in a second when he returned to his workbench. A whip sat on the bench. It was the real thing, not a sex toy. It was a tool. A weapon.

What had made her think she could take this guy? He was bigger than her, stronger than her, and not doped into submission. What skills did she possess? None. And this son of a bitch was an unknown quantity. He could be a martial-arts master or military trained for all she knew. He'd captured Holli and her without much effort, hadn't he?

What was her plan? To charge in there and knife him before he could fight back? That was crazy. She couldn't run ten feet before falling on her face. Even if she surprised him, he could take her down with the whip. If she went in there, she wouldn't be saving Holli, she'd be getting both of them killed.

She looked over at her car. That was the better weapon. Jump in the car, find cops, and let them storm the place. Going for help would save them both and would send this bastard to jail. That was the smart plan.

But for whom? For both of them or just for her?

Zoë peered inside again. Holli was in bad shape. Zoë knew leaving her friend was a risk. It might be too late for her already, but she didn't think so. Holli was bleeding, but none of it looked serious. If Zoë slipped away unnoticed, then she could do something.

Zoë stopped trying to convince herself and sagged, exhausted from the strain of the situation. They were screwed. No decision was the right one. Whatever she chose could turn out bad for them. The only thing she knew for sure was if she went in that room, they'd both die.

Then Holli's glassy-eyed gaze fell on Zoë. Her eyes widened, and the daze left them. Zoë thought she saw hope in her friend's face. Holli saw a rescue, while Zoë saw a suicide mission.

Zoë shook her head.

The hope in Holli's face deserted her as quickly as it had arrived and shock replaced it. Zoë recognized the shock for what it meant: shock that her friend would abandon her to save her own ass. Shock that she would surely die.

Zoë mouthed the word *sorry* and dropped out of sight. As she darted over to her car, she heard Holli scream, "No, no, no. Help me, Zoë!"

Each word cut into Zoë as she ran. Tears poured down her face.

"I'm so sorry," she murmured.

She tugged on the door handle, and it opened. Thankfully, the keys were inside. She slipped behind the wheel and twisted the key in the ignition. She slammed the car into drive and it leapt forward.

"I'll come back for you," she said, knowing full well her escape had condemned her friend to death.

CHAPTER TWO

Fifteen months later

The therapist's room was cramped and uninviting. Maybe she'd seen too many movies where psychologists conducted their work from something resembling a gentlemen's lounge, with floor-to-ceiling bookcases, knee-deep shag carpeting, and a leather couch. Maybe some of these people had offices like that, but not the ones provided by a charity for victims of violence. David Jarocki worked out of a twelve-by-twelve box with furniture liberated from an Office Depot display. The walls were painted a depressing off-white shade that erred on the side of gray. She sat on a sofa that failed to be comfortable. Jarocki sat across from her in a chair that had been pilfered from the waiting room.

"You've cut your hair again," he said.

She'd been keeping hers short for the past year or so. Not mannish short. She kept it all one length in a feminine bob. Reflexively, she touched the nape of her neck. It felt exposed.

"I thought you were letting it grow out."

"I wanted to, but long hair is a problem for the job."

Jarocki nodded, but his expression said he didn't believe her. It wasn't surprising. Even she didn't believe her. To have kept her hair long would have made her vulnerable. She had learned that in her defense classes. She kept it short for one reason and one reason only—so there wasn't enough of it for someone to grab. She knew it, and so did he.

"Maybe we should do a systems check," Jarocki said.

A systems check was Jarocki's little phrase for a self-assessment he had her perform before every session. Zoë hated it when the therapist made her jump through his hoops, but that was his job.

"OK, let's go."

"Sleep?"

"Good."

"Nightmares?"

"Yes. One. Last Sunday."

"Sobriety?"

"I've been a good girl. No benders."

Jarocki smiled. "Glad to hear it. Impulse control?"

"In check. No spur-of-the moment events."

"Good. Panic attacks? Anxiety?"

"Just one incident. I got a little freaked out but did your breathing techniques, and it calmed me down."

"Excellent. How's your week been?"

As much as Jarocki could irritate her with his tactics, she liked him. He might twist her arm in therapy to get her to open up, but he never judged her. Or at least he never showed it. He had to be evaluating her in some way. He was a psychologist. Assessing people and making judgments about them was in the job description, but he'd never uttered a personal opinion. He didn't pity, resent, or revile her for what she said, did, or thought. He offered her alternative perspectives, suggestions, and insight—and all with a passive, calm-seas expression. She marveled at his ability to do this. Her emotions were always an inch from the surface. His were always hidden. No, *hidden* was the wrong word. *Off-line* was a better word. It made sense, she supposed. What use would a therapist be if he or she showed shock, disgust, or contempt at the slightest remark made by a patient? Still, his passivity had irritated her at the beginning. She'd wanted his contempt and disgust. Now his disapproval wasn't something she craved.

In the year or so she'd been his patient, she'd come to trust him. She felt safe with her thoughts in this room, with him as referee. But she didn't give him carte blanche to all her emotions. As much as he was the expert on all things to do with the mind, he fell down in one aspect—experience. He hadn't abandoned a friend to her death. He hadn't fought against cowardice and lost. He wasn't a worthless piece of crap like her. When he posted *those* qualifications on his wall, then they really could shoot the shit about everything.

"OK."

"Anything you'd like to discuss today?"

"Nope. Not really."

"That's going to make today a little slow."

"I can't help that."

Jarocki squeezed out a humorless smile. She knew her lack of openness was irritating to him. "We seem to be sparring today."

That was code for "you're pissing me off."

She wished Jarocki would let rip at her, take her to task, anything to show he had some fire in his blood. She guessed it was in some therapist rule book that they couldn't lose their temper with a patient. A flash of emotion might actually do wonders for their relationship. Unflappability got to be annoying.

"I'm not trying to spar. I'm just not up for talking today."

He tapped his left temple, then pointed to hers. "Anything to do with that?"

Reflexively, her hand went to her temple, where she ran a finger over a large bruise. "No. That's got nothing to do with it."

"How did you pick it up?"

"At the mall. I was handing a shoplifter over to the cops. She swung an arm, and I caught an elbow."

Jarocki winced. "Nasty."

"All in a day's work for a mall cop."

She injected some levity into her response and received a polite smile for her effort.

Jarocki flicked through his notes. "Speaking of careers, today is a special day."

"It is?"

"Yes. A year ago, you dropped out of your PhD program. You said you wanted to give yourself time to heal, which was a decision I fully supported. We agreed on a year. Well, it's been a year. Ready to go back?"

"No. I don't think I'm up for that." She hoped her answer was concise and delivered with a sense of finality that would cause Jarocki to move on to a fresh tack. He didn't.

"The mall-security job was supposed to be a stopgap job—your words—while you got yourself back on your feet, before finishing your environmental-policy degree."

She felt Jarocki inching under her skin—worming his way into her thoughts so he could question her every decision.

"And it is. A year sounds like a stopgap to me."

"It sounds like a symptom of your trauma. Working as a security guard puts you in a potentially dangerous situation again."

"Being a mall cop is nothing like what happened to me." She hated the shrill tone that had entered her voice. It proved that Jarocki was getting to her.

"Isn't it?"

"No."

"I think we both know that isn't true. You were a victim of violence, and now you're in a job where you can be a victim of violence again and again."

"It's not the same."

He pointed to her bruised temple again. "Then what's that?"

"It's a bruise. It's hardly the same."

"Isn't it?"

"No, not remotely. Fifteen months ago, I was a victim. Now I'm a warrior and a protector. I stop people from being victimized."

Silence filled the air between them. She felt the pressure change in the room. It had intensified while they argued, but she felt it bleed off now and return to normal.

"I would dispute that, Zoë. Why did you go for a security job at the Golden Gate Mall?"

"They were hiring."

"It has nothing to do with it being the mall with the highest crime rate in the Bay Area?"

She said nothing.

"I understand your need not to be viewed as a victim. I understand your desire to stop crime and do good, but mall security isn't the answer. You're putting yourself at unnecessary risk. A mall-security officer is unarmed and undertrained. If you wish to fight crime and protect people, then why not apply to be a police officer? At least that way, you'd have proper training and an infrastructure that supports you. With your science background, you'd be a good candidate for a forensic role."

"I don't know. I'm not sure I'm ready for that."

"But you're ready to be a security guard where there's a good chance the bad guy will be better armed than you."

"Hey, that's not fair."

"You're still putting yourself in the firing line, Zoë. Where the rest of world avoids the crosshairs of danger, you step in front of them."

She shook her head. "Not true."

"It is and for a very good reason—he's still out there, living a guilt-free existence."

For all of Jarocki's desire to help her, he really knew how to pick at an old wound. She wiped away a tear before it had a chance to streak her face and embarrass her. "Why are you being so mean?"

"I'm not trying to be mean. I'm trying to help you. Post-traumatic stress is a powerful force with the ability to change us. Even the strongest of us. It's a tidal wave that can't be avoided. It will hit you and hit you hard. I outlined how it would affect you when you first came to me. We've worked together to recognize the signs and how to combat them."

"I can't just flip a switch and get over this."

He smiled. "That's right, you can't, but the Zoë who walked into this office last year wouldn't have known that, so you've made progress. There's no way to just circumvent PTSD. You have to work through it, and some do that more easily than others. No two people will experience the same thing the same way and for the same length of time. All I can do is support you and guide you through the issues as they present themselves. PTSD is like a serious wound. It'll take time to heal. That said, I think you're hindering the healing process."

"What do you mean?"

"When you came to me, you were close to completing your PhD, with a view to working for the EPA. You were on the verge of graduating."

"Still am."

"Great. What have you done about that?"

"You might have noticed that we're in the middle of a global recession. Environmental-policy positions aren't exactly falling from the skies."

"But you've been looking? Have you been keeping up with your schooling?"

She thought about her dissertation, sitting on her computer, collecting cyberdust. She'd opened the file once since Vegas and never looked at it again. Had environmentalism really been her life's goal? What an uninspiring future she'd had in mind for herself. She'd dropped out of school, and her books now had dust on them. She'd also walked out on her internship at the Bay Area Clean Water Agencies. She hadn't lasted a day after her sick leave ended. She couldn't deal with the stares, the questions, and the assumptions her coworkers made. She could barely look herself in the mirror. How could she face them?

"No, I haven't been looking."

"If you need help with a job search, I can put you in touch with someone."

She raised a hand. "I'm not sure about environmentalism anymore. I don't think it's for me."

"Then what is?"

That was a really good question. One she didn't have an answer for.

"Maybe you should brainstorm about what you'd like to do. Don't limit yourself. Think about a career that would give you pleasure or bring you satisfaction."

She frowned.

"Seriously think about it and we'll discuss it next time. I don't think you want to be a security guard at a mall for the rest of your life. You have a lot of potential. You can do anything you set your mind to."

God, the idea sounded like an exercise a high school career counselor would ask you to do. But it was something she needed to do. Environmentalist wasn't her, but neither was mall cop. "I'll try."

"Good."

They both got to their feet and he saw her to the door.

"See you next week, and don't be reckless."

Recklessness was Jarocki's little joke. Money was the root of all evil and recklessness was the root of all PTSD.

"I'll do my best," she said, "but no promises."

CHAPTER THREE

Kristi Thomas popped her head through Marshall Beck's door. "The fighting dogs are here, Marshall."

Kristi was the founder of Urban Paws Animal Rescue, and the rescued fighting dogs were a big deal to the center. The Fremont Police had busted a professional dog-fighting operation, and the injured dogs had been destroyed. The same fate had awaited the uninjured dogs, but Urban Paws had appealed the kill order and had volunteered to take them in an attempt to rehabilitate them. The judge granted the charity their shot, but if any dog couldn't be turned around, it would be destroyed. Urban Paws wasn't the ASPCA, but they had a solid reputation for saving lost causes. The publicity behind the court decision had brought in a flood of donations.

Beck got up from his desk and followed her into the hallway. Rescue-center staff and cops were bundling eighteen caged pit bulls and pit-bull mixes onto dollies and then rolling them down the corridor toward the Assessment Annex. All surrendered animals went for assessment before being made available for adoption. All the preexisting animals in the annex had been fast-tracked through in order to make room for the fighting dogs, and only the fighting dogs.

He watched the animals as they rolled past him. Some fought their steel confines, scratching at the frame or biting it. Others lay still, defeated and accepting of their fate. It was a sorry state of affairs, and another example of man's inhumanity to anything and everything around him. It would be a different case in a couple of months. With the love and support of the behavioral trainers here, most of these dogs, if not all, would be rehabilitated. It always astounded him that animals possessed the ability to forgive and forget after all they'd endured, but he'd seen it again and again in the eight months since he'd joined the charity. He knew he didn't share that ability.

On his way out, one of the cops said, "You're doing a good thing here."

Not me, he thought. He didn't work with the animals. He managed the money. He did payroll, banked the donations, wrote the grant proposals, found the tax breaks, and negotiated the contracts and discounts. The problem with charities was they were founded and run by people who operated on high emotion. That garnered donations, but passion was useless when it came to dealing with the IRS and other government agencies. That was where he came in. He spoke pure bureaucrat. His fact-and-figure sensibilities ensured these guys could keep their quest alive.

He stopped Kristi on her way by, after seeing the cops out. "How many of these dogs will you be able to save?"

"I want to say we'll save them all. I like to be positive," she said with a smile, then chased after a couple of trainers.

"Glass always half full?" he called to her retreating form.

"I like to think of it as completely full."

He returned to his office, a large room that he had to himself and that gave him a bird's-eye view of the street corner below. The four-way intersection of Fillmore and Washington gave him insight into how the world was changing. Pedestrians jaywalked, forcing drivers to jump on their brakes. Those who did wait for the crosswalk pushed others aside so they could be at the front. Drivers ran red lights because their lives were in such high gear, they didn't have time to stop. Bums panhandled instead of getting a job. People dropped their trash on the sidewalk or tossed it from their car windows. All these actions said the same thing: my shit is more important than yours. The world was a self-centered place and he hated it for it.

This attitude was the main reason the cats and dogs here at the shelter amazed him so much. They could be subjected to the worst of circumstances and yet give their love to the first person who showed it back. If people could learn that simple aspect, there might be a chance of saving this world.

His heart rate was climbing, and he felt his blood pressure rising. He didn't need to be angry right now. He exhaled and let the stress of the moment bleed out of him.

He cut himself off from the shelter's day-to-day operations by closing his door and zeroing in on his work. If he was honest, the charity's success and failure didn't interest him. He'd taken the Urban Paws job for the autonomy it afforded him. Kristi and her staff left him alone to take care of the money side of things, which gave him the freedom to do what he had to do.

Unfortunately, an hour later, as he came out of the break room with a cup of coffee, his peace was broken by a moan of "Christ, she's back again."

He didn't have to ask who. He knew it was Laurie Hernandez without leaving his desk. He got up and went into the hall just in time to see her disappear into the cat enclosure.

Kristi blew by him on a collision course.

He hooked her arm. "I've got this. You've got those dogs to attend to."

"You sure?"

"Of course."

"If she touches one of those animals . . ."

". . . then I'll kick her out."

"Thanks, Marshall."

He waited for Kristi to return to the Assessment Annex before moving in on Ms. Hernandez. He kept his distance from her. The shelter's layout afforded him that luxury. The building had been divided up into annexes. Two for cats, one for small dogs, one for large dogs, and one for rabbits, chickens, and more exotic animals. Each annex was closed off to keep the sound down but glass-fronted to keep it bright, which also made observation easy. Animal theft was an issue. He leaned against the wall of the large-dog annex and observed Laurie Hernandez at play.

Beck guessed Laurie Hernandez was in her late twenties. She was fairly attractive, although a little rough around the edges. The dark rings circling her eyes and her sickly pallor added years to her age.

She'd gone into Cat Annex Two and seemed oblivious to anyone watching her. Not that Beck guessed she cared. This wasn't her initial visit here. It was her fourth in the past two months. At first glance, she'd seemed like every other prospective pet adopter. She'd ooh and aah at the animals and put her fingers through the cages so that the animal would sniff or lick them. But then she'd switch from pet lover to pet tormentor with no warning. Once she'd gained the animal's trust, she'd flick it with her finger, poke it with something, or squirt it with a water pistol. She carried out her offenses without any concern of being seen. Beck got the feeling she wanted to be caught. It was part of the fun for her.

Laurie Hernandez dropped to her haunches in front of a cat and urged it to come over to her. The animal edged forward from the recesses of its cage as she reached into her pocket. She produced a toothpick and jabbed it at the cat just as it got within poking range.

Beck opened the door to the annex. "I think it's time for you to leave—again."

Laurie Hernandez grinned. "I have a right to be here."

"Not with that toothpick, you don't."

"What if I said I wanted to adopt this cat?"

"I doubt that would happen. We're trying to prevent animal cruelty, not encourage it."

"OK, I'll go." She stood, but not before flicking the toothpick at the cat. Luckily, it bounced off the cage. "You people are no fun."

He walked her out, then grabbed his coat and followed her. Only he knew her name was Laurie Hernandez. She always ran off before anyone could get a cop. He'd learned her name by trailing her.

The second she was on the streets, she plugged in the headphones to her iPhone.

He tailed her down Fillmore, lagging only a half block behind her as he watched her cut her way through the world. Her self-absorption always allowed him to stick close without any fear of being spotted.

He'd started these surveillance missions after her second visit to the shelter. The first time, he'd put her behavior down to that of a mean-spirited person, but her return put her on his radar. This was a woman with contempt for the world and everyone who lived in it. That kind of behavior deserved to be punished.

His observations had unearthed a few interesting tidbits. Urban Paws wasn't the only animal shelter she visited. She tormented the animals at most of the shelters around the city. On weekends, she liked to hit the clubs and steal from wallets and purses left out in the open, then get drunk on the take. She let any guy who showed her the slightest attention fuck her. She worked at one of those cheap jewelry boutiques in the Westfield Centre. His estimation of her was that she was a despicable human being who got her kicks from tormenting small animals and making people miserable. He wondered how she'd feel if someone tormented her. He'd made his decision. It was time for her to learn something about respect. He thumbed the knife in his pocket. It had been eight months since he'd left his mark on someone, and he would again tonight.

"See you later, Laurie," he murmured to himself.

*   *   *

Other than a couple of kids making fools of themselves and someone trying to use a stolen credit card, Zoë's shift at the mall was quiet. The downside of that was it gave her plenty of time to replay everything Jarocki had said during their session that morning. She knew he was challenging her, forcing her to examine her behavior and her mental mindset, but she didn't like it. Jarocki made it sound so simple: event A resulted in behavior B, and if behavior B wasn't modified, it would lead to result C. She wasn't a machine. She was a person and far too complex to be pigeonholed, as Jarocki had pointed out.

Am I, though?

Completing her final walk through of the mall before she clocked out, she looked at her workplace with fresh eyes. Had she really chosen this place because it was the most dangerous mall in the Bay Area? Had she become a rent-a-cop just to put herself in harm's way? Was it all done to punish herself? That theory made her sound so shallow and childish.

She didn't buy Jarocki's psychobabble. She had taken the mall-cop job for good reasons. People treated her differently when she returned to UC Davis after the abduction. A label had attached itself to her—victim. Everyone knew what had happened to her, and that event redefined her in their eyes. She had to get away from it. She could have switched schools, but she wanted to start over and do something as different from her PhD as she could get. Mall security was it. She had also found the job attractive because it didn't require any qualifications or life commitment.

She protected the mall one day at a time. When her shift ended, so did the work. You moved people on when they needed it, and if you caught someone stealing, you handed them off to the cops. No fuss, no muss, no strings. There was no mental conspiracy to harm herself. She believed the job was one that wouldn't tax her, and truth be told, she liked the idea of punishing those who broke the rules. She knew what Jarocki would say to that.

She thought about Jarocki's cop suggestion. He'd picked that up from her. They'd talked a few times about what she wanted to do with her life, and she'd mentioned law enforcement. She wanted to stop people like the man who'd abducted her and Holli. It wouldn't make up for leaving Holli behind, but maybe she could prevent others from being victimized.

Could she really become a cop? It would take years. She didn't have the time for that. She needed instant gratification. Also, she didn't know how long her interest in it would last. Jarocki prattled on about PTSD being a passing phase. She could quite easily lose the desire to fight crime herself, so following the cop angle would be a total waste of time for everyone.

She smiled at the thought. She'd use that argument on Jarocki the next time he pulled that one from his psychologist's arsenal.

She went into the staff locker room and changed out of her stiff, barely comfortable uniform. She clipped her pants onto a hanger. They managed to maintain their shape, whether she was wearing them or not. That was polyester for you.

In her own clothes, she slipped unnoticed from the mall. She rode home on her aged motorcycle. The VW had to go after the event. It had brought back too many memories. It was just another of those life adjustments she had to make. She never called what had happened "her escape" or "attempted murder." She hadn't escaped, not really. And she didn't like to remind herself of how close she'd come to death. She always thought of it as "the event" or, if she felt brave, "the abduction."

The motorcycle was efficient in the rush-hour crush from Richmond to San Francisco. While everyone sat in endless rows of traffic, she could lane split. She made it home to her apartment complex before 8:00 and jumped into the shower. She spent the next hour doing her hair and makeup before squeezing into a cherry-red cocktail dress, which rode the rail between sophisticated and slutty. It was short enough and plunging enough to show off her assets, but cut conservatively enough to be flattering. The night was cool enough for nylons, but she went without. She wanted people to see her bare skin.

She called for a cab. No drinking and driving for her. Besides, a dress and heels didn't work well with a motorcycle.

While she waited for the taxi to arrive, she checked herself out in the mirror. She looked good in the dress. Seeing how good she looked pleased her. If she wanted to get Jarocki-technical about things, looking good boosted her self-esteem, and wasn't that a good thing?

The therapist was wrong about her. She didn't hit the town to put herself in danger or reinsert herself into the same situations that had led to her abduction. She went out to have fun. Plain and simple. She was alive, and that was worth celebrating at least once a week and twice on holidays.

Her cell phone rang. The cab was outside. She told the driver she'd be down.

She checked herself out one last time. She smiled. She was dressed to kill.

CHAPTER FOUR

Laurie Hernandez was dead. She dangled from her wrists, her body slack, her head canted forward. Beck shined a light on her face. Her expression was peaceful. Gravity took hold of a strand of bloody spittle, pulling it toward the ground. She had no doubt bitten through her tongue. He'd put her out of her misery after a couple of hours of punishment, with a thrust of his knife to her heart. He wasn't a monster.

The abduction and punishment had gone perfectly. He'd snatched Laurie Hernandez after work. She'd been so absorbed with her cell phone, she hadn't noticed him following her on BART and on the street. He knew her route home. It had been easy to just walk up on her, tranquilize her with an anesthetic pilfered from Urban Paws, stash her in a Dumpster while he got his Honda Pilot, and then transport her to his skiff to drive out to the pier. Every step had been planned and calculated.

"I hope you've learned your lesson."

No reply came from the dead woman, but he thought she had learned. She said she had while he flogged her, but most of them did. They were willing to say anything just to make the pain stop.

But there always came a point, usually just before he ended the punishment, when the sinner either confessed to their crimes or remained defiant. In Laurie Hernandez's final minutes, she'd begged for forgiveness for all she'd done.

She'd almost thanked him when he put the whip down and stood before her, placing the knife over her heart. She had surprised him. He'd expected a fight with thrashing, kicking, and screaming. Instead, he got only surrender. She just closed her eyes, and he drove the blade home with a hammer blow to the butt of the knife.

"People are unpredictable creatures," he said and stretched to pat her cheek with his gloved hand.

He left Laurie Hernandez to hang while he got down to the important business of cleanup and disposal. When he'd lived in the open country near Bishop, it had been easy to operate. Bishop had afforded him the isolation, time, and space to be casual with the housecleaning. Here in San Francisco, he had to be more precise and refined with his punishments. These were skills he needed after the debacle in Bishop. Losing one of the two party girls he'd collected there was a mistake that he was lucky to have gotten away with. The city wasn't so bad, though. San Francisco was a city with benefits. While the desert was his friend before, the ocean was his friend here. He could simply bundle Laurie Hernandez up and sink her body out there. If she ever washed up, the water would have done its damage, leaving no ties back to him.

And while the city was short on open space where he could work in relative privacy, it did have reconstruction projects. The waterfront was going through a big change with many of the piers under redevelopment. It amazed him how many of these sites went unsecured at night, with no security patrol and often no more than a chain-link fence and lights for protection. But these people forgot one thing—access from the water. It wasn't hard for him to drift in on a skiff and work in relative quiet. This was why he'd chosen Pier 25 as his new workplace. It was intended to be an arts and entertainment center after the America's Cup tournament. He got a thrill out of handing down his punishment in this place, knowing full well that dozens of construction workers would be literally covering his tracks and destroying the crime scene the following morning.

He pressed a gloved hand to Laurie's chest and tugged the knife free with the other. Little blood escaped from the wound, courtesy of her dead heart, but what there was dripped onto the plastic sheeting he'd placed over his work area. He bagged and double bagged the knife in Ziplocs and placed it in his backpack. He crouched before the whip on the tarp. In its half-coiled state, in the dim light, it looked like a dead snake. He liked its unassuming nature. It was little more than a length of braided leather, but it possessed the power to devastate the human body. Just ten lashes wrecked most people. It was an elegant device. He picked the whip up, carefully coiled it, and placed it inside another bag. There was no disposing of this. He would clean it and ensure it was ready for the next offender.

Other than the plastic sheeting and the cuffs, the whip and knife were all the equipment he required. He liked the efficient setup. It was uncluttered. Clean. Simple. It was the way he lived his life, and the way others should live theirs. He believed you should go through life causing other people as little inconvenience as possible. Sadly, that wasn't the attitude these days. The world needed a mirror held up to itself to teach it a lesson. Laurie Hernandez was that mirror.

It was time to take her down, wrap her up in plastic, and send her to her final resting place. He had her raised up on a simple block-and-tackle rig he'd found at the job site. He shined a light across Laurie Hernandez's back and buttocks. The whip had done its job. Each lash was an open wound. Skin gone. Flesh exposed. Nerve endings raw. He was impressed with his handiwork. He'd gotten good coverage with little overlap. Impressive considering he'd flogged her more than forty times.

He'd always tried to be precise with the lashings, ensuring each one connected with virgin skin. Once the whip did its damage, there was no advantage of retreading on torn-up real estate. After forty strikes, there was little chance of finding untouched flesh.

A sudden noise from the entrance of the construction site caught his attention. It was the slap of a footfall on concrete. It bounced off the skeletal steel structure. A laugh followed. More footfalls.

People. Was it someone returning to work? Was it security? Had he misjudged the place? No. He'd watched this site for two weeks before selecting it. He caught a glimpse of movement in the distance. It was a couple kids, hoodies covering their heads. Beck dropped to a crouch behind a steel column.

His heart galloped in his chest. It didn't matter who his intruders were. He couldn't be found. He had to go.

He looked up at Laurie Hernandez. There was no time to take her with him. He'd have to leave her. He snatched up his backpack, which had the knife and all her possessions in it, and slung it over his shoulder. He didn't run. He slipped into the shadows and cut a path back to his skiff. His movements were silent and precise as he clambered down the cat ladder to the dock and untied his bow rope. It made the noises of his gate-crashers all the easier to hear. They were screwing around—looking for mischief and not finding it. Their plans would change when they discovered Laurie Hernandez. It would be a tough lesson for them as well as for him. Some nights didn't go your way.

*   *   *

Zoë had the cab drive her over to Russian Hill. The neighborhood was awash with restaurants and bars. She went stag because friends were another casualty of the event. None of them treated her the same. Some blamed her for leaving Holli behind. It wasn't that she disagreed with them, but she would have liked to know how they would have handled the situation. Others felt the need to treat her as though she possessed a terminal disease. No, it was better to seek the company of strangers. That way, she came without baggage and left without attachments.

She walked into Ferdinand's. It was one of a dozen bars and restaurants she hit on a regular basis in the area. It had an upscale restaurant that served a professional clientele. Certainly not the kind of place for a mall cop making minimum wage, but she was an attractive, young woman. If she made a "friend" fast, she never had to pay for more than one drink or her meal.

The place was packed shoulder to shoulder, which was busy for a Tuesday night. She squeezed her way to the bar and ordered a cosmo, then grabbed a barstool when one opened up.

It didn't take long for someone to fill the empty seat next to her. She put him in his early thirties. He wasn't bad looking, but he let the expensive suit elevate his importance. He'd tugged his tie to one side in some manufactured attempt to prove he worked hard, but just one glance at his manicured hands said that perfecting his appearance was the closest he came to manual labor.

"Is this seat taken?" he asked.

She glanced at the watch on his wrist. Three minutes had elapsed since she had walked in. That was a near personal best for someone to hit on her. "No, it's free."

"Great. I've been on my feet all day. I'll get up as soon as your people get here."

"I'm hooking up with a couple of girlfriends later." She smiled, which was something that came easy with strangers.

She liked how his smile widened when she made no mention of a boyfriend. Guys were so easy to hook. She pretended she hadn't noticed the smile and continued with her tale.

"But knowing those two, they'll be late. I don't understand why I bother making plans."

Lies came to her just as easily as the smiles. When she talked to strangers, she was a blank sheet. She could be anything she wanted to be, and men would believe it.

"Hey, we've all got friends like that. Have you paid for that drink?"

"Not yet."

"As an apology for having lousy friends, that drink is on me."

He signaled to the bartender. He told him that he was buying and that he'd have some Japanese beer she had never heard of. She liked how he insisted that he'd drink from the bottle in an obvious attempt to enhance his masculinity. They clinked the glass and bottle together in a toast.

"I'm Zoë."

"I'm Rick," he said and they shook hands. "Rick Sobona."

"You said you were on your feet all day. What do you do?"

"Advertising. I've had Apple in the office all day for a pitch meeting. I say 'I,' but I really mean my team and I."

She guessed it was real panty-lowering stuff for most airheads, but she saw through his star quality. If his firm had Apple in town, they'd be wining and dining them, and if that was happening and he was anybody, he'd be wining and dining along there with them. She didn't bother pointing out the holes in his story. It wasn't as if she was averse to exaggeration.

"And what do you do?"

"Accounting."

He looked her up and down. "You don't look like much of a bean counter."

She pressed a hand to her chest in mock surprise. "Should I be offended? Are you saying I don't look smart enough to be an accountant?"

"Oh, no, you look plenty smart," he said with a sheepish smile, which quickly turned lascivious, "but you look plenty hot too."

With a comment like that, he took it to the end zone a little too quick, but she guessed coming in alone, dressed the way that she had, she'd invited the first-to-the-finish-line type.

She smiled his compliment away. "You're very sweet."

The bartender came by and asked them if they wanted to see a menu. The offer elevated their relationship from people talking to people on the verge of something. They ordered food and a second round of drinks, and a third round when the food arrived. The meal helped soak up the alcohol. It was rarely her friend, and she was already feeling the effects of the three cocktails.

Sobona proved to be just as much of a lightweight as she was when it came to booze. The Japanese beers had dulled the sharp edge to his speech and forced his eyelids half-closed.

He leaned in close. "I was thinking, I don't live far from here. Why don't we grab a cab—hey, that rhymes—and go back to my place? What do you say?"

This was where things came to the tricky part of the festivities—the letdown. Rick Sobona was good for a free drink and making a dull weekday night interesting, but that was it. For all his bravado and desire, he wasn't her type, and she wasn't going home with him. She never went home with anyone. Not anymore.

One of the many flat screens above the bar caught her attention. The news was playing, the volume barely above a whisper and drowned out by the bar's noise. *Breaking news . . .* chased across the bottom of the screen. The main shot was of a police cordon in front of one of the piers along the Embarcadero. In typical crime-scene fashion, uniformed officers held a perimeter, while onlookers crowded around in the hope of a glimpse. In the far distance, men in suits, probably inspectors, roved in and around the building. An inset showed a news anchor talking with their reporter on the scene. She wouldn't have given the report a second glance if it hadn't been for the headline—*Murder victim found suspended.*

Alarm bells rang in Zoë's head. Her chest tightened up on her, and she found it hard to breathe. The lack of oxygen intensified the effect of alcohol in her bloodstream. It seemed to converge on her brain. Every time she tried to grasp what the TV was showing, the booze knocked her understanding loose, sending it skittering into vague recesses she couldn't find. She took long, deep breaths. It stemmed the rising panic, but just for now.

Zoë snagged the bartender's arm as he went by. "Can you turn the TV up?"

He looked at her as if she were crazy.

"I need to hear this."

"Hey, I'm talking here," Sobona whined.

She ignored him. "I need to hear this," she repeated to the bartender.

He picked up the remote and raised the volume. There was a collective groan from the majority in the bar, who turned to see why the TV was allowed to cut into their lives.

She was making fists, tightening, then loosening. "Louder, please."

"Planet earth to Zoë. Planet earth to Zoë. Rick speaking."

"Just to conclude," the field reporter said, "the body of a woman was found at Pier 25 earlier tonight. Details are vague right now. The SFPD hasn't released any information, but according to eyewitnesses, the victim was naked, bound by the wrists, suspended from the structure, and possibly whipped."

The fear slammed into her, the impact of it forcing her to grab the bar. The world spun, and when it stopped, she wasn't in the bar or even San Francisco, she was naked, alone in a shed in the desert. It was happening again. It was happening here.

She grabbed her purse. "I have to go."

"What?" Sobona said. "What's going on here? Did I suddenly get boring? I thought we were moving this party."

"I'm sorry. Another time."

She spun around on her barstool and hopped off. She had made her way about halfway to the door through the wall of patrons when a hand grabbed her trailing arm. She whipped around to find Sobona holding her wrist.

"We aren't done."

The grasp was a mistake. She wasn't the hapless victim she'd been in the past. She had learned the skills to defend herself.

Zoë didn't argue or complain. She acted on instinct. With her free hand, she grabbed his thumb and jerked it back. He yelped and released his grip on her. She maintained the pressure. The simple maneuver drove his arm into his chest and him down to his knees to prevent his thumb from breaking. Zoë released her grip.

"You bitch." The hatred behind the word seemed born more out of the public embarrassment than anything else.

Sobona lunged and met the heel of Zoë's hand coming in from the opposite direction. It smashed into his nose with enough significant force to bring tears but not enough to break it.

"You never, ever touch a woman like that again," she screamed in his face. "Do you understand me?"

CHAPTER FIVE

Neither Rick Sobona nor anyone from Ferdinand's chased after Zoë. That didn't mean someone wouldn't call a cop. She couldn't deal with that noise right now. There was too much going on in her head as it was. She needed the police, but not for this. She had to know if the murdered woman was linked to Holli. Had she known Holli?

She moved fast and grabbed the first cab to come her way. She told the driver to take her to Pier 25. One thing about the killer choosing an obvious landmark like Pier 25 was that it was easy to find.

She leaned forward in her seat, her hands balled into tight fists. Her body thrummed with the adrenaline coursing through her. She wished it was just a side effect of taking Sobona down, but it was pure fear. Fear of what had happened to her and Holli. Fear of what had happened to this murdered woman. Fear that it could be starting all over again for her.

Fear is the enemy, she thought. It was one of Jarocki's phrases. Fear clouded the mind, obscured judgment, and ruined recovery. She was in a state of panic and needed to calm down. She performed one of his breathing techniques. She sucked in air and held it for a second, before releasing it. She repeated it ten times and felt the fear ebb away with each breath. She wasn't sure if Jarocki's party trick worked because the forced injection of oxygen brought clarity to the brain or because the simple act of controlling her inhalations took her focus off her panic. Either way, it worked. She wasn't calm, but she was in control of herself.

She caught the taxi driver eyeing her in his mirror. She must have looked crazy to him. Was she? Her reaction to the news story certainly felt nuts. She'd seen dozens of murder reports since the event and had never reacted like she had tonight, but the way this woman had been suspended screamed a connection with her case. She had to know if that connection was real. She didn't care if she embarrassed herself in the process.

The cab stopped two blocks short of where she asked to be dropped, but with all the cops, camera crews, and onlookers, it was as close as anyone was getting. She paid the cabbie and jumped out.

She raced up to the crowd, but the wall of people in front of her gave her only glimpses of the developments beyond.

"Have the cops said anything?" she asked the people around her.

"They ain't saying shit to us," the man next to her said.

"All we've seen is people go in and come out," the woman directly in front of Zoë said. "The body's still in there because no one has brought it out."

"Did anyone here see the body?"

She got a round of nos and head shakes.

"Did we see the body?" a woman snapped. "What's wrong with you? Don't you have anything better to do?"

Zoë could ask her the same thing.

"Where's the person who found the woman?"

"The cops have them," a guy in his twenties said.

"Them?"

"I think two people found the body."

"I heard it was just one person," someone else chipped in.

This was pointless. No one knew anything, and if they said they did, it would just be speculation at best.

Zoë pushed her way through the crowd, then waved down a cop behind the cordon.

"Can I help you?" the officer said.

"I need to speak to whoever's in charge."

"Why?"

"I need some answers."

"I'm sure you do, but this is an active investigation. There will be no press releases."

She should have known she'd get the wall of silence. "I'm not asking just because I'm curious. I may have information."

She held off from saying she might have encountered the killer, because her conversation was drawing too much attention from the now-interested crowd.

"Like what information? Did you know the victim?"

"Yes. No. That's why I want to talk to someone. I might know something. I have information."

The cop gave her that I've-heard-it-all-before look. "Please step back, miss."

"No."

Her blunt reply shocked him. He seemed lost for a moment, but he soon recovered. He looked her up and down. He took in the dress, the bare skin, and the makeup. He leaned in and sniffed her breath. "Have you been drinking tonight, miss?"

She groaned inside. "Yes, but what has that got to do with anything?"

"Look, if you don't leave, I will arrest you for public intoxication. If you'd like me to call a cab, I'd be happy to do it."

This cop was wasting her time. She shouldn't go home and wait for the answers to come out in the news. Not knowing the truth would eat her up. There was no way she was waiting to find out, and she as sure as shit wasn't letting this guy get in her way.

She spotted a couple of men in suits emerging from the building. Both of them were pulling surgical gloves off their hands. They had to be inspectors or at least have better knowledge of the case than this cop.

"Sure."

She made a pretense of leaving, and just as the policeman turned his back, she ducked under the crime-scene tape and bolted for the men in suits. A cry went up from the crowd, followed by the cry of the cop, telling her to stop. She heard the thump-thump of footfalls on the pavement behind her.

"Excuse me, are you in charge?" she yelled out to the men.

A second later, both men raced toward her.

"I need to talk to you."

"Stop," the cop's voice rang out from behind her again.

He sounded close and he was. He slammed into her, driving her to the ground. The cop took the brunt of the impact on his shoulder, protecting her, although her purse went flying and one of her heels shot off into the distance.

The younger of the inspectors wrenched Zoë to her feet.

"What the hell is going on, Acosta?" the other detective said.

Acosta rose to his feet gingerly. "She's a drunk."

"I'm not. I need to talk to you about this murder."

The detective who'd helped Zoë up hadn't released his grip. "Do you know something?"

"Yes, I might. I just need to know some details."

"Goddamn it," the other detective said. "Are you a reporter or a blogger?"

"No."

"What's your name?"

"Zoë Sutton. Fifteen months ago, a man abducted me and killed my friend. I saw the news. This is the same guy."

She expected this information to unlock a door, gain their confidence. Instead, she got blank looks. Honesty should have bought their trust, but it seemed to have done the opposite.

"I'm not crazy."

"No one is saying you are," the younger detective said.

"Ms. Sutton, do you realize what you've done?" the other man asked. "You've just contaminated an active crime scene. Do you know what damage that can do to our case?"

"I'm trying to help you."

"Well, you aren't. Take her in, Acosta. Book her on something. I don't care what."

Acosta took out his cuffs, and a cheer went up from the crowd.

No, they were going to listen to her. She shook off the younger detective's arm and reached for the zipper on the side of her dress. Both detectives reached for their guns. Acosta leapt back from her. She ignored the peril she had placed herself in and tugged the zip down. She yanked the dress to one side to reveal the letters *IV* carved into her hip.

"Does the woman in there have a scar like this?"

Their stunned silence told them she did.

*   *   *

Marshall Beck sat in the dark in the Assessment Annex at Urban Paws. Only light from the streetlights lit the room. The fighting dogs were quiet. They'd been rechristened. Many had never been given names and the ones that had wore moronic fighting ones, like Killer or Beast or Diablo, given to them by their moronic *owners*.

He came here most nights, after hours, to hang out with the animals. He enjoyed the solitude. The creatures helped him decompress when people and their attitudes overwhelmed him and he needed somewhere to escape. When the noise of his thoughts threatened to split his skull, they offered him silence. They didn't bombard him with their problems and petty squabbles. They gave him space. He liked that about them—they weren't sentimental, and they didn't judge. If one of them died, they didn't mourn. They moved on. He felt a special kinship with these fighting dogs. It was why he'd chosen to sit with them instead of the others. Life and death were all they knew. They'd understand the enormity of the problems he faced now.

Beck leaned against the wall, watching Brando—one of the pit bulls—in his cage. While all the other dogs slept, this one remained awake. He sat upright and stared back at Beck. Of all the fighting dogs the shelter had taken in, Beck felt an instant connection to Brando. Life had dealt these dogs a shitty hand, and it had taken its toll. The ordeal had broken some, driven others crazy, and left some frightened, but not Brando. He still possessed the soul he'd been born with. The behavioral trainers at the shelter would be able to rehabilitate the other dogs, but not him. Brando wasn't the type to change. He was a universal constant. The instructors hadn't seen it or hadn't wanted to, but Beck did. Underneath the lacerations and scars, the truth about Brando shone bright in the dog's eyes. And what he recognized in the dog, the dog recognized in him. They were both survivors. They'd both suffered, but they hadn't succumbed.

A lightning flash of his past arced across his mind—him, a child, in the foster home, whipped again for an infraction.

He winced at the memory. Brando bristled at the sign of his weakness and growled. Beck smiled. "That kind of reaction will get you killed," he said.

The dog stopped growling.

"Not that it matters. You know they're going to have to put you down, don't you?"

Brando just stared.

One of the dogs whimpered at the sound of Beck's voice and retreated to the corner of its cage. Except for a twitch of an ear in its direction, Brando remained statuelike.

"It's a sorry state of affairs when you have to pay the price for the person who put you in this predicament."

The dog neither agreed nor disagreed.

"Hardly seems fair. But life is like that."

The whimpering dog settled down.

"I bet you wish you could even up the score, don't you, Brando? Of course you do. If you're lucky, you might even get the chance." He sighed. "I'm not sure I'll get the chance to continue my work, though."

After tonight's fiasco, he was in virgin territory. His work had been discovered. Where did he go from here? He felt as trapped as these dogs.

"I screwed up, Brando. I got it wrong again. There's a chance I could end up in a cage now."

The damage had been done. He'd given the cops an opening. Laurie Hernandez was a big chunk of evidence and so was the construction site. They had the beginning of a trail.

But could it lead back to him?

He didn't think so. At first, panic had told him that it was a foregone conclusion the cops would be beating down his door, but the feeling had changed in the tranquil surroundings of the rescue center. Logic had replaced panic—thanks to Brando's soothing influence. When he picked apart his earlier actions, he saw that he was safe. He'd been careful. The cops would be hard-pressed to make any connection between him and Laurie Hernandez. He hadn't left any prints at the scene, and even if they found any DNA, they had no comparison source. Other than the plastic sheeting and Laurie Hernandez herself, he hadn't left anything behind. He still had his whip and knife. The police had a corpse, and that was it. Despite his screwup tonight, he was indeed safe. He smiled.

Brando stiffened.

Beck nodded. "Can't be too cocky about these things. I suppose I should check the situation."

He clambered to his feet, and the sudden movement set off a sea of reactions from the dogs. He let his absence settle them.

In his office, he switched on his computer. He looked up all the local news channels on the web. Laurie Hernandez was their collective top story.

"Let's see how bad it is," he said and clicked a video link.

It was the typical news report. The field reporter, Dinah Ortiz, stood in the foreground and cops worked the crime scene in the distance, while a crowd of onlookers gawked and jockeyed for fifteen nanoseconds of on-air time. She relayed the scant facts: that the body of an unidentified female had been discovered naked and hanging from her wrists at the development site. She also intimated that the victim had been brutalized. Sadly for Ms. Ortiz, she had failed to secure a statement from the police.

The three-minute report told him little. That was good. It confirmed his feeling that the investigation wasn't leading the SFPD to his door.

He replayed the clip. His attention drifted from the reporter to the scene itself. There was an intensity surrounding the event, with the reporter's shot-in-the-dark speculation and the fervor radiating off the onlookers. This reaction to his handiwork took him by surprise. He'd always striven to keep his actions hidden from the public and police. Seeing this interest in what he'd done stunned him—and intrigued him.

Privacy had always been his watchword, but should it be? He did what he did for one reason—to punish those whose behavior was unacceptable. Until now, his message had been confined to those he taught a lesson to. That was small time. Media interest in Laurie Hernandez's death would change that. It would provoke discussion, speculation, debate. It could affect real change.

He smiled. He'd seen tonight as a screwup, but it was turning out to be serendipitous. From now on, he wouldn't attempt to hide his work. He would broadcast it and let it be a warning to others that their bad conduct would not be accepted.

He leaned forward on his chair and checked out the video reports from the other local affiliates. He was rewarded with different talking heads with the same backdrop. He absorbed the sights with pride.

The ABC affiliate had an updated report, and he clicked on that. The video started with an intro from the in-studio anchors.

"There was an interesting turn of events at the scene of a brutal murder of a woman at Pier 25 tonight when an onlooker charged through the police cordon. Our news crew was there to catch what happened," Mick Tolley said. "We go back to our own Dinah Ortiz for a firsthand account."

Dinah Ortiz stood in a different spot than in her earlier newscast, although the onlookers didn't seem to have changed. "Yes, Mick. While we were between reports, a verbal encounter between a bystander and police officers led to this."

Her segment cut to a video. A whip pan zeroed in on a young blonde woman in a skintight minidress breaking through the police cordon. The camera followed the blonde as she yelled and charged at a pair of men, no doubt detectives, who were leaving the construction site. She was too far away from the camera crew for the mic to pick up the details of what she was yelling. The out-of-control woman didn't get far before a uniformed cop tackled her to the ground. The camera focused on her as the cop brought her to her feet and the detectives moved in.

She looked familiar to Beck.

The camera captured a muffled confrontation with the detectives. Just as it looked as if the blonde was heading to the drunk tank, she unzipped her dress and pointed furiously at her lower hip just above her panty line.

A tingle of recognition crackled throughout Beck's body.

At a sickening speed, the camera zoomed in on what the woman was pointing to.

He knew what the lens would capture—his mark.

He fell back in his chair, tuning out the remainder of Dinah Ortiz's report. It wasn't important. Something amazing had just happened. It's her—the Vegas girl, he thought, the one that got away.

CHAPTER SIX

When the cops didn't cuff her, Zoë took it as a good sign. It meant they believed her or at least took her claim seriously. The inspectors simply put her in the back of their car and drove her to the Hall of Justice. They didn't talk on the short drive, not to her and not to each other. She guessed they wanted anything she had to say to be on the record.

They whisked her through the building and dumped her in an interview room. They took her driver's license, snapped a photo of the scar on her hip, and gave her a bottle of water. She knew the routine. They were checking up on her. Good. She wanted them to. Then they'd get past the bullshit and could focus on the case.

Of course, checking her out came with its own problems. They would confirm that she'd been abducted, but they'd also see she'd been drugged and drunk at the time. Credibility was everything, and hers was a little shaky. Maybe they were just taking their time to let her cool off. She had crashed a crime scene, after all. That was fine with her. She took long, cleansing breaths as Jarocki had taught her and felt her body calm down as she waited.

It was close to an hour before the younger of the two inspectors entered the interview room.

"Hello, Ms. Sutton. I'm Inspector Ryan Greening. Sorry to have kept you waiting. I hope you're up for answering some questions."

"Yes, and I have some of my own."

Greening took the seat opposite her. "And I'll answer them if I can."

She thought it interesting that only one of the inspectors was interviewing her, and of the two, it was the youngest. Did they think she'd connect with someone closer to her own age? Maybe she was overthinking it. *So suspicious, Zoë,* she thought.

He handed back her ID and smiled. "Your hair was longer when this was taken."

Reflexively, she ran a hand across the back of her head until she touched her bare neck. "Yeah, I keep it short now. Don't you like it?"

"Sure, it just makes you look different. Before we get started, I just wanted to inform you that this interview is being recorded. Is that OK?"

"Fine."

He eyed the scratches and bruises she'd picked up on her elbow and shoulder when they'd tackled her. "That wasn't a very smart thing you did tonight. You could have gotten seriously hurt."

"I needed to speak to the people in charge."

"There are better ways of doing it than breaking a police cordon and contaminating a crime scene. You could have called or checked in with a station."

She didn't like that Greening was trying to put her in her place. Cops always wanted things done the cop way. Newsflash, the world didn't operate the cop way, or she wouldn't have been abducted and they wouldn't have found a dead woman tonight. "Yeah, but I would have gotten the runaround if I'd done that."

Greening didn't have an answer. Instead, he eyed her left temple and winced. "It looks as if you've got a bruise coming."

She guessed the makeup she'd put on to hide the bruise had worn off. "You didn't do that. I picked that up at work."

"Really? What do you do?"

"Mall security."

Her answer spurred a raised eyebrow. "I wouldn't have guessed. How long have you been doing that?"

"About a year. Can we get back to what happened tonight?"

"Sure. Can you tell me what you were doing between 10:00 p.m. and midnight?"

"Just hitting a bar," she said and instantly regretted the answer. "Ferdinand's."

He nodded at her dress. "With friends?"

She was slow to answer. "No."

"Alone?"

She nodded.

She watched his expression change as he tried to work that one out. She willed him not to press the subject. She had information that would help their investigation. It didn't matter that she'd gone barhopping alone; she could help them find a killer. Thankfully, Greening heeded her mental urging and let the subject die.

"Can anyone confirm you were at Ferdinand's at that time?"

She was sure Rick Sobona and a few others could provide her with an alibi, but not the kind she needed right now. "It was busy. I doubt anyone would remember me."

"So, you were having a night on the town and you just happened across the crime scene."

More credibility testing, she thought. "No, I was in the bar and I saw it on the news. The second I did, I made the connection and came down."

"What connection?"

"The person who killed this woman tonight is the same person who killed my friend Holli and . . . abducted me."

"What makes you think that tonight's events are linked to your own?"

Christ, isn't the scar enough? He was testing her. If he'd checked her out, he knew what had happened to her. She guessed she'd have to jump through his hoops. "The news reported the woman was naked and suspended by her wrists. That was what he did to Holli."

An image of Holli hanging from that damn hook flashed through her mind. Now another woman was dead, and this time, in the city where she lived. The status quo had been broken. Her future was uncertain because her safety was uncertain.

She suddenly became aware of Greening's gaze on her. It was sympathetic, but she didn't feel any less uncomfortable under its weight.

"Tell me about your abduction, Ms. Sutton," Greening said.

Another cop, another retelling, she thought. Besides Jarocki, it seemed police were the only people who ever heard this story. She wasn't sure if it was the booze overtaking the waning adrenaline in her system, but a sudden wave of lightheadedness washed over her. She asked Greening for some water.

When he left to get it, she took the moment to compose herself. She needed to do this.

Greening returned with a bottle and cracked the top before handing it to her.

She unscrewed the cap and drank. The water touched her somewhere inside that produced a shiver.

"OK, Ms. Sutton, I've spoken to the Mono County Sheriffs, and I have the bare bones of what happened, but I'd like you to walk me through it. You and Ms. Buckner had gone to Vegas."

Zoë was silent for a minute. She felt the weight of Greening on her as she steadied herself against the past before speaking.

"Holli and I had driven there for a long weekend. We drove back on Sunday. The AC in my car wasn't all that great, so we set off late. We stopped at this little town to get something to eat. That's when he abducted us."

She found it a little easier to say the A-word this time around.

"And this was in Mono County?"

Zoë went silent again.

"Ms. Sutton?"

Her hands balled into fists.

"Zoë?"

She smashed her fists on the table, toppling the bottle of water onto its side. "I don't know," she bellowed. "I don't know, OK? It happened. I don't know where. I don't know when. And I don't know with whom."

Zoë saw the shock and surprise on Greening's face and regretted her outburst. It made her look unstable. And just to underline her mistake, it was all on tape for everyone to see. She could almost feel Jarocki's disapproval at her display.

"It's OK, Ms. Sutton. There's no need to get upset. We're just talking."

"I'm sorry. I'm sorry. I didn't mean to fly off the handle. I just remember so little from that night, and it pisses me off. That bastard is out there, and I saw him, but when I try to remember him, all I see is a smudge. If I'd identified him back then, this woman wouldn't be dead now."

"You don't know that, and you are not responsible for what others do."

"That's easy for you to say," Zoë replied.

Greening turned to his notes. "The officer I spoke to told me you'd been roofied. It's not surprising you don't remember much. The stuff is used for a reason—it's effective. Why don't you tell me what you do remember?"

She shook her head. "It's all in fragments. I remember that we stopped in a small town, but I don't know which one. It could have been Mono County or somewhere else. We were drinking. We flirted. With whom, I don't know. I remember waking up in a shed, naked, bound and bleeding from where he cut me." She touched her hip that held the scar. "Where that was, I don't know either."

"But something must have happened, because you were found naked and unconscious at the side of US 395 in your car."

"I escaped and went for help." She didn't have the courage to say she ran away like a scared little bitch, leaving her friend behind.

"How far do you think you got?"

"It could have been up the road from the bar or a hundred miles away. I have no idea."

"Holli was never found?"

"No."

"What do you think happened to her?"

"He killed her." Her words seemed to hit the walls of the cramped room and fall to the floor with a dull thud. "The last time I saw my friend, she was hanging from a hook in the ceiling of some tin-roofed shithole, like a side of beef, naked and bleeding while that psycho circled her with a whip, and do you know what I did? Did I help? Did I fight? No. I ran. I saved my own ass at her expense."

Zoë dropped her head in her hands and closed her eyes. Images of Holli filled the void, her dangling slack from the hook in the ceiling, with him standing behind her with his whip in hand.

"What do you think he did with her?"

She'd run through the possibilities a hundred times, none of them pleasant or respectful of the dead. "What do you think? He buried her. We were in the middle of nowhere. No one would ever find her. C'mon, you're just wasting time."

Greening raised his hands. "I'm sorry, Ms. Sutton. We can take a break and get some air if you like."

She shook her head. "No, it's OK. I'm fine. Sorry about this. Tonight has just been a shock."

"I totally understand, but anytime you want to take five, just say the word, all right?"

She nodded.

"Why do you think he took you and Holli?"

"I don't know. I remember him with his whip, asking Holli if she was sorry."

"Sorry about what?"

"God only knows. You'd have to ask him."

"That scar on your hip. Does it mean anything to you?"

She looked down at herself. "He did it, not me. It means something to him."

"I know, but I was wondering what your thoughts were about it."

"I assumed it was his initials—IV. That he marked me as his property."

Greening nodded. "Do you remember a similar marking on Ms. Buckner?"

Zoë closed her eyes and then shook her head. "I'm sure he cut her, but I can't remember if it was the same. That woman you found tonight, did she have the same mark on her? I know you can't tell me everything, but I just need to know that. I won't be able to sleep otherwise. I won't say anything. I promise."

"She had been cut on her left hip, just like you, but she wasn't marked with an *IV*. It was *VI*."

"He screwed up his own marking? That's crazy." She stopped. This guy wouldn't have made a mistake like that. "They're not letters, are they?"

He shook his head. "We think they're Roman numerals."

Zoë's stomach turned as the enormity of what that meant struck her. "That means she was number six."

*　　　*　　　*

Ryan Greening left Zoë Sutton again and walked into the observation suite. Edward Ogawa stood in front of the monitor to Interview Room Three. Zoë was sitting with her head in her hands but suddenly sat up, sneered at the bottle of water on the table in front of her, and batted it away.

"That's one angry young lady," Ogawa said.

"One damaged lady," Greening corrected.

Greening had pigeonholed Zoë Sutton as a drunken party girl when she had come busting through the cordon. That scar elevated her from some hammered chick to someone of great interest. She was a game changer. Their whole investigation had shifted in scope and emphasis because of her. They weren't dealing with an isolated case.

Greening flipped through his notes on Zoë Sutton and looked over the scant details he'd managed to get out of the Mono County Sheriffs. In the early hours of the morning, the duty officer had managed to track down a case number but couldn't release the file without the investigator's approval. He'd gotten lucky that the duty officer had been one of the responding cops, who'd been called to the scene of a naked, semiconscious Zoë found at the side of the road. The officer had been able to give him a snapshot of what had happened to Zoë and her friend, which highly suggested that the Jane Doe at Pier 25 and Zoë were connected.

"What do you think?" Greening asked.

Ogawa shook his head. "Something doesn't smell right. The Mono Sheriffs never found the location where the girls were held, the friend, or anything else to support her account. There was also no sign of sexual congress, consensual or otherwise."

"She was doped. She's not going to be reliable on facts."

"That's my problem." Ogawa tapped the papers with his finger. "Reading between the lines in this report, these guys couldn't determine what was fact and what was fiction."

Greening had also gotten that feeling from the account. "I've got a call in with the lead investigator on the case. Hopefully, he can shed some light. In the meantime, just looking at the similarities, she is tied to this. Her scar matches ours, and no one outside of the investigation knew that detail. Her friend was supposedly suspended and flogged. Ditto for our girl. No sexual assault in her case, and it looks to be the same with ours."

"Most of her story is uncorroborated. Anything could have happened."

"But a few things support her story. One, the friend has disappeared. No one has seen her since the trip, and there's no record of her since that weekend. So, where is she? Two, while the Mono Sheriffs wrote her off as an unreliable witness, they found Rohypnol in her bloodstream, so something definitely happened. And three, she has the scar on her hip. That scar cinches it for me at this stage."

Ogawa leaned against a wall of the cramped room. He stared at Zoë Sutton on the monitor. "That scar. Goddamn that scar."

That wasn't the kind of reaction Greening was expecting. "Why are you all bent out of shape?"

"If that scar is connected to all this then we're looking at a serial killer and I don't want that."

If the case went multistate, they'd forfeit it to the Feds, but Greening had worked with Ogawa long enough to know that losing the case wasn't upsetting him. He didn't care about jurisdictions and credits. He cared about getting criminals off the street, and a serial case would be hard to solve and suck up thousands of man hours. Serial cases made careers, and they also destroyed them.

"I don't like this twist in the tale," Ogawa said. "Zoë Sutton could be the break we need or a pain in the ass. If she is connected, we don't know how."

"She could be our best lead."

"Or our prime suspect."

It was a theory that Greening didn't buy. Ogawa was tossing out all possibilities, and they couldn't ignore any of them, but Greening didn't believe that they were staring at the killer.

"Right now, she's a distraction. Zoë Sutton isn't our case, the Jane Doe is, and the clock is ticking. That has to be my primary focus. So I want you to run with this, find out if there really is a connection here. That's your top priority, OK?"

"Sure thing."

"I'm going back to the scene. You talk to her. Get everything you can out of her and report back to me."

"Will do."

On the way out of the observation room, Ogawa patted Greening on the back. "I think this one is going to get ugly."

*   *   *

Marshall Beck sat in his SUV waiting for Number IV. He had parked between a couple of bail-bond outfits and had a clear view of the Hall of Justice, which was home to the superior court, the DA's office, and the SFPD, to name just three. He had no idea if she was inside there, but there was a good chance she was, since the Hall of Justice was home to the SFPD's major-crimes division. She was no longer at the crime scene. He'd checked. The cops were there, doing their cop thing, but Number IV wasn't. The police might have sent her on her way, but he didn't think so. They would want to question her, even if it was to dismiss her as a nut.

Since seeing Number IV on the news broadcast, he'd been scouring his brain to remember her name. Snatching her and Number III had been a spontaneous thing, so he hadn't done his usual due diligence. He hadn't thought it was necessary at the time. The two of them were just passing through town. They were strangers with no ties. That had been his foolproof thinking, until Number IV escaped. He'd gotten a look at their IDs only once before he'd disposed of them. He remembered Number III. Her name was Holli Buckner, but Number IV was just out of his memory's reach. He closed his eyes and pictured himself reading her ID. A name came into focus.

"Zoë Sutton," he said. "How nice to renew our acquaintance."

He wasn't concerned that Zoë would be spilling her guts to the cops. She didn't know anything that would send them to his door. If she did, she would have told them after her escape. The only damage she could do to him was to provide the police with a second data point. Then they'd realize they weren't dealing with a single case, but two and possibly more. Even that second data point didn't help the investigators much. You needed three or four to yield direction, and that wasn't anything Zoë could provide.

No, his interest in Zoë was one of personal pride. She was unfinished business. He'd been lax, and she'd gotten away because of it. She hadn't paid her dues. She'd gotten only a taste of what was coming to her. It was high time he made her endure her full comeuppance.

But he couldn't rush things and let his emotions rule over good judgment. He'd taken all precautions with Laurie Hernandez, and something had still gone wrong. He needed to use stealth and cunning if he was to close his account with Zoë. He had to track her and observe her. But for that, he needed his own data points, and at the moment, he had none. He knew only her name and that she lived in this area. A quick Internet and phone-book search had failed to reveal a home address or any active social-media links. If she'd gotten married, she might be going under a new last name, but he didn't think that was the case here. That dress wasn't the dress of a married woman. No, Zoë Sutton was single. And that told him something. She was living as far off the grid as someone could these days. Who avoided Facebook and Twitter and didn't have a listed phone number? Unabomber-style technophobes? Yes, for sure. People hiding from the world? Most definitely. Zoë was hiding, and hiding from him. He could have tracked her down right after she had busted out, but he'd had other things on his mind. He'd accepted her escape and moved on. It looked as if Zoë hadn't. He had to give her props for that. She'd learned from their previous encounter.

He eyed the dashboard clock. He'd been here two hours already. Had he missed her? He hoped not. He pieced together a timeline. Working from the time of the news report, he estimated Zoë had engaged the cops approximately three-and-a-half hours ago. To hustle her from Pier 25 to this office wouldn't have taken long, but they would have most likely put her on ice for a while so they could run a background check. Maybe he was being optimistic, but he could see them grilling her for a couple of hours if she'd told them something worthwhile. It was still in the realm of possibility that she was in there. The thought buoyed him. He decided he'd give it another two hours before he called it quits for the night.

But he didn't have to wait that long. Forty minutes later, Zoë emerged from the slab-sided building. A man in his thirties, wearing a suit, escorted her down the steps to the sidewalk. Beck guessed he was either a plainclothes cop or a district attorney. Zoë and the man were talking, but he was too far away to catch any of the conversation.

A car that appeared to be an unmarked police vehicle drew to a stop in front of them. The man held the door open for Zoë, and she climbed into the back of the car.

Beck started his Honda Pilot and pulled onto Bryant Street behind them. Tailing the unmarked was a trickier proposition than normal. Now that they were into the small hours of the morning, traffic was scarce, giving him little in the way of vehicles to hide behind. All he could do was hang back and hope for the best. He liked to think his cause was helped by driving the ultraordinary Honda. It was practically urban camouflage. He wondered if cops looked for a tail as a matter of course. He imagined they scanned for illegal activities, but he doubted they figured they were being surveilled. He put that down to the arrogance of their position. Police saw themselves as untouchable, even bulletproof. He guessed he'd soon know if his tail had been spotted or not. The cop driving Zoë wouldn't do the dirty work himself, not with a person of interest in the car. No, it would be called in, and a separate unit would try to pull him over.

The unmarked cut across the city. He mentally crossed off neighborhoods as they passed through them. He was starting to wonder if this was a wild-goose chase when the unmarked slowed and turned into an apartment complex. The security gate eased back as the cop car approached. It was a small complex, maybe less than thirty units, and Beck chose not to follow them inside. Instead, he pulled over, jogged across the street, and stopped in front of the gate just as it closed. He watched the uniformed cop walk Zoë to her door on the second floor of the unit. It was too dark to make out the number, but he memorized the location. He'd come back during the day to establish her full address. As Zoë let herself in, he turned around, smiling. He knew where Zoë Sutton lived. He had his first data point. Now he could begin planning her recapture.

CHAPTER SEVEN

The following morning, Greening was deskbound while Ogawa attended the Jane Doe autopsy. He developed his background check on Zoë Sutton. The databases told an interesting story about her, throwing up a number of red flags he wasn't expecting to find, namely a number of misdemeanor charges. In the past fifteen months, she'd picked up two disturbing-the-peace charges in San Francisco and a misdemeanor battery charge in Oakland. Reading the police reports, the incidents shared a common thread—Zoë's temper. She'd gotten into an altercation with someone at a bar or club, which had led to words before turning physical. She pled guilty in all three cases and served her sentence with community service.

The convictions had all happened in a seven-month period. Seemingly, she'd kept her nose clean for the last six months, at least as far as the courts were concerned. However, her name appeared on a number of field interview cards, which had resulted in warnings instead of arrests. There were four during those months, and judging by the addresses, they'd all occurred in and around her neighborhood. The interesting feature to these call outs was the responding officer. Officer Javier Martinez had answered three of the four calls, and he was the arresting officer in one of the disturbing-the-peace cases. He'd also tagged Zoë's name, asking to be contacted if she was picked up on a charge. It looked as if Zoë had a guardian angel. Greening picked up the phone and left a message for Martinez to contact him.

Greening ran Zoë's name through the national crime databases, and her name came back clean, other than her and Holli's abduction. Databases were limited in their reach. They gave him the official account of a person—what they'd done, how much they were worth—but they didn't tell him about a person. Social media was the place to get a window into someone's personality. While some saw social media as a twenty-first-century scourge, it was a godsend to law enforcement. People forgot how public they made their lives—even criminals. You were what you retweeted, for better or worse.

He plugged Zoë's name into Facebook, Pinterest, Tumblr, Google+, Twitter, and all the other usual social media suspects. Zoë had Facebook and Twitter accounts, but both were dormant. The two had been pretty lively until fifteen months ago. Zoë's last post on Facebook simply said: *Vegas, baby!* In the string of replies was a comment from Holli that said: *What happens in Vegas, stays in Vegas.*

And it had, he thought sadly.

Zoë hadn't posted since. Others had. There were comments from friends, asking where she was and what had happened, but no responses from Zoë. Michaela Shannon looked to be a persistent friend. Every few weeks for the past year, up until three months ago, she'd dropped a note on Zoë's status page. Messages included: "How are you doing?" "Hope you're OK." "Call me." "Where are you?" Her last message had been: "I'm worried about you. Please call." All her pleas had gone unanswered.

Greening shot Michaela Shannon a private message from his account, introducing himself and asking her to get in contact with him about Zoë.

Greening saw a shadow descend over him. He turned to find a uniform containing a barrel-chested man in his fifties with thick salt-and-pepper hair.

He smiled. "You know, I can cite you for social networking on police time."

Greening smiled back. "It's work stuff. Honest."

"Javier Martinez. You called?"

Greening stood and shook Martinez's hand. He gestured to his one and only visitor's chair, and Martinez sat.

Greening didn't know Martinez but instantly liked him. His friendly manner put Greening immediately at ease. It was such a great asset for a beat cop. Invariably, people encountered the police at the worst moments in their life. It made all the difference if the officer was viewed as someone who was there to help.

"What can I do for you, Inspector?"

"Zoë Sutton."

Martinez's smile disappeared. "She in trouble again?"

"Yes, but not in the way you're thinking," he said and explained the events from the previous night.

"Poor kid. Is there a connection?"

"Possibly. I'm checking into her, and I see you've been asked to be contacted in case of trouble—may I ask why?"

"I picked her up on a disturbing-the-peace thing a year ago. It should have been for assault. She'd gotten into it with some guy who was hitting on her in a bar, and she hit him when he wouldn't back off."

"Why didn't you push for the assault?"

"I felt sorry for her. I could tell there was something more to the situation than a girl who wasn't slow when it came to throwing a punch. I got her to open up, and she told me what'd happened to her friend. It was still raw for her back then and continues to be so. The girl needed help, not prison time, so I changed the dynamic of the situation. I asked the guy—a real asshole—if he really wanted to go to court and testify that a chick half his size put him on his butt. That cooled his jets and I took her in on disturbing the peace."

"I see there've been a few field incident cards with no charges."

Martinez shifted in his seat. "Yeah, I've been trying to keep the girl out of trouble. She got put through the wringer and survived, but no one was there to help her handle what came next. She's got a hair trigger. I just try to talk her down from the ledge when she hits a red zone and assist her with assholes that aren't worth going to jail for."

"Where's her family in all this?"

"I reached out to her parents. They're good people, and they did their best to be supportive. They even got her younger brother to act as emissary, but she cut herself off from them. Embarrassment and the shame factor are at play there. That's when I got her some outside help. There's a women's victims-of-violence charity that funds therapy. I hooked her up with them, and they got her a shrink."

Greening picked up his notebook and flipped it to a fresh page. "Got a name?"

"Yeah, Dr. David Jarocki." Martinez brought out his cell phone and thumbed through it. "He's got an office on Spear, but this is his number."

Greening took the phone, jotted the details down, and handed it back.

"Therapy working?"

"I don't know, but she's certainly more stable than when I first met her. She went through something horrific. That shit don't fade overnight."

Greening smiled. "Are you a knight in shining armor for lots of damsels in distress?"

Martinez colored. "I do my best for everyone I encounter, but Zoë's different. With a little help, she can get her life back on the right track. Did you know she was halfway through her PhD when this happened? She wanted to work for the EPA and clean up the planet."

"She's a mall cop right now."

"Yeah, I know. She's turned her back on life, love, friends, career, dreams—everything. It's a real shame."

Martinez had confirmed what Greening had established for himself. All signs pointed to Zoë's life taking a complete left turn after the abduction. But that was underplaying the situation. Zoë's life hadn't changed—she'd changed. Effectively, she had died when Holli Buckner had, and someone else had been resurrected.

"What do you think happened to her in the desert?" Greening asked.

"She and Holli ran into one of life's brick walls."

"So you think they ran into a tall, dark stranger?"

Martinez's expression tensed, and he sat a little stiffer in his seat. Greening had touched a nerve and Martinez was tightening up on him. He was used to seeing that with suspects and witnesses, but it was strange to see it from a cop. "What are you getting at?"

Martinez might be a brother officer, but in these situations you had to push to get the truth, even if that meant hurting a few feelings. Playing to his own healthy sense of cop skepticism, Greening picked up all the FI cards on Zoë. "Zoë Sutton has a history of violence. Could she have harmed Holli Buckner and invented this abduction?"

Martinez was already on his feet. "Like I said before, Zoë Sutton needs our help. She's the victim here."

Greening watched Martinez stride out of the investigation unit and thought, nice going. He might have burned a bridge there. He'd upset one fellow officer. Now it was time to see if he could upset another. He went through his messages and dug out the note from Deputy Greg Solis. Solis was the investigating officer in Zoë's abduction case from Mono County. Following up on Greening's request to the duty officer the night before, Solis had faxed over his complete report with a call back number.

He picked up his desk phone and punched in Solis's number.

"Deputy Greg Solis, Mono."

"Hi, this is Inspector Ryan Greening, San Francisco Police Department. I wanted to talk about one of your cases." He recited the case number. "Zoë Sutton and Holli Buckner."

"I know the case. Do you have something for me?"

"To be honest, I don't know what I have. Zoë Sutton claims her case is connected to a homicide we had in the city last night."

"Really?" Solis didn't sound that impressed. "Anything to it?"

"That's what I'm hoping you can confirm. If possible, I wanted to request a copy of the case file."

"Shouldn't be a problem, but before I go wasting my time, what do you have?"

From his tone, it seemed that Solis either didn't have a high opinion of the SFPD or of Zoë Sutton. "Last night we had a murder of an unidentified woman in her twenties. She was discovered at a construction site, naked, suspended by her wrists. She'd been flogged repeatedly before being stabbed in the heart."

"Flogged?"

Greening heard surprise and interest in Solis's voice. Now he moved to totally hook him. "Yes. Our victim also had the Roman numerals *VI* carved into her left hip. We think he's numbering his victims."

Silence. That said plenty.

"I have Ms. Sutton's account, but could you give me your take, Deputy?"

"We responded to a trucker's 911 call that he'd found a woman unconscious on the shoulder after spinning out in her car. We found Ms. Sutton naked and semiconscious. At first glance, we thought we were dealing with a DUI. A blood test revealed she was under the limit, but the drug panel revealed Flunitrazepam. This tied into her assertion that she and her friend, Ms. Buckner, had been abducted and held captive."

Greening didn't like the way Solis gave his account. He sounded like he was giving evidence in court, not talking cop to cop. Something was off here.

"What did you learn about the abduction?"

Greening heard Solis exhale down the line.

"Not much. Ms. Sutton could provide very few details. She couldn't give us her whereabouts leading up to the abduction or after. Nor could she provide more than a very generic description of the man who kidnapped her. No one could corroborate her account. Essentially, the case ran out of steam."

Greening understood Solis's frustration. There was nothing worse than landing a case with no leads. It was like trying to capture a cloud in a jar. What Greening still didn't understand was the dismissive tone he was hearing.

"Did you ever get anything from Ms. Sutton's car?"

"We found fibers and hair belonging to Ms. Sutton, Ms. Buckner, and an unknown male."

Trace evidence was one thing Greening didn't have. It showed the guy had gotten careful since Zoë, but if he proved to be careless, a comparison match would nail this guy for both crimes. "If we get anything on our end, I'll share results with you. Did you ever get a line on this workshop location this guy took them to?"

"We canvassed the area looking for buildings matching the descriptions of the building she mentioned, but we never found a match. That's if she remembered it right in the first place."

That was the problem with Zoë. Her account was Rohypnol distorted. A workshop could be an office building or a church basement, for all she knew. "What about Holli Buckner? Did you look into her?"

"Yes. It appeared that Ms. Buckner had reserved a room with Ms. Sutton in Vegas, but we couldn't confirm or deny whether she was with Ms. Sutton. Proving the validity of her claims was difficult. We couldn't find any eyewitnesses to prove Ms. Buckner had traveled with her, despite appearances that she had."

Appeared and *validity* were interesting choices of words. They fell into the same category as *alleged*. They implied disbelief.

"Holli Buckner hasn't been seen since this incident."

"I know." The words came tight and clipped.

"What do you think happened that night?"

"I don't know," Solis said with less tension in his voice. "Ms. Sutton was an unreliable witness. She provided us with a confusing account that made it impossible to pursue a case of any kind."

Considering Zoë had been roofied, her imprecision wasn't surprising.

"What's the case's status?"

"Open."

Not a surprising classification under the circumstances, but Greening knew these guys hadn't done enough on the case. He could rub Solis's nose in it, but he threw the man a bone instead.

"Just between us, what are your instincts telling you?"

"It could have gone down just as Ms. Sutton says."

"I hear a *but* in there."

Solis gave Greening a grunt of appreciation. "This could be a tale to cover a catfight gone bad or a cover for Holli Buckner to disappear."

Zoë as perpetrator. It was an interesting theory. Solis was as suspicious as Ogawa. "But her wounds?"

"Easily self-inflicted."

"And the Flunitrazepam?"

"Possibly self-administered."

"That's pretty convoluted."

"It's just a theory. With so little evidence, everything is in play."

No love lost here, Greening thought. Zoë must have made a real impression on these guys, as he didn't feel they were giving her the benefit of the doubt. He could see Solis's predicament and possible resentment. He had a case built on vapors. There was nothing solid for him to hang his investigation on. He didn't have a crime scene, and he didn't have a victim, per se, because everything hinged off a single, unreliable witness. Holli Buckner's disappearance said something had happened that night, but without some other piece of evidence, the case had stalled.

"In light of a potential new victim, what's your read now?"

"Nothing's changed—yet."

Greening smiled. "If I drove out there, do you think you could show me around?"

"Not sure that I can show you anything that would help your case, but you're welcome to visit."

Ogawa walked into the office, carrying a newspaper and a pissed-off expression. Greening thanked Solis and told him he'd be in touch.

Ogawa parked himself on the corner of the desk. "I've got good news and shit news."

Greening leaned back in his seat. "Give me the good."

"We have an ID on the Jane Doe—Laurie Hernandez. She made it easy for us. She has a rap sheet. Check her out for me."

"And the shit news?"

Ogawa tossed the newspaper on Greening's desk. "Someone talked, because the press has given him a name."

Greening found the name easily in the story. Because he numbered his victims, they were calling him the Tally Man.

CHAPTER EIGHT

At Urban Paws, Marshall Beck was catching up with the morning news in his office. He scanned the headlines for updates on Laurie Hernandez. He didn't expect the police to show their hand, but he did expect them to reveal a few case details to quell any public tension. As yet, the police hadn't revealed Laurie Hernandez's identity or that of his little runaway, Zoë Sutton. He found it interesting that the cops hadn't revealed her name or said much about her. None of the network affiliate websites or SFGate.com had reported any updates on her breaking through the police cordon last night, and none of the police statements mentioned her. He took their radio silence as a sign they believed her. She'd persuaded them that she was of value. A tingle of fear passed through him, but he knew he had nothing to worry about. She couldn't tell them anything. If she'd been able, the police would have tracked him down long ago.

SFGate.com might not have mentioned Zoë, but they did mention him—by nickname. Inspired by the numbers he'd carved into the women, the press was now calling him the Tally Man.

Talentless hacks, he thought. They'd boiled down what he did to a catchy moniker to sell more newspapers. *With unimaginative thinking like that, no wonder journalism is in the state it is.*

He reined in his contempt. As much as the dumb label irritated him, the revelation that someone had worked out his marking system irritated him more. The Tally Man name was a journalistic invention, but he had his doubts they'd figured out his numerals. That was a police discovery, which meant the SFPD had leaked the numbering of the punished to the press. He didn't think that was smart of them. Now he knew they were on to him and his point of view. No matter, though; it wouldn't change anything. He would keep on numbering the punished. Now that it had been revealed, maybe the public would understand what he was doing.

He smelled Kristi Thomas's perfume a second before she leaned over his shoulder. He hated it when she did that. He didn't like people invading his space. It was a minor irritation, not serious enough to earn her a *number.* The woman had dedicated her life to saving animals, after all.

"Isn't it terrible what happened to that woman?" Kristi said.

"Yes, terrible."

"They say she was flogged and branded."

They. What trash. The unnamed sources always knew more than anyone. He hadn't branded anyone.

"Have the cops worked out who she was?" Kristi asked.

"No, not yet. Can I help you with something?"

"It's that time of the month—payroll," she said with a smile. "Is it ready for me to sign off on?"

"Not yet. By lunchtime."

"Lunchtime." She nudged him with her elbow, which he didn't like. "You're slipping."

A cacophony of barking exploded throughout the center. It was angry and hostile. Kristi raced out of the room. Beck chased after her.

Dogs in the viewing areas barked in their pens, but that wasn't the epicenter of the commotion. That was coming from the Assessment Annex. It sounded as if a war had broken out in there. Beck's thoughts turned to Brando. Had he been provoked?

Kristi pounded on the door. "Is everything OK in there?"

She was smart. If one of the fighting dogs had gotten free, the last thing she could afford to do was let it loose in the visitors' area.

"Yes," Tom Fisher yelled back.

Kristi opened the door and went in. Beck followed and closed it behind them.

Tom and Judy King were valiantly attempting to get Nero back into his pen. He was growling and lashing out at them, trying to clamp his teeth down on anything that got near him. They were using an animal-control pole and brute force to try to get the dog back behind bars.

Beck was surprised to see this particular animal at the center of the trouble. He'd always seen it as one of the more docile ones. Then again, it was a fighting dog. That's what it was trained to do.

In a corner, Bonnie Moebeck had Lilith, another of the pit bulls, pinned in a corner with a second animal-control pole. Kristi rushed over to offer her assistance.

The other fighting dogs barked and snarled in their pens, all except for Brando. By the way he circled his tight confines, he was clearly agitated, but he seemed to recognize that nothing he could do would change his situation. Beck took pride in Brando's intelligence.

Tom and Judy finally wrestled Nero into his pen and locked the door. They then helped Kristi and Bonnie get the other dog confined.

"What the hell happened?" Kristi demanded.

"We had Nero out for his socialization test, and he did OK," Tom Fisher said. "We brought Lilith out for hers, and as we were bringing him back, he went for her."

"Goddamn it," Kristi said. "You know you can't take any chances with these dogs until they're fully assessed. One dog out at a time. That's the rule."

The animal-behavior trainers looked suitably chastised, with bowed heads.

"That means Nero just failed his assessment," Kristi pounded the wall with her fist. "Goddamn it."

Beck knew what a failed assessment meant for Nero and probably Lilith—euthanasia. A sad end for doomed lives.

"OK, let this be a wakeup call. Carry on with our good works," Kristi said sarcastically.

Beck got it. She was frustrated by how futile it all was.

Kristi headed back to the door. He stepped in front of her.

"How's it looking for these guys?"

"Not good." She cast a look back over her charges. "I don't think many of them will get a stay of execution."

"How about Brando?"

She flashed him a quizzical look. "I don't know at this point—why?"

He flushed under the weight of her stare. "I like him. He seems like he has potential."

"How would you know?" she asked, genuinely interested.

"I've been checking in, seeing how they've been getting on. He's different from the others. Proud. Regal, even."

Kristi smiled. "Are you interested in adopting him?"

He flushed again and didn't understand why. "Well, yes."

"Are we turning you into an animal lover?" she asked.

He recalled their conversation during his interview when Kristi had asked him how he felt about animals. He remarked that he had little interest, but respected the center's work, and that his primary goal was in doing a good job on their behalf.

"I don't know about that, but I am sure about Brando," he said.

"Let's go into my office."

Beck flashed Brando a look before following Kristi.

She sat at her desk. He chose to stand.

"Marshall, have you owned many dogs?"

"A few when I was growing up," he lied. There'd been no boy-and-his-dog moments in his life. There'd been no pets allowed at Jessica's Palomino Ranch foster home.

"Brando isn't just an ordinary dog. He's a fighting dog. He'll be a challenge for an experienced owner, let alone a novice. That's even if he's allowed to be adopted."

"Do you think he'll make the cut for adoption?"

"Hard to say, but his chances are probably less than fifty percent."

He hated the idea of Brando being euthanized. The animal had so much power and presence that he deserved a shot at life on his terms. He wouldn't allow him to be put down. He'd get Brando one way or another.

"This dog means a lot to you—why?"

"I see something in him and I want to nurture that."

Kristi smiled again. "Look, if you're really serious, I'll have you work with Tom. He'll show you how to handle a dog like Brando."

"Thank you."

"I can't make you any promises. If Brando fails his assessment, then there'll be nothing I can do. My hands will be tied."

I can assure you they will be if Brando dies, he thought.

CHAPTER NINE

Zoë stared blankly into the mall from her seat at the information kiosk. Shoppers passed back and forth across her field of vision, but she barely noticed them. A single, recurring thought played across her mind—*He's out there*. It was the same thought that had kept her awake all night and preoccupied her throughout her shift at the mall. She'd always known the man who'd abducted her and Holli was out there somewhere, but she'd never known where. He existed in the formless shape that was someplace. But last night had changed everything. He was in the Bay Area. She was within his grasp again. It had taken her a long time to lose that feeling, but now it was back. She ran a hand over the gooseflesh on her arms. It had been a near permanent feature since the cops had released her and the enormity of the situation had sunk in.

Jeff Hall, her fellow security guard, said something that jerked her from her thoughts. "What did you say?"

Jeff tapped his watch. "Time to make a sweep. You want to take it?"

It was the first thing he'd said to her in an hour, which was fine by her. She hadn't wanted conversation, and Jeff was good for that. He possessed the personality of a pet rock and was half as talkative. Normally his silence irritated her, but today it made him the perfect partner.

Zoë glanced at her own watch. Just thirty minutes until her shift ended. By the time she finished the patrol, it would be time to knock off.

"Sure. I'll do it."

She slid from her stool and made the pretense of conducting a sweep of the mall. She walked the upper and lower concourses and wandered through the stores. Her presence was enough to provide security for people who looked for it and to spook anyone who was loitering.

Questions filled her head as she patrolled. Why was her abductor here? Had he come looking for her? Did he know where she lived? She couldn't come up with answers. He could be in the Bay Area to finish what he'd started, but she'd moved since escaping him. Her rented apartment was in her parents' name because she had needed them as guarantors on the lease. And if he'd wanted to finish what he'd started, why had he left it so long? Wouldn't he have tracked her down as soon as she escaped? Why wait? It had to be merely coincidence. *Coincidence*—the word crumbled and fell apart as soon as she assembled it in her mind. The raw truth of the matter was that he was close. How close didn't matter, she just needed to protect herself against the possibility of another attack.

Just as she was coming to the end of her sweep, a small woman, no more than thirty, moved in from Zoë's right to block her path.

"Hi," the woman said with a smile. "I wonder if you could help me. I'm looking for the Starbucks. Could you point me in the right direction?"

Zoë didn't want to. She was off the clock, and the staff locker rooms were just fifty yards away. In there, she didn't have to be helpful, break up fights, or stop thieves. In there, she wasn't beholden to anyone but herself. But as much as she didn't want to, it was her job.

"Sure," Zoë said, forcing a smile. "You want the next level up." She pointed in the direction of the coffeehouse. "You see the Claire's? Turn left there."

"Thanks. I really appreciate it."

"No problem," Zoë said and sidestepped the woman, but she grabbed her arm.

"You're Zoë Sutton, aren't you?"

Zoë didn't recognize the woman and just stared at her in silence.

"You were at the crime scene at Pier 25 last night. You claimed you know the killer."

Zoë looked down at the small hand grasping her upper arm. Despite the light grip, it held her securely to the spot. "What?"

"I'm Lara Finz from the *Chronicle*. I wonder if we could talk?" She increased the wattage of her smile. "I'll buy you a coffee."

Fear knifed through her. It wasn't Lara Finz that frightened her. It was how easily this reporter had tracked her down at her job. If she could do it, *he* could do it.

Zoë backed up a step, jerking her arm free. "Stay the hell away from me."

"Look, Zoë, I just want to get your side of the story."

"I don't have a story." Zoë recognized the note of panic in her voice. She hated the sound of her own vulnerability.

"You do, and I want to get it out there."

Zoë continued to back away.

The journalist made a mistake. She stepped forward and grabbed Zoë's wrist. The impertinence of the woman's action ignited a primal instinct in Zoë. She didn't think. She reacted. She slammed the heel of her free hand into Lara Finz's shoulder. The impact sent the reporter tottering back on her heels. Not even her grasp on Zoë's wrist could keep her on her feet, and she crashed to the floor on her back. The contents of her purse exploded across the concourse. The spectacle forced everyone to turn and stare.

Zoë was frozen in the moment. She didn't know whether to help the journalist up or run. Shoppers were moving in. Damn the woman for cornering her like this. This was her fault.

Zoë felt the heat of stares on her. She backed away, then bolted for the staff locker room. Once there, she swiped her key card and burst inside. The door, with its pneumatic hinge, slowly wheezed closed and she threw her weight against it to close it just a bit faster. She released a breath when the lock snapped into place.

She staggered over to the bench opposite her locker and dropped down onto it. Her hands trembled. She clasped them together in an attempt to cancel out the shakes. It didn't work.

"Screw it," she said to herself.

She shouldn't have lashed out, no matter how much that woman had deserved it. She focused on one of her breathing exercises. It worked, but it was a couple of minutes before the shaking subsided. She unlatched her locker and pulled out her bag, then changed from her rent-a-cop uniform into sweats and a T-shirt.

Just as she was slipping her hoodie on, the door to the locker room opened. Jared Mills filled the doorway. At six-three and 220 pounds, it was hard for him not to. He was here to take the next shift. He was the one guy who could handle any of the assholes the mall cared to throw their way. He smiled at her and she smiled back. She liked Jared. He was a good guy and fun to be around. He managed to make a shift pass with ease. Sadly, they didn't get to work alongside each other as much as she would have liked.

"Hey, girl." He looked her up and down. "You got your self-defense class tonight?"

"Yeah."

"Be careful. There's some action out there. Some chick fell on her butt or was pushed or something. Jeff's dealing with it, but you don't want to get sucked into it on your way out."

She slung her sports bag over her shoulder and slammed her locker shut. "I'm in stealth mode."

Jared laughed. "Take it easy."

Zoë wished she could.

She slipped out of the locker room. There was a small group surrounding Lara Finz, including Jeff. She didn't think she had too much to worry about since Ms. Finz wouldn't want to reveal herself, but Zoë wasn't taking any chances. While everyone focused on Lara, she went in the opposite direction.

In the parking lot, she breathed a sigh of relief. There would no doubt be repercussions from what had just happened, but they'd be tomorrow's problems. All that mattered to her now was getting to her class.

She jumped on her motorcycle and joined the slow crawl on the freeway back into San Francisco. The traffic was thicker than normal, but she managed to make it to The Female Warrior in time. The studio was in the SoMa district off Howard Street. At night, it was a dark and desolate location, and probably not the best spot for a women's self-defense studio, but then again, maybe it was if you wanted to put technique into practice. For once, she found parking close to the entrance. She jogged across the street and pressed the buzzer to be let in.

The Female Warrior was a private-members' studio. A lot of the women who attended the self-defense classes were victims of violence or knew victims of violence. This wasn't the place for the latest exercise fad. This was a place where women learned to defend themselves, which might just be the difference between life and death.

Classes were limited to twenty, and Zoë was the last to arrive, judging by the number of women in the workout room already. She quickly peeled off her hoodie and stowed it with her sports bag and helmet.

Karen Haldane owned the studio and taught the classes. She walked to the head of the workout room and called everyone to order. "Ladies, we're going to get started in five minutes, so warm up however you like."

While some women stretched, others practiced defense moves one-on-one. Zoë made a beeline for BOB. BOB was a sparring dummy consisting of a life-size head and torso made of plastic and foam, sticking out of a post. BOB stood with his semifeatureless face staring blankly at her. This was how she saw her abductor. The drugs he had dosed her with had reduced a positive ID to a less-than-defined face that could have belonged to anyone. That piece of shit had done that to her. He'd done worse to Holli and now to this dead woman. How dare he do this to anyone? How dare he ruin her life? There'd been things she'd wanted to accomplish, and he'd wiped them all away. Her hopes and dreams had ended in that desert. Now she was left to live this half life because of him. Well, fuck him. She drove the heel of a palm into the underside of BOB's chin, jerking the dummy back on its post. When the punching bag rocked forward again, she drove the heel of her hand into its nose. It deflated and reinflated. In real life, the nose would have splintered, with a satisfying crunch.

She worked the dummy using a combination called *ichi roku*. First, she drove a vertical fist to BOB's solar plexus. Using the momentum of her body and her close quarters to the dummy, she slid her arm across its chest and drove an elbow into the same point on BOB's solar plexus. This brought her close to BOB, so close she could smell its funky rubber smell. She turned her body and chopped it across the neck with the same hand. It was a nice little move that took only a couple of seconds to deliver but would disable most attackers.

She repeated the combination again and again, each time a little faster than the time before. With speed came elaboration. The four-point combination became five, six, seven, eight, and more, with the inclusion of a palm strike to the underside of the dummy's jaw, a haymaker to the side of the head, rabbit punches to the gut, and a knee drive to the rib cage. Keeping her guard up as Karen had taught her, she pounded all of BOB's vulnerable points. BOB recovered from them all. A real man wouldn't have. He'd be in an ER.

"OK, ladies, let's get started."

As Zoë left BOB and crossed to the center of the studio, she noticed Karen watching her.

This was an intermediate class, with most of the women in training for over a year. Zoë had been coming to The Female Warrior just short of twelve months, although she'd advanced further than many of the women who'd been there longer.

Regardless of the class level, Karen started it the same way, with ten minutes of stretches and lunges that helped warm up the body and unknot muscles. She followed with self-*kumite*, or self-fighting, where everyone essentially shadow sparred with an invisible foe, using strikes and counterstrikes. This warm-up reinforced the basics until they became muscle memory.

Zoë went through the drills. She didn't like her performance tonight. It was unfocused and clumsy. She wasn't in the zone. She blamed Lara Finz for undermining her focus.

At the top of the hour, Karen had everyone circle around her. "OK, ladies. Over the last few weeks, we've been practicing scenarios involving attacks from behind. Tonight, we're going to look at a move that deals with an oncoming, charging attack. Jennifer, can you give me a hand with this one?"

Jennifer nodded and stepped forward.

By all accounts, Jennifer was a long-time attendee of Karen's classes, so Zoë knew this had to be a tough combination.

"OK, Jen, freeze for me in a charging attack."

Jennifer stood in a wide stride, as if running with her arm raised.

Karen stood to one side and simulated a side kick to Jennifer's knee in a stomping fashion. Jennifer feigned collapsing to a knee. Karen followed this with double palm heels to Jennifer's nose. She ended the move by turning again to deliver a second side kick to the same knee using her trailing leg. Karen demonstrated again, this time with movement. Jennifer attacked in slow motion, and Karen repeated the three-point technique to show its fluidity. She performed it several more times, each time with a little more speed and with a few options thrown in.

"Done right, I guarantee that your attacker will be coming away with a busted knee and broken nose. OK, does everyone see how this combo works?"

Karen received a round of yeses.

"Good. Now, pair up and let's see how everyone does."

Zoë partnered with a woman she knew only as Monica. Monica had been coming to the studio a little longer than Zoë, but Zoë knew little about the woman other than that she'd been mugged a couple of years earlier.

"What do you want to do first—attack or defend?" Monica asked.

"You choose."

"I'll defend. I want to try this move out."

Zoë nodded and took up an attacking position, albeit a static one. Just as Karen had demonstrated, Monica followed the steps as Karen called them out. Monica repeated the combination until she'd gotten a handle on Karen's new combo.

"OK, let's try this for real," Monica said.

Zoë made a slow-motion lunge at Monica. She followed the three-step move, dropping Zoë to the mat, then made several more attempts with the same result.

Karen moved from pair to pair, providing assistance. She stopped to survey Zoë and Monica's progress. She gave Monica a couple of pointers and had Zoë go at Monica with more speed than before. The end result was the same. Zoë ended up on the mat. Zoë knew, as the attacker, she was the fall guy, but she wasn't making for a worthy opponent. She should have at least made it a challenge for Monica. Her head wasn't in the game tonight.

Lara Finz had deceived her so easily. It made a mockery of everything she did in this class. She was supposed to keep her guard up at all times, and at the first true test, she'd failed. And the journalist was nothing compared to a real predator. She needed to get her shit together, especially with that son of a bitch in the city.

"I think I've got this," Monica said. "Wanna take the reins now?"

Zoë nodded.

Monica played statue while Zoë followed the steps. Karen provided adjustments until Zoë had the move down. Then Karen moved on to the next pairing.

"Let's try this with some movement," Zoë said.

Monica came at Zoë slowly, but moving complicated the action. She missed with a side kick, lost her balance, and fell.

"Damn it," Zoë hissed.

"Don't sweat it. Let's try again."

The second time around, Zoë didn't get herself positioned correctly before Monica was on top of her.

"C'mon, Zoë. You can do this."

Zoë nearly told Monica what she could do with her encouragement. Monica didn't know anything about her.

"Do you want me to show you the move?"

"No," Zoë barked.

Monica blinked in surprise.

"No. Sorry. I've got this."

"OK," Monica said. "Let's try it again. On your call."

Zoë nodded and Monica came for her. Again, Zoë was too slow with her reaction and clumsy with her delivery, and Monica caught her off balance, sending her crashing to the mat.

"Shit."

"It's OK," Monica said and offered a hand.

Zoë reluctantly took her classmate's hand. "Let's go again."

"Sure."

They went again and Zoë made the move work, but Monica had definitely backed off to make it easier for her to defend herself.

"One more time, before we review this combination," Karen said. "So make it count."

"You heard the lady," Monica said.

"This time, no soft sell."

Monica smiled. "Sure thing."

She charged Zoë. Zoë saw the opening she needed to pull off the initial side kick and missed it. Monica brought down an imaginary knife slash and clipped Zoë across the jaw. It was an accident. Zoë knew it was an accident. But her reaction was immediate and impulse driven. She backhanded Monica. The slap froze Monica to the spot. It was all the opening Zoë needed. She followed the backhand with a palm drive to Monica's sternum. The impact sent her crashing to the mat with a scream. Zoë drew back a fist, in case Monica retaliated.

"Zoë!" Karen screamed.

Karen's shout jerked Zoë from her daze. Everyone was staring at her, shock and disgust on their faces. Monica was crying. Two women rushed forward and helped her up.

Zoë opened her mouth to apologize, but the words didn't come. She was just as shocked at what she'd done as everyone else.

Karen pointed at the door. "Get the hell out, Zoë."

Zoë nodded. It was the only thing she could do. She stood and turned to see Inspector Ryan Greening standing at the reception desk.

Shit, she thought.

When she passed him to collect her things, he said, "I think we need to talk."

CHAPTER TEN

Inspector Greening held the door open for Zoë, and they walked out into the night. The sounds of her classmates' dismay and disgust filtered through the studio's frosted-glass windows. She crossed the street to her motorcycle to get away from her screwup. Greening followed her.

"How did you find me?" she asked.

"I went by the mall to see you, but you had already left. One of your colleagues told me where you were."

Greening could have easily called ahead or even made an appointment, but he'd dropped by unannounced so that he could catch her in her natural habitat. She didn't have to ask him if she was a suspect. The fact that he'd witnessed her little display in class had probably done nothing to shake his suspicion. When she screwed up, she really screwed up.

"You want to tell me what just happened in there?" he asked.

"Nothing. I just got carried away. It happens. What do you want?"

"I have some things to tell you about our investigation, but I have some questions too. Do you have some time to talk?"

The question sounded more like a request. "Sure. Where do you want to do this?"

"I want to go over some of the events from last night, so how about we go to that place you were drinking at, Ferdinand's?"

Zoë groaned inside. The last thing she wanted was to go back to the scene of her crime. She tried to think of an excuse why they couldn't return there but came up short. She surrendered and said, "Sure. Whatever."

He insisted on driving, so she left her bike where it was. She felt he was controlling the situation in a passive-aggressive way. That was the cops' MO—make you feel like you had a choice when you didn't.

It was another busy night on Russian Hill. The area around Ferdinand's was packed and it took Greening three blocks to find parking. They walked together. A casual observer might have mistaken them for a couple, if he didn't look very closely.

Ferdinand's was as busy as the night before. It was a crush all the way to the door, and the restaurant didn't have much in the way of tables.

"It's a war zone in there," she said. "Sure you want to discuss police stuff with so many people around?"

"I think we'll be OK."

She conceded there was no avoiding this and walked inside with him.

Stepping into the restaurant, she felt uncomfortable. Ferdinand's didn't have a dress code, but no one else was slumming it in workout gear. They'd have to trade off Greening's suit and badge. Last night she'd come in here dressed to kill, and here she was in sweats and a hoodie.

But her workout look also worked for her. She recognized a couple of faces among the staff, but they didn't recognize her. Last night, she'd looked like a million bucks. Tonight, she looked like fifty with change. No wonder no one recognized her. That helped shift a load from her shoulders.

Greening asked the hostess for a table. As she picked up her clipboard to get his name, he casually flashed his badge. They were seated immediately, although immediately didn't mean a good table. They ended up with a two-top in the window by the door. He took the seat facing the door—the seat she wanted. She never liked having her back to the entrance. You never knew who might creep up on you. It wasn't something that had bothered her before the abduction.

"Come here often?" he asked, looking around before turning to the menu.

"Now and again."

Has it been only a day since I was here last? It seemed like a lifetime ago. She wished she was as carefree as the other customers. They were happy, laughing, and joking, as if a murder hadn't happened just a handful of miles away. But it hadn't happened for them, had it? People recognized death only when it touched them. She bet that if she asked any of them if someone had been murdered last night, they wouldn't know. No one really took notice. No wonder killers could operate for so long with impunity.

"You eaten?" he asked.

"No."

"Me neither. I'm starving. Order whatever you like. This is on me."

She didn't like the idea of a free meal from a cop. It would come with strings. "We can split the bill."

"It's on me." He smiled. "Actually, I should say it's on the department."

She didn't know much about police department expenses, but she doubted they covered dinners with persons of interest. "That's OK. I'm not that hungry."

He frowned. "Suit yourself."

Their server introduced himself and set down a bottle of water. He asked if they wanted anything from the bar. Both of them said no, but Greening ordered a number of small plates.

"Feel free to pick from my plates."

She wasn't sure if this was an interrogation or a date. The latter was unlikely, but Greening was certainly buttering her up for some reason—and it couldn't be good.

"You said you have an update."

"I do." He straightened in his seat and leaned forward. "There have been a few developments."

"Like what?"

"We've identified the woman from last night. Her name was Laurie Hernandez. Did you know her?"

Zoë shook her head.

"Didn't think so. It was a long shot," he said. "I have a more serious question. Have you spoken to the press?"

"No," she lied. It was a white lie. The press had tried to talk to her. She hadn't wanted to speak to them. As much as it would be gratifying to set Greening on Lara Finz, the potential backlash from an assault charge prevented her.

"Have you? It's important, Zoë."

"No. Why?"

He removed a copy of the *Chronicle* from his pocket and put it on the table. "They've given him a name."

She looked the story over, and Lara Finz's name was on the byline. *Bitch*, she thought.

She scanned the rest of the article and stopped when she reached her killer's public identity. He didn't have a face, but he had a name—the Tally Man. She exhaled.

"Yeah, not exactly original, but potentially accurate."

"How did this happen?"

"You were caught on the TV news last night, flashing us your scar."

Reflexively, her hand went to the spot on her hip. She colored at the obvious tell.

"But you guys came up with the theory about him numbering his victims."

Greening sighed. "The feeling is that someone within the department leaked that detail. It's not unheard of for someone to sell information to the media. Rest assured, when the person is found there'll be some serious butt kicking."

Rest assured? What a joke, she thought. *What else has Greening's department leaked? Was that the reason Lara Finz found me so easily?*

"My name can't be released to the press. He might recognize me."

"Yes, I know. Inspector Ogawa is in contact with the *Chronicle* over this point. Please don't worry."

"That's easy for you to say." She slammed her hand down on the table. Heads turned their way. She lowered her voice. "He doesn't have unfinished business with you."

"Yes, I know. I'm sorry."

"Tell me one thing. Is it the same guy?"

"Yes, we think it is. Laurie Hernandez was stripped, strung up by her wrists, and viciously whipped before this guy killed her. Obviously, we can't do a handwriting comparison, but the scars look to have been cut by the same person."

It was somewhat of a relief to hear it. For so long, people had viewed her as some party girl who'd gotten so wasted she didn't know fact from fiction. But she'd been victimized, and no one could deny it anymore. It just felt wrong that her vindication came at the price of another person's life. It was a sad victory.

It really was *him*. The Tally Man was in her city. It didn't matter if her name appeared in the newspapers or on TV, she'd already drawn attention to herself at the crime scene. All he had to do was look at the news to know she was close. The son of a bitch had the advantage on her. He knew what she looked like. He could stand in front of her, and she wouldn't recognize him.

"So Laurie Hernandez was number six, Holli was number three, and I was number four. What about one, two, and five?"

"We're looking into it. We're running searches on similar victimology."

Zoë winced. *Victimology* was a hard word to hear when you were a previous victim.

"Sorry. Cop speak. Not always easy on the ear."

"It's OK."

"The problem is the search range. The suspect won't be local, considering where he abducted you. The other victims could be anywhere in the country. That's going to be tough to narrow down, and it will take a while. The law enforcement machine is thorough but it's also slow."

The plates Greening ordered arrived. He cherry-picked from all the appetizers and encouraged her to do the same. Despite her bad mood, she was hungry. Apparently, kicking the crap out of a classmate did that to a person. She grabbed a couple of spring rolls.

"I don't think you'll find the other victims," she said.

"What makes you say that?"

"No one ever found Holli, and I was with her to report the abduction. I don't think he wants his victims found. I bet you wouldn't have found Laurie Hernandez if he hadn't been disturbed."

"Maybe, but mistakes are how cases are broken," Greening said. "Most crimes are spur-of-the-moment and improvised. I doubt if most criminals plan more than a couple of hours ahead at any point. Even someone as organized as this guy won't have all the angles covered. Nobody does. He's one man against the might of the SFPD and all the other branches of law enforcement throughout the Bay Area and the country. Have a little faith in us. This Tally Man screwed up with you and again last night. That makes me feel confident of our chances."

She liked his analysis, but did feel a certain amount of salesmanship in his pitch. The Tally Man had managed to remain hidden for years, so chances were he could for years to come. As much as a single person was no match for a police department the size of the SFPD, the Tally Man had an advantage over an organization that big. He had the ability to go unnoticed, the flexibility to move quickly and change plans. That maneuverability was hard to beat.

She kept her thoughts to herself. It would have come off as uncharitable. After all, she had to believe in the SFPD because she desperately wanted the Tally Man to be caught. She needed to have his spell over her broken.

Greening grabbed a couple more items from the appetizer plates before saying, "I spoke to a couple of your friends today."

Friends? She didn't know she had any of those.

"Dr. Jarocki and Officer Martinez."

Did a shrink and a cop count as friends? If that was the best she could do, she was in trouble.

"What did Dr. Jarocki say?"

"Not a lot, due to patient confidentiality. I told him about last night."

That was good. She had meant to call him but hadn't been up to the task.

"Cockteaser," someone yelled outside.

Neither Zoë nor Greening took any notice until a fist struck the window close to Zoë's head. She jumped in her seat.

On the other side of the window was that jerk, Rick Sobona, the high-flying ad exec. A purple bruise stained him under his eyes and stretched to the bottom of his nose where she had punched him. He jabbed a finger at her.

"Cockteaser," he yelled again.

Zoë shook her head.

"What the hell?" Greening said.

Sobona glared at Zoë, waiting for her to acknowledge him. When she said nothing, he stormed into the restaurant. The hostess raised her hands and blocked his path, but he brushed her aside.

He loomed over Zoë, standing directly against her table. Her skin prickled at the invasion of her personal space. Since Greening was there, she fought the impulse to smash him in the balls with her fist. She had a straight shot, but Greening had already seen her assault someone tonight.

"I can't believe you're back here after you played me last night," he said. "I see you're up to your old tricks, eh, cockteaser?"

"Watch the mouth, pal."

"What did she promise you? Whatever it is, don't believe it. She gets off on flirting and playing the game, but it's all show. When the show's over, she does this." He pointed to the damage her single blow had done.

Zoë felt Greening staring at her.

Greening stood and faced Sobona. "OK, you've said your piece. Now it's time to go."

Sobona snorted a derisive laugh. "We are far from finished. We're sorting this shit out now."

Greening reached into his jacket and produced his badge. "No, we're finished here, unless you want to make it much worse for yourself."

Sobona rolled his eyes and clapped his hands dramatically. "Fantastic. A cop. So that's how you get away with it—police protection. You're a piece of work."

He couldn't have injected any more contempt into his voice if he tried. If his intention was to shame her, it had worked. She wanted to disappear.

The hostess returned with the chef and two waiters. They crowded around Sobona.

"Sir, you are not a customer here. Please leave."

"This bitch nearly broke my nose and thumb last night."

"That isn't any of our concern. It's time to go."

One of the waiters, a broad-shouldered guy, placed a hand on Sobona's arm just to reinforce the chef's point.

Sobona raised his hands in surrender, dislodging the waiter's hand. "OK, OK. I'm going. I know when I'm being screwed over."

The waiter ushered Sobona to the door, in case he changed his mind about leaving. Greening remained on his feet, no doubt in case his cop powers were needed.

"Sir, you are not welcome here in the future," the chef said.

"I wouldn't waste my time with this place. Your food stinks." Sobona couldn't resist leaving without pounding the window one last time and screaming, "Bitch."

The chef moved to the center of the restaurant with hands raised. "Sorry for the commotion, folks. We're not impervious to the occasional drunk making trouble. I hope it hasn't spoiled anyone's enjoyment."

He got a round of applause on his way back to the kitchen.

Greening retook his seat. "Never a dull moment in your life."

The hostess came over to Zoë and Greening. "I'm so sorry about that. Are you guys OK? Is there anything I can get you?"

"No, I'm sorry," Zoë said. "I'm really embarrassed."

The hostess placed a hand on her shoulder. "Please don't be. Whatever you did, he deserved it."

"I think we'll take the check," Greening said.

As the hostess returned to her station, Greening leaned in. "And you said no one here would remember you. Would you like to amend your statement, Ms. Sutton?"

*   *   *

From across the street, Marshall Beck watched Zoë take the man's double-barreled outburst. He had quite a temper on him, which was something Beck didn't like. Emotional displays in public disgusted him.

As much as Beck wanted nothing to do with the man, there was a story here that might give him an edge against Zoë. Targeting someone was all about research. The more you knew, the more likely you'd have the upper hand.

Tracking Zoë proved to be a straightforward affair now that he knew where she lived. One of the advantages of working at Urban Paws was he was allowed to set his own hours. Instead of going in this morning, he'd staked out Zoë's apartment building. He'd waited until she'd left and followed her to the Golden Gate Mall. He'd determined the shift she worked by making the pretense of applying for a security guard's position. He'd gone into work and left early in order to catch Zoë on her way home. She was tough to follow on that motorcycle of hers in the rush-hour crush. She took plenty of risks cutting in and out of traffic. It had forced him to drive in the carpool lane, just to keep up. He'd thought he'd lost her until he'd spotted her bike outside the self-defense studio. She was quite the GI Jane now. He put that down to his influence. Now his tracking skills had brought him here. He'd followed Zoë and that cop who'd seen her off from the Hall of Justice the night before. The irate man provided yet another wrinkle to this evening's surveillance effort.

This is going to be very easy, Beck thought. He crossed the street, putting him on a collision course with the angry man. Still cursing and muttering to himself, the guy was totally unaware of Beck zeroing in on him. Beck's casual demeanor was more to disguise his actions from everyone else on the street than for his target.

Beck strode straight at the guy. The man was looking at him, but his rage blinded him to what was directly in front of him. Beck removed his cell phone and pretended to be reading texts as he walked. He positioned himself so he and the man struck shoulders.

The impact knocked Beck's cell from his grasp, sending it skittering across the sidewalk.

"Look where the fuck you're going," the man barked.

Zoë's irate man was a good six inches shorter than Beck. He popped up onto his toes in order to put his face in Beck's. The guy might have anger on his side, but Beck had size, strength, and skill on his. He could break this man where he stood, if he wanted.

Beck raised his hands. "Sorry, sir, it was just an accident. We just bumped into each other. No harm, no foul."

"Wrong. There is harm. There is foul."

Beck furrowed his brow in mock intrigue. "Are you OK? I mean we just bumped. It's not a big deal."

"I'd be a lot better if assholes like you watched where they were going."

"OK. Sorry. Not trying to pick a fight. Just wanted to make sure you're fine."

A woman picked up Beck's phone and held it out to him. "Here's your phone." She glared at the irate man. "I think it's broken."

Beck examined his phone. The screen was cracked. In the scheme of things, it was a small price to pay.

The man stared at the damage, mouth open to hurl more insults, then all the tension went out of his body. "Hey, fuck it, I'm really sorry. I'm not pissed at you. I'm angry at someone else." He jerked a thumb over his shoulder at the restaurant where Zoë and the cop still sat.

Beck pointed at the man's bruised face. "It looks like someone got angry with you."

He touched his swollen and bruised nose. "Yes. Hence my mood. Let's just agree that I'm the dick here. I'll pay for the phone. It's the least I can do under the circumstances."

Beck knew in that moment that he had this guy.

"Don't sweat the phone. I got suckered into buying one of those insurance plans where they replace it with the next-generation phone for free. So, you actually did me a favor."

The man laughed. "At least I did something right tonight."

"Look, if you want to make it up to me, buy me a drink."

"I'll do you one better. I'll buy you two drinks."

Beck put out his hand. "Brad Ellis."

The other man shook his hand. "Rick Sobona."

They walked half a dozen blocks to Poison, a bar that Sobona had claimed, "You'll love."

It wasn't a place Beck could love. It was much too brash. Backlights behind the bar placed a heavenly glow on the expensive brand-name liquors, as if they possessed magical powers. Poison didn't have bartenders. It had mixologists. The way people whooped and high-fived when the mixologists made a cocktail smacked of the desperation of trying too hard to have fun.

"Great place, right?" Sobona said.

"Very cool," Beck lied.

Sobona cut through the people lining the bar in front of them. He flagged down Nick, one of the mixologists, who was sporting a prohibition look with gelled-down hair and a pencil moustache.

"What's your poison, gents?" Nick asked.

Beck guessed that was the marketing slogan for these guys.

"This man is a cocktail genius. Give me that thing you gave me over the weekend."

"That would be a John Gotti," Nick said.

Beck rarely drank. He never possessed a hunger for it, so he drank only when social niceties required him to do so. Like now.

"Sounds like something I need to try," Beck said.

Nick rapped the bar. "Two Gottis coming up."

While Nick put on a show, making the cocktails, working a couple of shakers at the same time, Beck and Sobona shared small talk: where they lived, worked, hung out, and so on. Beck had to lie about the more social aspects of his life. His main social activity was teaching irresponsible people a lesson. This forced him to steal from conversations he'd had with his more gregarious coworkers.

Nick finished his performance and set the two drinks down in front of them. Beck asked for a water chaser and sipped the drink. It was a clash of sweet and sour. He assumed that was the point of a John Gotti.

"So, can I ask you a personal question?" Beck asked.

"Sure. We're pals now."

"Why the attitude on the street?"

Sobona frowned and shook his head. "I had just run into some bitch who pissed me off."

Beck didn't like the word *bitch* when used as a slur. He didn't like name-calling in general. People might deserve a derogatory epithet, but it showed the mudslinger in just as bad a light. If people were bad, the appropriate reaction was to teach them a lesson. Insults were for children. Retribution was for adults.

"She did this to my face last night," Sobona said, indicating his bruises. "I tried calling her on it, but she had some cop with her to cover her ass."

Beck had to give Sobona props for admitting Zoë had done that to him. Most guys wouldn't have admitted to taking a beating from a woman. Maybe Sobona wasn't the blowhard Beck thought him to be.

"This bitch"—the word tasted as sour on his tongue as the John Gotti—"tell me all about her."

CHAPTER ELEVEN

Zoë found a message from David Jarocki on her answering machine when she got home from her awkward dinner/interrogation with Inspector Ryan Greening. "Zoë, I had a police officer here, asking questions about an incident involving you. Could you drop by my office sometime tomorrow? I have appointments during the day, but I can see you anytime after 7:00 p.m. Come by whatever time works for you. Hope you're well."

She felt like she was being summoned to the principal's office. She could try ducking Jarocki's message, but he'd only track her down at work. He'd done it before.

After a low-key day at the mall, where customers behaved themselves and Lara Finz hadn't reported her for the assault, she arrived at his office at seven thirty. She found the psychologist alone at his desk, writing up patient notes. At least, she guessed as much, because he switched his computer monitor off the second she walked in.

"Thanks for coming in. Take a seat."

She took the sofa, and he switched from his desk chair to his armchair.

He clasped his hands together and leaned forward. "The police came by yesterday and asked me about you. Naturally, I told them nothing, but they told me about the incident at Pier 25. I watched it on the web."

"Not my finest hour."

"That's not important. I was concerned about you after I watched it. How are you doing? Want to tell me about it?"

The answer was no, but this far down the road in her therapy, Jarocki didn't take no for an answer. "I was out at a bar. I caught the news about a murder. Something about it told me it was very similar to my abduction. I went to the scene to get some answers, but the police gave me the runaround. That wasn't acceptable, so I ran through their cordon."

"What made you think this murder was connected to you and Holli?"

She shook her head. "Instinct and the circumstances. The fact that this woman had been suspended naked and whipped. It just spoke to me. It sounded just like what had happened to Holli. I had to know if this woman was killed by the same attacker. If it is the same guy, I have information that will help them catch this person. I can make a difference."

"And?"

Jarocki was on to her. He knew she wouldn't have run down there just out of some sense of altruism. He knew as well as she did that she'd gone there for selfish reasons. "And I can see Holli's killer pay for what he did."

"And?"

"There aren't any more ands."

"Are you sure?"

Zoë's hands turned to fists. She leaned forward in her seat, her feet bouncing in agitation.

"Zoë?"

"And if they catch this bastard, he can tell them what he did with Holli."

"You're in search of answers. To some people, that may seem selfish or self-centered. It doesn't matter. You need answers to move on with your life. Don't feel you have to hide your agenda, Zoë."

She breathed a little easier at his validation.

"Is there any connection between this woman and you?"

"Her name was Laurie Hernandez." She didn't like her to be thought of as an anonymous victim. People forgot the anonymous.

"I'm sorry, yes. Laurie Hernandez. Any connection between you and Laurie?"

"I didn't know her, but she has the same thing carved into her hip as I do. Roman numerals. The press is calling him the Tally Man because he numbers his victims."

"Yes, I saw that in the *Chronicle*. How do you feel about all this?"

How do you think? she wanted to say. It was a dumb question, but it was how Jarocki operated. He asked seemingly obtuse questions to provoke a response and give her room to open up.

"Frightened. Nervous. Upset. Angry." She looked down at her balled hands and unclenched them. "The son of a bitch who tried to kill me is here in the Bay Area. That scares me. He's always been a bogeyman who existed out there in the ether, but now he's real, and that upsets me. I'm angry that he did to someone else what he did to Holli and me. I'm angry because he thinks he can keep on killing women. I'm angry because if I'd done more when I had the chance, Laurie Hernandez wouldn't be dead. And that pisses me off more than anything."

Jarocki was silent for a moment. "You are not responsible for his actions."

"Only my own—and those have had consequences."

"What consequences?"

"I left Holli behind. No one knows whether she's alive or dead. I couldn't take the cops to his little killing playground, so they never found him. He's been free to continue killing since then, and that's partially my fault. Don't tell me it's not."

"And there's an airliner that went missing, the new Bay Bridge is cracked, and the national deficit hasn't decreased. Those are all on you too, I presume."

"No, of course not."

"Are you sure? These things happened, and you did nothing to prevent or alleviate them, so you must be responsible for them too, going with your logic."

"You're being ridiculous."

"Maybe, but I'm illustrating that you are not responsible for the world's ills. You can't carry the blame for others or their future consequences. None of us can. That's the road to self-destruction. Look, we've talked about this many times during our sessions, and I know it's hard, but you have to forgive yourself. People can't function without forgiveness. It's why the Catholics have confession and the Jews have Yom Kippur. You recognize your failings, and you move on."

"Sounds like guilt-free living."

"It's sane living."

"That's all fine and dandy, but you're forgetting punishment. If I go to confession, there's no getting off the hook. I have to do penance by saying Hail Marys or whatever. There's a punishment to be paid. Where's my punishment?"

"Haven't you punished yourself enough?"

It was a low blow, a good one, but still a low one.

Jarocki got to his feet. "I'm going to make myself a cup of coffee. Can I get you any?"

She nodded, and they left his office for a closet masquerading as the staff break room. He made them both coffee, using one of those pod machines.

"I get stuck in that office all day. Do you mind if we walk and talk? Everyone's gone for the day. No one will overhear us."

"Sure."

They walked the quiet, narrow corridors. It reminded her of her rounds at the mall. She resisted the urge to check doors to see if they were locked.

"Despite your unorthodox approach, how did the police treat you?"

"Like cops."

He smiled and nodded. "I got that from the inspector who came by to see me. He knew I couldn't share anything, but still he came on a fishing expedition."

"Actually, if I'm being honest, they were good. Once I got them to listen, it helped calm me down. I won't say they made me feel like I was helping, but I know I have. Because of me, they know the case isn't a one-off."

"Isn't that great? You said you wanted to help and you have. You've put the police on the right course that will help catch this killer."

"But I can do more."

"I'm sure you can, but it's not your job. You're not the police. You've done what you can. Now let them do their job."

That was easier said than done. It was hard to sit on the sidelines when she was connected to all this. There were still more answers locked inside her head. She needed to dig them out and not just for their benefit. She needed to know what had happened to her and Holli when they left Vegas. She wasn't willing to let it be lost in the murk anymore.

They reached the end of a corridor and stopped to look out the window. They weren't high enough to get the full panorama of the city, but she got a decent look at Alcatraz, the Golden Gate Bridge, and could even make out the top of Pier 25. She sipped her coffee and found it tasted more bitter than it had a moment ago.

She didn't like it when Jarocki got all parental with her and tried to teach her life lessons, but his genuine concern for her well-being took the sting out of his mild badgering.

"You know I have to take you to task," Jarocki said. "When you rushed to that crime scene, you were in crisis and you didn't call me."

An image of her bursting through the police cordon played across her mind. It had been a long time since she'd been that out of control. She took a breath and exhaled. "There wasn't time. The police interviewed me for a long time."

"And that could have been avoided if you hadn't acted so impulsively. You should have called me first, and I could have been there with you. As we've discussed many times, impulsive behavior isn't good for us. Do you think you could have handled the situation differently and achieved the same results?"

Impulse control was one of Jarocki's many hobbyhorses, but to Zoë it smacked of emotional repression. She understood that it wasn't. Feeling fear wasn't anything to avoid, but letting it overwhelm her behavior was. It had taken a year of hindsight to understand that. In the heat of the moment, she wasn't always rational.

"I panicked when I saw the news. I was back in that shed with him. I had to know whether it was him again, and I didn't care how I did it. I didn't give myself any time to deal with the shock, and I should have."

"I'm a resource you should never be afraid to use."

"I'll make sure I do that next time."

"Several other aspects of what happened that night concern me. First, you came from a bar."

"Oh come on, Dr. Jarocki. I'm not a drunk."

"I never said you were. There's nothing wrong with the occasional drink, but as I've discussed with you before, alcohol doesn't help PTSD."

"What else?" Zoë asked.

"You were provocatively dressed."

She'd told him in the past that she dressed suggestively and went out alone to pick up guys. It was a side effect of her trauma. She had to put herself back in danger by placing herself in the same situation that had gotten her abducted. It was her punishment for escaping when Holli hadn't. It hadn't even been a conscious thought until Jarocki had gotten it out of her during one of their sessions. And even though she understood it, she still kept doing it.

"I was just having a night out. It wasn't planned. It was just something I felt like doing. Are you now telling me that short skirts are no friends to PTSD?"

"No—and you're being combative, Zoë."

"What's the problem, doctor? Look, if you've got something to say, then just spit it out."

"You were out drinking in the middle of the week, dressed for a pickup. You were re-creating the scenario that got you abducted and putting yourself in the firing line again. Putting yourself to the test. Hoping for a confrontation. I thought you'd gotten past that behavior months ago. When did you slip—or have you just gotten better at lying to me?"

Zoë could tell Jarocki was angry, but he still managed to keep his tone to that of a disappointed parent.

"Look, you're making a lot of assumptions. I could have been celebrating a birthday with a friend, for all you know."

"Were you? Correct me. Tell me I'm wrong. What was the friend's name?"

Zoë didn't answer.

"Zoë, I have been your confidant for over a year. I know you. I understand the situation and the pain you are in, and I'm here for the long haul. It doesn't matter if it takes a year or a decade to help you, I will be here to support you. You don't have to lie to me.

You'll never disappoint me, but if you keep making bad choices, you'll disappoint yourself."

Yeah, he was a confidant. Confidants were great at listening and providing shoulders to cry on, but that was it. They were never there to offer any concrete help, help that made a change. And therapists were the worst kind of confidant. They tossed you all the materials for making a bridge but never provided the instructions. She was just about to drop this science on her *confidant* when the fight went out of her.

She couldn't chastise him for what he'd said, because he wasn't wrong. She was putting herself in harm's way. She was putting herself to the test. She wanted to see if she could repel someone like the Tally Man. She had skills she didn't have the last time. If she ran into another Tally Man, would the outcome be the same? She wanted to win, score one for the victims. And if she lost, she was OK with that too. It was the price she had to pay for surviving the abduction when Holli hadn't. These were crazy thoughts. *What's wrong with me?* At first, she hadn't been aware of her actions, hadn't recognized her dangerous thinking. Now she did. She was aware. Yet still she did the same thing again and again.

She slumped against the wall, slopping coffee onto the tile floor. "I don't know why I do it," she conceded.

He took her half-drunk cup of coffee. "We're complex machines. It takes us a long time to work out why we do the things we do, but once we do, we are better off for it."

He walked her back toward his office. "With so much that's happened, how do you think you're doing in general?"

She wanted to lie and say she was doing fine, but couldn't. She'd recently assaulted three people because a killer was at the back of her mind. She told Jarocki about lashing out at Monica at her self-defense class and the incidents with Rick Sobona and the journalist.

"Those are unfortunate incidents, but hopefully you recognize your situation. You are in a vulnerable state, and you need to take care of yourself. Don't spread yourself too thin. Be good to yourself and surround yourself with supportive friends."

It was all good advice, but advice was rarely that easy to implement. Being good to herself wasn't going to help her against a killer. Friends might help. But when it came down to it, there was just herself to count on. That was a sad indictment of her life.

"Have the police offered you protection?"

"No. Why?"

"I don't mean to scare you, but if I saw you on the TV, then there's more than an even chance that this killer did too, and he may have recognized you. That's not good. Watch out for yourself."

CHAPTER TWELVE

The following day, Zoë sat at the mall information kiosk, thinking. She hadn't stopped thinking since her session the night before. Many things swirled around in her head. The scariest of them all was that Tally Man could have recognized her. Her impulsiveness may have put a target on her back.

Sometimes, you're not too smart, Zoë thought.

When it came to personal space and safety, she'd upped her vigilance. The Tally Man could be anyone. That was the problem. He was a ghost to her. It was exhausting defending herself against a shadow.

The other issue that bugged her was Jarocki's assertion that she'd helped the police all that she could, and it was time to back off and let them do their work. Jarocki was right but not in one respect. She could help the police more by giving them a concrete account of what had happened to her and Holli. The only way she knew how to do that was to retrace their route home from the Vegas trip.

She'd attempted the trip once, not long after she started seeing Jarocki, but had gotten only as far as Livermore. The moment she'd seen the signs for I-5 south, she'd panicked. She'd broken into a sweat, hyperventilated, and ended up at the side of the road, unable to go forward or go back. She'd finally called a tow truck to take her home.

She wasn't ready then. She was now. It was important that she do this for Holli, Laurie Hernandez, and all the other victims—and for herself. Jarocki was always professing the need for her to do something constructive and positive. Going back to Vegas was it, for many reasons. In addition to helping the cops, she'd be facing an old demon, and that would help boost her self-confidence. Getting out of town would also put a lot of distance between her and the Tally Man, now that he was in the Bay Area. Retracing her steps was a good idea.

She played with Google Maps on her computer terminal in between shopper inquiries. She wasn't supposed to use the computer for personal business, but there was a lot of downtime, despite the mall's dubious reputation. Luckily, she was on shift with Jared and he wouldn't say anything. He'd seen she was preoccupied and was happy to do patrols while she manned the kiosk.

She examined the possible routes to and from Vegas. Her journey to Vegas was easy to map. She and Holli had followed the freeways—I-580 to I-80, hang a left at Bakersfield, pick up CA 58 for Barstow, then follow I-15 all the way to Vegas. The drive had been dull, the equivalent of motoring elevator music. It had been her idea to shake things up for the return by avoiding the freeways, but she couldn't remember the convoluted route they'd concocted. She'd been picked up by the Mono County Sheriffs between Bishop and Mammoth Lakes after she escaped, which meant she and Holli had been trying to come home via Yosemite. That narrowed their possible routes to only a couple of options. They'd either followed the roads up to Carson City or through Death Valley.

She zeroed in on the satellite image of the map. Somewhere along those roads, he'd held her. She didn't know if she'd find him, but she would find his workshop. Anger and excitement quickened her heart rate.

Her radio crackled into life. It was Jared. He was breathy. She could hear he was running.

"Zoë, need help, thief, upper deck, coming your way, Niners hoodie."

Jared's shorthand was all she needed. She grabbed the radio. "On my way."

She bolted for the escalators. Taking the steps two at a time, she propelled herself to the upper concourse in seconds. She staggered coming off at the top but recovered her footing in a couple strides and raced along the mall.

She didn't have to yell for people to get out of the way. They cleared a path for her so they could take in the show.

It took her only a moment to pick out the perp in the 49ers hoodie, sprinting toward her through the crowd, with Jared in pursuit. They were two hundred yards away. The thief had thirty yards on Jared, but the security guard was closing in.

If Jared didn't catch up to him, she'd stop him. The guy had boxed himself in. She stood between him and the exits on the upper concourse. If he doubled back, he'd run straight into Jared. She upped her pace, a hard thing to do in the bulky uniform.

The issue looked to be academic. Jared had caught up to the thief. He drove a hand into the guy's back, sending him sprawling to the ground. As Jared lunged to grab him, the thief reached into his pocket and whipped out a knife. He slashed the air in a sweeping arc, catching Jared across the chest, leaving a long red streak. Jared slapped a hand over it and dropped to his knees.

"Son of a bitch," Zoë snarled and ran on.

The perp leapt to his feet. It took him a second to realize he was sprinting toward her, then he ground to a halt. Zoë did the same. There was thirty feet between them. Shoppers ducked back into stores or pressed themselves against the railing.

She had an up-close look at him. He was no more than twenty and was taller than her, five-ten but skinny. She doubted he weighed 150 pounds. It made them evenly matched.

He flashed a look from her to the exits behind her, then back. She read his expression and knew what he was thinking: *The exit is right there and she's only a woman. I can take her.*

He thrust the knife out. She'd expected a switchblade, but it was a cheap-looking steak knife with a four-inch blade. It didn't make it any less lethal, however.

"Get the fuck out of my way," he barked, but a stammer shook every word.

Theft was the least of this guy's problems now. He'd cut Jared. There was no way she was letting him escape. No one who inflicted harm on others got to escape. Not this guy. Not Laurie Hernandez's and Holli's killer. She stood her ground. "Drop the knife."

"You're crazy. You don't get paid enough for this shit."

"Honey, it ain't worth it," a shopper said.

She took a deliberate step forward, and the guy rushed her. The onlookers around them scattered, causing others to gasp in surprise.

He was fast. He covered the short distance in a flash, with the knife raised, but she didn't panic. This was what all her self-defense classes had taught her. The move Karen had demonstrated a few nights earlier sprang to mind. She sidestepped him and lashed him with a side kick. She failed to connect 100 percent, but it was enough to drop him to one knee. She aimed a double palm heel at his face and caught him hard across the bridge of his nose. He yelled out, but to his credit, the blow didn't fell him.

He swung his arm, knife in hand. The wooden butt connected with her cheekbone. Pain exploded from the point of impact, sending shockwaves across her face. She staggered back and bounced against the safety railing, which kept her from falling down to the first story of the mall.

The thief jumped to his feet and broke into a loping stagger for the exit. Zoë had no doubt given him a dead leg with her kick. She chased after him and surprised him by chopping him across the forearm, sending the steak knife skittering across the polished floor. Before he could chase after it, she stamped down on the back of his leg, driving him to his knees again. She'd gained the upper hand and pounced on it by wrapping her arms around his neck in a sleeper hold.

He toppled forward, either in surprise or in an attempt to dislodge her, but she maintained her grasp. The both of them went down. He thrashed, but she maintained her hold. He flipped them over, throwing himself on top of her, but his scant weight did little to deter her. She knew she had him and wrapped her legs around his waist. He drove an elbow into her ribs. She bit back the pain. His blows were losing their power, and she could feel his strength going out of him. It was just a matter of time now. An uncomfortable gurgle slipped from his lips before he went slack in her hold.

Jared appeared with a hand to his chest where he'd been cut. He grinned and pulled the thief off her. "You got the prick, Zoë."

She clambered to her feet to cheers and applause.

She looked down at the thief in his Niners hoodie. *Yeah, I got the prick*, she thought. *Now I just have to get the one who counts.*

*   *   *

The mall turned into a circus filled with police, paramedics, supervisors, shoppers, and a small media presence. Marshall Beck had taken up a satellite position on the periphery to observe. The police had the suspect in cuffs now that he'd come to. They'd also rounded up a bunch of eyewitnesses and cordoned off the area where Zoë had choked the kid in the 49ers hoodie. Paramedics worked on both Zoë and her fellow security guard while a couple of cops tried to get statements from the two. Mall management stayed close to

Zoë and her coworker. The aftermath took place under the hungry gazes of dozens of onlookers. A couple of news crews were interviewing shoppers and a spokesperson from the mall. From Beck's point of view, it was all very satisfactory, considering he'd masterminded the whole thing.

After finding out that Zoë was taking self-defense classes, he'd needed to establish whether she'd learned any actual fighting abilities. It looked as if she had. She certainly hadn't fought like that when he'd taken her. She'd been shown the error of her ways, and she'd changed because of it. He liked that. He'd affected change in someone for the good. He wondered what other changes Zoë had made to her life. If she had made enough, maybe he'd leave her alone in favor of someone else who needed reeducation.

This performance had taken some wrangling, but it had come off without a hitch. He'd wanted to put Zoë to the test but hadn't been sure how to do that until he'd discovered she worked at the Golden Gate Mall. It had a reputation for pickpockets and shoplifters, thus providing the perfect environment for assessing her. He couldn't afford to hang around waiting for criminal inspiration to strike of its own accord so he'd walked around the mall, being sloppy with his wallet and iPhone. He'd made himself an obvious target and it had paid off. While he was in Macy's, he'd put his phone down to pick up a shirt, and the kid in the 49ers sweatshirt had grabbed it. It couldn't have worked out better if he'd wanted it to.

Zoë had gone through her trial by fire. Now it was his turn. He had to know how much she remembered. He was risking everything, but it was a calculated risk, so sure was he that she had no solid memories of that night. He squeezed his way through the crowd and announced himself to the first police officer he encountered.

"Hi, it was my cell phone that guy stole. Who do I talk to?"

"Come with me," the officer said and waved him through.

The policeman walked him over to a sergeant to make a statement. Beck performed his account for the official record. He made sure he injected shock and dismay to add a human element to the story. He couldn't be a nothing-but-the-facts guy. He'd just been robbed. It was a life-altering moment, and he needed to act accordingly.

There was a bored and dissatisfied aspect to the sergeant's demeanor. He showed no excitement at taking a criminal off the streets. It was what it was. Just another one for the crime stats. Beck didn't blame him. He guessed the cop had seen this a thousand times. To him, it was probably just another sad indictment of human society.

Between the sergeant's questions, Beck snatched quick glances at Zoë. There she was—the one that got away. He never caught her looking in his direction. She was too busy with the cops and paramedics.

"We'll have to hold on to the phone as evidence."

"Really? I suppose you would."

"We should be able to release it back to you in a couple of days."

"Sure. Whatever you need. What happens now? Do you need me to stick around?"

"No, I've got your details. You're free to go, and we'll be in touch about your phone in the next day or two."

"Thanks. Is it OK if I say a quick thank-you to the security guards? Those guys went the extra mile, and it's the least I can do."

"Sure."

Beck couldn't deny the tingle of excitement coursing through him as he crossed the short distance to his would-be heroes. Here was his moment of truth.

The paramedics had finished up with Zoë but were still working on her colleague. He gingerly inserted himself in between the paramedics and cops.

"Hello. Sorry to disturb you guys, but I wanted to say thanks. It was my cell phone that got stolen and you two recovered."

He purposely made eye contact with Zoë and didn't get a reaction from her. He couldn't decide if she was hiding it or not.

"I really don't know what to say other than thanks. You two are great."

"It's our job," Zoë said. "He broke the law and he shouldn't get away with it."

Her tone was hard and unforgiving.

Bravo, Beck thought. He'd made a woman of her, although part of him wondered if her remark was a coded message to him.

"It may be your job, but I'm just sorry you two got hurt. Are you guys going to be OK?"

Zoë touched her cheek where she'd been hit. She looked like a before-and-after photo for implants. One side of her face was twice the size of the other. Her cheek was red and inflamed right now, and he guessed there'd be some pretty impressive bruising by the end of the day.

"We're going to be fine," Zoë's colleague said in fine, superhero style.

Beck guessed he was still flush with adrenaline. Zoë seemed dazed by her encounter. Her stare was glassy and unfocused. While her colleague was ebullient, she was withdrawn. Was that why she didn't recognize him?

"What about that gash?" Beck said, pointing at the security guard's chest.

"It looks worse than it is," the paramedic attending to Zoë's colleague said. "There's no muscle damage, which is good. Luckily, the knife wasn't sharp enough to do any real harm. We'll be taking them to the ER for a proper checkup."

"We need to get these two to the hospital now," the other paramedic said.

"Again, I can't thank you enough for what you did today. My name is Brad Ellis," he said and put out a hand to Zoë's coworker.

"Jared Mills," he said, taking Beck's hand and giving it a powerful shake.

"Good to meet you, Jared."

He held his hand out to Zoë. She took it. Her hand was warm but dry to the touch. Not a hint of nervous sweat. "Zoë Sutton."

"Nice to meet you too, Zoë." He made eye contact and looked for a flicker of recognition, but saw none. Zoë didn't recognize him. He smiled, and it turned into a grin.

CHAPTER THIRTEEN

Greening stood at the whiteboard that served as the Laurie Hernandez murder board, adding information about the victim herself. At the beginning of any investigation, especially a murder, all he had to work with was a snapshot. There was no narrative, no story, just the circumstances. In Laurie Hernandez's case, he had a body, a location, and the manner of death. Before he or Ogawa could move forward, they had to go back and build a series of pictures of the past.

He didn't like to judge a victim. To him, no one ever "asked for it" or "had it coming," or "got what they deserved." Victims deserved justice regardless of their characters, and he gave every case 100 percent. That wasn't to say his personal feelings didn't seep into his thinking. After a long and depressing day talking to coworkers, family, and friends about Laurie Hernandez, he'd come to the conclusion that she wasn't a very nice person.

Coworkers—present and past, of which there were many as she didn't seem to hold on to a job for long—struggled to find a good word to say about her. "Difficult" had been the most complimentary thing anyone could offer. She ducked her duties, leaving others to pick up the slack, and was rude to customers. Rumors circulated that she stole money from purses and wallets in the staff locker room, although no one had anything concrete. She looked to be cut from the same family cloth as her siblings and parents. All but one had a rap sheet consisting of minor crimes, running from passing bum checks to DUIs. Her father had asked him if there'd be a payout from the city and the property developer since she'd been killed at Pier 25. Her friends squeezed out crocodile tears for their Mother Teresa-esque friend, while ignoring her laundry list of petty offenses, which included shoplifting, disturbing the peace, and public intoxication.

The picture he'd built up was of a young woman who skated through life with little drive or concern for anyone other than herself. Regardless of her failings, she hadn't deserved the brutal death she'd endured—and she had endured. The coroner's preliminary report estimated she'd suffered forty lashes. Even though a flogging like that seemed as if it would have been enough to kill her, it had been a knife wound to her heart that had been the cause of death. The coroner surmised she would have blacked out at some point during the whipping. He couldn't imagine the pain and torment she'd endured.

Poor kid, he thought.

The Tally Man was a sadistic piece of shit. He couldn't wait to arrest the bastard. The unfortunate side of the justice system was that the Tally Man would never experience the same level of pain as his victims had. Society was supposed to be better than its criminals, never stooping to their level of depravity. In the Tally Man's case, he wished society could make an exception. He deserved to suffer like his prey had and then some.

He stepped back from the whiteboard and perched himself on the corner of Ogawa's desk to get a look at the big picture. The murder board looked distinctly lopsided. It was divided into columns with information on the various persons of interest. Columns for

Zoë Sutton, Holli Buckner, and Laurie Hernandez were fleshed out. Little information existed for the Tally Man, other than his murder weapons and methodology. The columns for Victims I, II, and V were blank. Ogawa hadn't liked there being real estate on the murder board dedicated to victims outside their investigation and, more than likely, their jurisdiction, but Greening thought they deserved mentioning. If they managed to put names to the numerals, the potential correlations could help connect them to the Tally Man.

Ogawa walked in. "Hey, I thought you'd left for the Mono County Sheriffs'."

"I will when I've wrapped this up."

Ogawa pulled up his chair and sat alongside Greening. The two of them stared at the board.

"Tally Man, really? You had to use the name the press gave him?"

Greening had tired of just seeing "Perpetrator" up there. In most cases, they had suspects with names and identities to put on the board. In this case, they had nothing other than a nickname. Despite the cheesiness of the nickname, it kept him mindful of this guy's agenda—a killer who kept score.

"What would you prefer—*perp* or *evil-doer*?"

Ogawa snorted. "I prefer *douche*, but I'll take anything over what a journalist invented."

"Got anything to add to the board?"

Ogawa shook his head. "Our guy is a careful son of a bitch. He left nothing at the crime scene, other than Laurie Hernandez."

Considering he'd notched up six victims without being caught, it wasn't surprising. He would have gotten good at his craft.

"He gained access to Pier 25 by boat," Ogawa said. "No security cameras pointed out at the bay. His choice of weaponry is bad news for us. We've yet to create a national database for whips, and the knife he's using is a common hunting knife. If he'd used a gun, at least we'd have ballistics to point us somewhere."

"He's not infallible. He already screwed up the Sutton/Buckner kill by letting Zoë escape. He'll screw up again."

"So it'll be lucky number seven for us, is that what you're saying?"

The truth of the matter was that a seventh victim would help them catch this guy, but that was too steep a price to pay. "No. I'm just saying there's evidence out there that'll lead us to him, and it's his mistakes that'll do it."

Ogawa was silent for a moment. "I've been trying to get a handle on this prick. The numbering thing—whose benefit is that for?"

"Killers like this feel the need to signify their work some way— either by collecting or marking. Our boy is a marker."

"I wish he was a collector. If he kept souvenirs from any of his kills, it would make nailing this guy a damn sight easier. But why number these people? It's not like he's leaving the bodies out for us to find."

Ogawa is right about that, Greening thought. They'd plugged the numerical scarring into every national and local database and got nothing matching the Tally Man's MO. "He's obsessive-compulsive. He's keeping score, even if he's the only one who knows it."

"We need something else." Ogawa went to the murder board and pored over the information.

"There's got to be something in his victims. Guys like this have a type. They kill the same person again and again."

"So what's his type?"

Female, as far as Greening had determined so far. At least with Zoë Sutton coming forward, they had a better grasp on the situation. Without that, they'd really be scrabbling for a thread. He pushed himself off Ogawa's desk and went to the whiteboard.

"There isn't much in the way of similarities between these three. All three can be considered attractive and are in their twenties, but that's where the commonality ends. Laurie Hernandez didn't graduate high school, while Zoë Sutton and Holli Buckner were in PhD programs. Zoë and Holli have no association with Laurie Hernandez. Zoë is blonde, while Holli and Laurie were brunettes. Zoë is on the short side, Holli was tall, Laurie was average height. Laurie and Zoë both have criminal records, albeit misdemeanors, while Holli had none."

Ogawa tapped the dates of the charges against Zoë's name. "And all Zoë's convictions came after her abduction, so that doesn't jive with anything."

Greening nodded. If the Tally Man had a type, not having a type was his type. If only they had some information on Victims I, II, and V. It would either make or break that theory.

"The Tally Man is an equal-opportunity killer. He goes for good girls and bad ones."

Then something clicked in Greening's head. "That's not strictly true. As far as he's concerned, they're not good girls. He grabbed Zoë and Holli after they'd been rowdy at some restaurant, and Laurie Hernandez seemed to be pissing someone off at all times."

Greening shook his head at his own conclusion. It had seemed as if he had something when he'd thought of it, but the idea went stale as he said it. "Maybe that's it. Maybe he goes after bad girls. Zoë remembers the Tally Man asking Holli if she was sorry."

"It kicks up some interesting ideas," said Ogawa. "If we use Zoë and Holli as models for all the victims, it would go a little something like this: he witnesses a woman behaving inappropriately—he dopes her, abducts her, and kills her at a prearranged kill site. If we apply this to Laurie Hernandez, what have we got? We know where he killed her. The coroner found a puncture mark, and the tox screen, when it comes back, will more than likely tell us she was doped. What we don't know is where he witnessed her bad behavior."

"She worked at that costume-jewelry-and-ear-piercing joint in the Westfield, which I can't see being a regular Tally Man haunt. Although, considering no one saw her after she left work, he more than likely snatched her on her way home. That means he knew where she worked."

"Which means he watched her long before he snatched her. That's a change from Zoë and Holli. It seems like he was opportunistic there. Whatever unsavory thing he witnessed Laurie Hernandez doing, he probably saw it at some place they both frequented. See if you can establish a list of her regular haunts, and we'll check them out for any incidents." Ogawa put his hands together. "Let's pray to the gods of CCTV for it to be caught on camera."

"We're focusing on his victims, but what about him? If this guy is so sensitive to improper behavior, there's a chance he would have gotten into it with someone at some point, resulting in a police call."

Ogawa smiled. "Yeah, I like that. I'll check the FI reports. They brought down Son of Sam on a parking violation. I'd love to see an asshole as pious as this one brought down because he gave his information during a field interview."

Greening looked at what they had again and shook his head. "I can't believe this guy is on a crusade against girls going wild."

"I'm guessing he's no fan of *Sex and the City* either." Ogawa shrugged. "Like you were expecting anything more from this guy?"

CHAPTER FOURTEEN

Zoë's heart fluttered when Las Vegas appeared small on the horizon. It glowed in the night, thanks to a million lights and miles and miles of neon. The sight of the city at the end of the freeway announced her task was just beginning. Until now, she had just been driving, a passive pursuit, just travel. Her destination was now within arm's length. It signaled the true beginning of this trip. The prospect of what she'd discover both exhilarated and frightened her. Jarocki was on speed dial, in case events overwhelmed her.

At least she'd gotten farther than she had last year. Once she'd left San Francisco city limits, her bravado had waned, but the real test had come when she'd reached Livermore. The invincibility she'd shown in Jarocki's office had seemed to desert her as she'd reached the stretch of road she hadn't managed to broach last time—her palms had been damp and butterflies had swarmed in her stomach. She'd breathed deeply, pushed down on the accelerator, and blew past the spot, trying not to think about it. As soon as she'd made it past that point, her confidence had risen. Breaking that barrier told her she wasn't the same person she'd been last year. She was better. Stronger. With purpose. That monster who'd driven her life, hopes, and dreams onto the rocks no longer controlled her life. She couldn't completely move on until he was in jail, but this was the tipping point, the moment where she started taking back her life.

"Your days are numbered, Tally Man," she murmured to herself.

When she reached the outskirts of Las Vegas, she eyed the clock on the rental car's dashboard. It was close to 11:00 p.m. The drive had taken her close to ten hours. She'd learned all over again how dull six hundred miles of road was. At least before, she and Holli had had each other to talk to when they'd done it. This time, she was alone with her thoughts. Memories of that previous trip seeped into her mind—the conversations, the gambling, the nightclubs, and the drinking. She teared up when she hit the black spot where the memories dissolved and the nightmare took over. The wounds were still raw. If she let them bleed before she was ready to face them, she'd never reach Vegas. She put the car on cruise control and did the same with her thoughts. She focused on the road and the changing scenery, listened to the radio and sung along with the songs. She forced herself to live in the moment and not the past. And it worked. She was here—the halfway point.

She navigated her way onto the Strip, and pulled into the parking garage for Caesar's Palace, where they'd stayed before. If she was replicating her movements, it meant overnighting at the same hotel.

"We have you for just the one night," the desk clerk said.

Mall management had given her the week off after taking down Brad Ellis's iPhone thief, but a single night was all she needed for this excursion.

"That's barely enough time to have fun here in beautiful Lost Wages," he said with a smile and a wink.

Zoë bit back the urge to tell him she wasn't here for fun. That would have been an impulsive response, and Jarocki wouldn't have liked that. "I'm just passing through on my way home."

The clerk smiled. "Then you've picked a good pit stop. One night is plenty of time to get into trouble."

"I don't want trouble."

The clerk's gaze lingered on the bruising on her face. Zoë watched potential story lines play across his expression. *Abused wife on the run, maybe? Hooker escaping her pimp?* She almost smiled at the thought. His jovial demeanor collapsed, and he turned businesslike. He handed her two card keys and told her the room number before wishing her a good stay.

Her room was small, and cramped by the presence of two beds. It was the same configuration as last time. She looked out the window at the view, which consisted of the parking structure with the Palms and Rio in the distance. Out there, thousands of people were having fun. The thought depressed her.

"Shake it off, Zoë."

She felt bad for throwing a barb at the desk clerk. Maybe she should have fun. She deserved to celebrate. Jarocki liked to talk of breakthroughs and how she wouldn't necessarily recognize them until they struck. This was striking time. She was claiming her life back.

She tossed her overnight bag on the nearest bed, pulled her things out, and hung up the red minidress she hadn't worn since punching Rick Sobona. She jumped in the shower and washed off ten hours of road and recycled air. She shampooed her hair and styled it to make it more edgy and dangerous. She worked the makeup hard to hide the bruising. The careful application of foundation and blush gave her stunning cheekbones.

Before she slipped into the dress, she examined the blotches of purple and blue mottling both sides of her rib cage where the iPhone thief-not-so-extraordinaire had pummeled her. She stared at the damage before applying concealer. How many times had she picked up injuries like this in the last year? Five? Six? She thought it was closer to nine. They were nothing serious—always superficial. Nevertheless, Jarocki was right. She did put herself in the firing line. No one she knew got hurt as routinely as she did. She blamed it on the fact that people underestimated her. She was female and slight, which made them think she was unsubstantial, a paper target. Those people learned that she was a force to be reckoned with and wouldn't make the same mistake twice. She pulled up the zipper and smoothed her dress down over her hips.

It was midnight when she reached the casino floor. Although it was a weeknight, the casino was bustling. She guessed that if you were in Vegas, you didn't have a day job to wake up to in the morning.

She changed two hundred bucks into chips, although she didn't plan on spending more than half. She couldn't afford to lose more than that.

She hit a packed craps table. She liked craps because of the decent odds and the community spirit. It wasn't long before she had forty bucks on the pass line, a cosmo in one hand, and the dice in the other. People cheered when she rolled and willed her to do well. She liked the thrill of the unknown and the unforeseeable consequences. Each cast of the dice could lead to fortune or ruin.

She rode her luck for as long as she could, but the crazy train came to an end when she threw a seven before her point. Boos and moans followed, and the stickman clawed back all the money everyone had been making during her sweet run. Not all was lost, because she'd pocketed three hundred and fifty dollars before she'd sevened out. That was enough to cover the costs of this expedition.

Just as she walked away from the craps table, two guys in their forties sidled up to her. Both sported the same Men's Wearhouse look, simple dress shirts and slacks. Neither were Brad Pitt in the looks department, but they weren't entirely hard on the eyes either.

"Hey, you're not going, are you?" one of them asked. "The night is young."

She glanced at her watch, which told her it was close to 2:00 a.m. "Yeah, a girl has to get her beauty sleep."

"Have a drink with us first," the other said.

"Why would I get a drink with a couple of strangers?" She smiled to let them know she wasn't being mean.

They smiled back.

"A stranger is just a friend you haven't met yet," the other said.

A stranger is also someone who'll abduct you, hang you from a hook, and lash you with a whip, she thought.

"I'm Jack," the first of them said, "and this is Rob."

"And you are?" Rob asked.

"Zoë."

"The stranger spell has been broken," Jack said. "As new friends, let's toast the occasion with a drink."

She felt the weight of their stares passing over her body. "Why would you want to have a drink with me?"

Rob held a fist of chips. "You won us a lot of money. It's only right to thank you. Blame my Texas upbringing."

"So, what do you say?" Jack asked.

She was going to say no, but then considered how stressful tomorrow was likely to be—finding the places that had wrecked her life and cost Holli hers. Regardless of what she discovered, it was going to be brutal on the soul. A cocktail with strangers would be a nice distraction.

"Why not?"

The three cut across the casino floor to Mark Anthony's. They were trying to impress her. Mark Anthony's was the kind of bar where complex lighting accentuated the extravagant decor, to justify the high prices, and a pair of bouncers protected the entrance. They grabbed a high-top table in the middle of the place.

Their waitress came over the moment they sat. She introduced herself as Jade, a name Zoë suspected was fake. Zoë guessed they were similar in age, although the waitress's makeup made it hard to tell. The black cocktail dress Jade wore was low in the front, backless, and high on the thigh. It was all designed to get men to act like fools and spend recklessly in order to impress. Zoë couldn't really judge. Didn't she wear the same type of outfit, for a similar effect?

"So guys, can I interest you in a cocktail? Our crew can rustle you up anything you care to name. Or, better yet, can I interest you in a bottle service?"

"Champagne," Jack announced. "We're celebrating."

"I can go for that," Rob added. "What do you say, Zoë?"

Neither of them seemed like champagne guys to her, and she certainly wasn't into it. She shrugged. "You said you guys were buying, so I leave it to you."

"Champagne, it is," Jack said.

"I'll bring that right over, guys," Jade said.

"With a glass of water," Zoë said.

She'd snacked during the drive, without a real meal, and she was already feeling the effects of the two cosmos she'd knocked back earlier.

"We're here for the medical-devices trade show," Jack said. "You here for it too? I'm thinking you're a rep. Am I right?"

She was half tempted to tell them she was. It wasn't the first time she'd lied about her profession during a pickup. No one wanted to hear she was a mall cop. Instead, she told them she was just on a minivacation.

Their faces lit up at this reveal. Zoë knew what they were thinking—no blowback. If something sexual happened, it wouldn't hurt their working relationships. She should have told them she was part of the trade show. It would have helped keep them at bay.

The champagne came, and Jade made a big fuss of filling their glasses. They toasted their good fortune. The guys drained their glasses, while Zoë sipped hers. Rob poured refills all around.

Zoë drank more from her water glass than her champagne glass over the next ten minutes. She didn't know what was wrong with her tonight. Normally, she would have been matching the guys drink for drink, but she just didn't have the thirst for it, in more ways than one. She didn't know if it was Jack's and Rob's dull attempts to impress her with their jobs and big-boy toys back home, or the trip she was on that was bringing her down. She had thought a carefree evening at the casino would give her the respite she needed before her journey, but she was wrong. The idea seemed so tawdry and meaningless. She was here to find a killer's lair. Getting picked up by a couple of random guys just didn't play into it. The weight of her stupidity rested heavily on her shoulders.

Smarten up, she thought. *This is the kind of shit that got you snatched in the first place.*

"You know what, guys?" she said, cutting Jack off in the middle of some story about his boat. "I have to call it a night."

Both Jack and Rob hit her with a chorus of nos and expressed their general disappointment.

She hopped off her stool. "Duty calls, guys."

Rob caught her wrist. "Look, stick around. We'll get another bottle, have some fun, and see where the night leads us."

Rob said more but she didn't hear him over the roar of blood rushing through her ears. She went from zero to pissed in an instant. All she saw was his grip on her wrist. His attempt to restrain her. His misguided belief that he had control of her. All she had to do was chop him across the throat with her free hand, and he'd learn how misguided he was.

The simple defense move was in her head, ready and primed to go, but she didn't unleash it. These guys weren't worth it, and she didn't need any trouble. What she needed was to get back to her original plan of retracing her steps. The rage left her in a long exhale.

"Rob, don't make this unpleasant. We all won some money and we had a drink. Now I want to leave."

He snorted. "What if I don't want you to leave?"

She felt the rage bubbling back up. She pushed it down. "If you don't let me go, I'll scream, and that will bring the bouncers, then the cops, and finally, a night in jail."

Rob froze.

"I feel a scream building."

"Christ, Rob, do as she says," Jack said.

Rob released his grasp, and she strode from the bar, never once bothering to turn around.

On the way back to her to room, she reexamined what had just happened. She'd put herself in a vulnerable position and walked away without hurting anyone. She knew what Jarocki would have called it—growth.

*   *   *

Marshall Beck slipped into Zoë's apartment complex unnoticed, helped by the cover of night. He'd been watching the place for the past couple of hours, and he was pretty sure she wasn't in. No lights were on in her residence, and no one had come and gone.

He climbed the stairs to the second floor and strode up to Zoë's door as if he had good reason to be visiting. That was where so many people went wrong. They looked as though they were there for nefarious reasons. It was an easy disguise for him to assume. He wasn't acting nefariously. He was acting with good intent.

He brought out a shave key and slipped it into Zoë's lock. He'd made it himself and practiced on the doors of his home. He had a pick gun too, but he didn't need it. The shave key worked its magic, and he let himself in.

He flicked on the lights. The apartment's floor plan was simple—one bed, one bath, with a living room connected to an open kitchen and dining area. The furnishings, or lack of them, gave the place an uninviting feel. Zoë's place possessed the bare minimum for making a home. In the living room, there was a loveseat and an armchair separated by a coffee table. A TV, not even a flat screen, sat on a stand. The bedroom consisted of just a bed with no headboard pushed against a corner of the room with a nightstand on the exposed side.

This is no single-girl's love nest, he thought.

The place didn't feel feminine. There was nothing ladylike about the furnishings; they were purely functional. And something else was missing. It took him a second to realize what it was—pictures. No paintings or prints gave the rooms personality. No photos gave insight as to whom Zoë held dear. It was such a minor thing, but it made such a difference.

He couldn't decide if the austerity was a sign of Zoë's reformed ways or not. When he'd encountered her last year, she'd been a loud and bawdy party girl. Now she lived like a nun but was a gung-ho rent-a-cop, willing to put her life on the line for a stolen cell phone. But that wasn't strictly true. Rick Sobona's run-in with her clashed with the nun image, as did that skimpy dress he'd seen her wearing the night of Laurie Hernandez's death.

He went into the bedroom and slid back the closet door. Among the mall-security uniforms, he found jeans and T-shirts, workout clothes, and four skintight dresses fit for a slut. He touched one and fingered the material.

"You're a conundrum, Zoë Sutton," he said, closing the door.

He sat down on the corner of the bed and took in this window on Zoë's life. He'd come here purely for scouting purposes, but he'd come prepared to take matters to a final conclusion, if needed. His Taser was in one pocket, as was a chloroform-soaked rag. It would be nothing to take her the second she walked through the door.

But should I?

That had been the big question plaguing his thoughts since seeing her on the news. His investigation had revealed a changed woman. Part of him said let her go. He'd made a difference in her. Besides, there were worse examples of human life out there that needed reeducating.

But . . . there was always a *but*. Those whore dresses in her closet. He couldn't get past those damn dresses. They shrieked of Zoë's failure to reform. If she hadn't changed, after getting a second shot at life by the skin of her teeth, well, she deserved his originally intended outcome.

Pursuing her now came with great risk. The cops were watching her. He couldn't come at her with the same freedom he had with the others, and she wouldn't be a clean kill. The best thing was to leave her alone. He'd left his mark on her, and it was more than just a scar. Forgetting her was the smart move, but he felt his personal pride picking at him. He'd screwed up and she'd gotten away. He needed to finish what he'd started. That was his failing and his strength.

He moved to the living room and waited for Zoë. And he waited. The clock on the cable box went from midnight to 1:00 a.m., then to 2:00 a.m. At 3:00, it was clear she wasn't coming home tonight. He could just imagine what she was up to in one of those *dresses*, with someone like Rick Sobona. That red getup he'd seen on her was missing.

"Where are you, Zoë?" he said with contempt. He had the feeling she'd gone somewhere. He'd dropped by the mall earlier in the day, and she hadn't been there. Had she skipped town? That absent red dress said no. No one skipped town leaving all her clothes but taking her party dress.

Any thought of sparing her left him. He let himself out, knowing he would return.

CHAPTER FIFTEEN

Zoë waited until a couple of hours prior to dusk the following day before leaving Las Vegas. That was when she and Holli had left for home, so it was when she left this time. That meant she'd been forced to spend the day kicking around the Strip, but that had been fine. Vegas had plenty to keep her occupied before she'd begun her long journey of discovery.

She remembered the route they'd started with for their trip back home. It was one of the few things she did recall. They took US 95, which headed to Indian Springs, then threaded between Creech Air Force Base and Death Valley. Eventually, they had planned to cross back into California and return to San Francisco by cutting through Yosemite, a drive that showed the changing landscape of California and Nevada. It should have been fun, not the nightmare it had become.

She had to retrace only the first 250 miles of the 600-mile drive because the police had found her in her wrecked Beetle on US 395, halfway between Mammoth Lakes and Bishop. Confusingly, she'd been heading in the wrong direction, away from San Francisco.

What does that mean?

It meant she'd been doped up enough not to know left from right, north from south. God knows where she'd thought she was going. She replayed the smudged memories of that night. All she remembered was just trying to get away. The shameful thought brought tears to her eyes.

She had used the spot where she'd wrecked as the center of her search. What happened to her and Holli would stem from the point where the cops had found her. How big a radius she was looking at was hard to determine. There were a number of factors to consider. In her dazed condition, how far had she driven from those old sheds? How far had her abductor driven them from the bar they'd been in? Where was the bar? She guessed she was looking at a fifty-to-eighty-mile radius, and she'd drawn the ring on a map that she'd picked up with her rental car. She'd focus her search in that circle. It was a lot of road, but she was helped by the fact that it wasn't a densely populated part of the country. Towns were few and far between in the large expanse of land. However, it made the task no less daunting.

She didn't trust herself to remember the bar just from seeing it from the outside, which meant stopping at every town to check out every bar and restaurant that fell within her search radius. The first town she hit was Big Pine, which turned out to be an Indian reservation. She pulled off at each road sign that pointed to someplace where there could be a bar or a restaurant. It was slow going. The hours slid by, but she didn't let that stop her. Everything else could wait. This was all that mattered.

She eventually came to Bishop. It was a small town but by far the biggest one she'd hit since leaving Vegas. She checked her odometer. She'd racked up over 260 miles since Vegas. She and Holli would have been hungry, low on gas, and only halfway home. It was a likely place for them to have stopped.

She slowed her pace. Bishop was a place out of time. US 395 served as Main Street and its spine, with everything else spreading out from it. From what she could see, it was a tourist town serving as a base for exploring the Sierras. She could envision Holli and her stopping here. It was kitschy, which was right up their alley.

But for all its kitsch and possibility, she didn't remember it. It was as unfamiliar as everything else had been during the drive. She didn't let her lack of recognition deter her. She'd known when she'd started this journey that the whole thing could be a massive blowout, but that was OK. The important thing for her was that she tried and didn't let the past stop her from finding the truth. Bishop meant nothing to her—*fine*—but she had to look under every rock.

She stopped at a place claiming to be a bar, restaurant, and gift shop. She asked for the manager and was met by the owners, a couple in their sixties, as round as they were tall.

She started with her opening gambit, "Do you remember me?"

It was an odd question to hit strangers with, but it got their attention, for better or worse. It had been awkward and humiliating at first, but after a dozen shots at this, the sting had gone.

The couple, Martha and Fred Blanco, shook their heads. She explained the situation and showed them a picture of Holli. That got her more head shakes.

The Blancos offered her a complimentary dinner, but she declined. Time was working against her. Places would be closing for the night in a couple of hours. In lieu of the meal, she asked for the location of all the other restaurants in town. They marked them for her on a tourist map.

She went to The Alley, a bowling alley with a restaurant; La Hacienda, a big Mexican cantina; Lucia's, an Italian place; a German hofbräu, and three other places, and struck out at every one. Nobody remembered her and she didn't remember them.

That changed when she reached the Smokehouse, a barbecue joint. It was a big place for the size of the town. It was a warehouse in scale and shape, but the whitewashed walls and colorful murals softened its appearance. The establishment meant nothing to her on the surface but struck a chord with her subconscious. Her palms were slick with sweat in an instant. Her body was telling her that this place meant something.

"Please don't be a delusion," she told herself and climbed from the car.

She walked in. The Smokehouse was a Wild West saloon on the inside. It had bare wood floors and a long bar. A brass foot rail ran the length of one wall, flanked by high-top tables. Booths resembling horse stalls with high wooden walls filled the other half of the restaurant. Antler and longhorn racks and cowboy garb decorated the walls. A small stage and dance floor were in the back. Country music played. She thought she felt a flicker of recognition, but she couldn't tell if it was genuine or was just the echo of some other barbecue joint or steakhouse she'd visited in the past.

A waitress spotted Zoë and walked up to her. She was short and in her late forties.

"How many, sweetie?"

"Just one, but I have a question first."

"Sure. Shoot."

"My name is Zoë Sutton. Do you remember me at all?"

A concerned expression spread across the waitress's face, and she shook her head.

Zoë ignored the look and plowed on. It paid to keep going. "It would have been fifteen months ago. I was here with my friend." She held up the picture of Holli. "My hair was longer back then."

The waitress kept shaking her head. "Hon, do you know how many people I've waited on in that time?"

"I'm sure we would have been memorable."

"Memorable or not, I don't recognize you."

"But you were here back then," Zoë said, pouncing on the implication. It was one of those things that worked to her advantage. In towns like this, away from the big cities, job turnover wasn't high.

The waitress put her hands on her hips and frowned. "Look, I don't mean to be rude, but do you want to be seated?"

She was losing this woman, and she needed to pull her back in. "I don't mean to take up your time, but it's important. My friend and I were abducted on the way home. I have no memory of what happened. I'm trying to piece together our movements for the police."

She spotted a heavyset guy who was wearing a Smokehouse polo shirt, carrying half a dozen dirty plates, and looking their way. He handed his load off to a busser and headed for them. His frown said she was about to be kicked out. She needed to make an ally.

She pulled out a newspaper clipping and showed it to the waitress. "I got away. My friend was killed. Are you sure you don't remember us?"

Shock entered the waitress's face.

"Do we have a problem, Karalee?" the heavyset guy demanded.

"No, Tom," Karalee said. "She needs help, that's all."

Zoë couldn't tell if Karalee meant general help or mental assistance.

"Are you the owner?" Zoë asked.

"No, the manager."

She handed Holli's photo and the newspaper clipping to Tom and hit him with the bare facts. His gaze remained on the article. She knew how she sounded. She could be a crank, but it was hard to ignore that story.

"What do you want?" Tom asked with a mix of caution and helpfulness.

142

"To ask your staff if they remember me or Holli. Is there anyone here who was working here back then?"

"Three or four of my staff. But look, I don't want you upsetting our customers. As you can see, we're busy."

Despite their size, the place was close to two-thirds capacity.

"I promise to be discreet and quick."

Tom exhaled and said to Karalee, "Sit her at the bar, and I'll send them over one at a time."

Zoë took Tom's hand. "Thank you. You don't know what it means."

"Yeah. Great."

Karalee sat Zoë at the end of the bar. The bartender came over and put a paper napkin down along with a menu.

"This is Andrew. He was here," Karalee said. "Andrew, this is Zoë. She has some questions. Please help her."

Andrew took the cryptic request in stride. "Sure. I can do that. Can I get you something to drink, Zoë?"

"Coffee. I've got a long drive."

"Coffee, I have," he said and retreated to a coffeemaker.

Andrew was somewhere in his thirties and not bad looking. He had an untidy thatch of blond hair, which needed a good brushing, but it worked for him. Zoë put it down to his laid-back manner.

He put a cup before her. "You have questions?"

She slid the clipping over to him. "I'm trying to find out if I was here fifteen months ago. I was traveling with my friend, Holli." She handed him the photo. "My name is Zoë. Someone kidnapped us and killed Holli."

"It says here that she's missing," Andrew said without scorn or judgment in his voice.

"Trust me, she's dead. The cops just haven't found her yet."

He handed back the photo and the clipping. "And you're trying to find her?"

"If I can, but what I'm really trying to do is give the police a better account of what happened. I want to help lead them to the bastard who did this or to anything that'll assist."

Andrew stared at her, expressionless.

"My hair would have been longer then. I was driving a VW Beetle."

"I remember you."

The remark caught her off guard. She was so used to people having no recollection that a positive answer had thrown her.

"You do?"

"I don't remember the date or anything, but I remember you and your friend."

A sudden rush of elation swept through her. This was a start. It was more than that. It was the beginning of the end for *him*—her kidnapper and Holli's killer.

Zoë hoped Andrew wasn't bullshitting her.

"How do you remember us?"

"You both made quite a spectacle while you were here."

She felt herself flush.

"You'd come in from Vegas. You were cash rich and manners poor. You were whooping it up. The two of you hit on every single guy in the room and a few that weren't that single. We had the band in that night, and you ladies got up on the stage for some impromptu karaoke."

She looked over her shoulder at the small stage and dance floor. She tried to picture the events Andrew was describing and saw nothing. She could imagine her and Holli doing things like he described. They'd been playing fast and loose in Vegas. That was the point of their trip. They were letting their hair down and blowing off steam.

"I'm sorry if we were jerks."

Andrew shrugged. "You weren't doing much harm. I saw you as a couple of girls having fun. You did upset some of the diners, but nothing too heavy. You were encouraging others to spend, so the manager liked that."

"Was that Tom?"

"No. Tom's only been in charge three months."

She thought of the people who'd gotten upset. "Did anyone get superpissed at our antics?"

"A couple of families with kids. Some of the older crowd." Andrew tapped the news clipping. "But angry enough to do this to you? No."

Her thoughts took her to the other end of the scale. "Did anyone get friendly with us?"

"You had quite a few admirers."

"Anyone special?"

"Yeah, one—Craig Cook."

The name meant nothing to her. "Is he local? Do you think I could talk to him?"

"Yes and yes."

Craig Cook . . . could he be the one? She played the name over and over in her head. Had she and Holli pushed his buttons, and when he hadn't got what he wanted, he'd taken it anyway? Had he done the same to four other women? Her hands tightened into fists.

"Where can I find him?"

"I'll do you one better. I'll bring him to you." Andrew brought out his cell and dialed a number. "Craig, it's Andrew. You busy? No? Good. Come by the Smokehouse. I have a lady who needs to talk to you. No, it's not like that, man. Get here, ASAP." Andrew hung up. "He's on his way. Get you anything while you wait?"

She ordered an appetizer she had no real interest in eating.

While she watched Andrew attend to the other customers sitting at the bar, an eerie feeling wormed its way into her. He was so smooth and easygoing. Nothing ruffled his nerves. People were normally taken aback when she asked them about her abduction, but Andrew hadn't seemed to be. It had all washed over him. She pictured the Tally Man from that night. The figure with the whip, standing over Holli's suspended body, was tall and blond. Andrew didn't match that drug-addled image. He wasn't big enough, but she could be wrong. In her state of fear, he could have seemed larger than life. People's recollections were often unreliable, and hers were even more suspect since she'd been full of chemicals. Had there really been just one man? Could there have been two? How easy would it have been for a single man to handle a pair of doped women? Not that easy. And how had they been drugged in the first place? Had their drinks been spiked? That wouldn't be an easy thing for a customer to do, but it would be child's play for a bartender. She looked down at her coffee. *Is there just coffee in here?*

She may have just put herself back in the firing line, but she was okay with that. She wanted the police to find whoever had abducted her, and she didn't care how it happened. If these guys were expecting the same Zoë, they were wrong. She had skills now. Skills they wouldn't be expecting. She was a fighter. Not a victim.

A man walked into the restaurant and Andrew waved to him. The man waved back. Andrew came back over to Zoë.

"That's Craig. Remember him?"

Remember him? No. Remember his outline? Yes. He was big, over six feet with broad shoulders and a tight build. His hair was thick and blond. He matched the mental sketch she had from that broken-down workshop.

Anger rose up, hand in hand with fear, which mixed to form panic. Her breaths quickened. A meltdown was coming, but she had to rein it in. She couldn't let them know she was on to them.

Breathe, she thought. *Breathe. Don't give yourself away. Let them believe they have the upper hand. Don't let fear take over. Just breathe.*

Craig smiled at her and dropped onto the barstool next to her. She managed one in return.

"This is Zoë," Andrew said. "She and Holli came through here a while ago. You three got friendly."

Craig creased his expression in reflection, and it didn't look as if he remembered. It was a long moment before his look changed. The smile returned as a grin.

Was it all a game? she wondered.

"Zoë and Holli. I remember you girls. You cut your hair. We had a great night."

Holli and I didn't, she thought and hoped her facade remained intact.

"Is Holli here?" he asked.

"No."

"Shame. You in town for a special reason?"

"Yes. To see you."

She put out her hand. As he put out his, she grabbed his wrist and jumped off her barstool, sending it toppling to the floor. She yanked his arm back and thrust it up between his shoulder blades.

"Hey," he yelped. "What the fuck?"

A ripple of shock and surprise went through the customers.

"Jesus, Zoë," Andrew said.

The disturbance brought Tom rushing forward. Zoë stopped him with a glare.

"Call the cops," she barked at him.

"I knew you were trouble."

"Just do it."

CHAPTER SIXTEEN

The Bishop Police Department was tiny. Zoë had been in doctor's offices that were bigger. Hell, the Smokehouse was bigger. She guessed their force couldn't have amounted to more than half a dozen officers, which wasn't surprising considering the size of the town. She doubted their department was equipped or skilled enough to deal with a killer. She'd told them so, and it had gotten her dumped in the cramped waiting room. That had been hours ago.

Inspector Ryan Greening emerged from a door marked "Authorized Personnel Only." He was in jeans and a T-shirt instead of his usual uniform—a suit.

Zoë leapt from the bench. "Well?"

He frowned at her demand.

She couldn't be too angry with him. He'd saved her. Chaos had ensued at the Smokehouse when the cops arrived to find her pinning Craig Cook to the bar. Accusations flew left and right from her, Cook, Andrew, and Tom. The simple solution was to take everyone in to the station to sort things out. Her claims weren't met by a sympathetic ear. Instead, she was looking at a couple of charges that included disturbing the peace and battery. Thankfully, she'd gone from being classified as a perpetrator to a victim when she got them to call Greening. He told them he'd be straight over, and she'd been confined to the waiting room and a wall of silence. The one surprise had been Greening's appearance all the way from the Bay Area in less than an hour.

"OK, sorry. Please just tell me what's happening?"

"Let's go outside for a minute."

They stepped out onto the street. The night was still and quiet. It was as if the town was holding its breath.

"What's going on?" This time she managed to keep the accusing tone from her voice.

"Nothing. They aren't the guys."

"They must be. Craig Cook was with us the night we were taken. We talked to him. He was close enough to slip something into our drinks. He even looks like the person I remember."

Greening raised his hands to cut her off.

"Sorry. Sorry. What? Just . . . just tell me. Please."

"OK, it's pretty simple. Craig Cook remembers you and Holli. He hit on you two, and you two hit right back. By all accounts, you guys had some fun, then you and Holli left at your own volition, giving Cook a nasty case of blue balls. His phrasing, not mine."

"That's it?"

Greening looked at her with fatherly disappointment. "I could add that both of you were pretty wrecked when you headed for your car."

"No. That can't be right. I'll admit we would sometimes drink and drive but never while we were over the limit—and especially not with how far we had to drive that night. It was him. I know it."

Greening held up his hands. "Trust me, it's not."

"How do you know? It's just his word against mine."

Greening shook his head. "It isn't. He's got an ironclad alibi. He was picked up on a drunk and disorderly less than an hour after you and Holli left the Smokehouse."

She couldn't believe it. Didn't want to believe it. She was no closer to the truth. She wanted to scream, cry, and laugh all at the same time.

"So this has been a gigantic waste of time," she said, disgusted with herself more than anything else.

"No. The one thing we have now is another point on the timeline. According to the bartender, you and Holli left about a half hour before they closed. That was 10:30 p.m. The Mono County Sheriffs picked you up at 5:47 a.m. Whatever happened to you occurred in that window. That's something we didn't know. So well done."

"Please don't patronize me. It's been too long a day for that."

"I'm not. I've been looking into your case, and we have so few details that something seemingly as unimportant as a timeline is a big step forward."

Zoë smiled, then shook her head as she realized something. She should have thought of it earlier, but it was late, and she'd been focused on Craig Cook instead of the bigger picture.

"You got here really fast. You were checking up on me, weren't you?"

"In part, yes. It's just procedure."

"And did I pass?"

"Zoë, it's late. I'll answer your questions tomorrow, but right now, Craig Cook wants to talk to you."

"He does?"

Greening nodded and led her back inside. As he was walking her to the interview room, a uniform was escorting Andrew out. He looked at her with the same unflappable expression he'd displayed earlier. This wasn't true of the cop, who glared at her. She guessed she was guilty of ruining a quiet night in Bishop.

Greening knocked on the interview-room door and the chief of police opened it. Craig Cook sat in the farthest corner with a table in front of him. With his size and the small room, he looked like an oversize kid in elementary school. He also looked ruffled. She guessed he'd gotten a hard time during questioning. The chief pointed to the chair opposite Cook, and she sat down. If Cook was expecting privacy, he wasn't getting it. The chief and Greening remained in the doorway.

"Zoë, they told me what happened to you, and I just want to say how sorry I am. I can't imagine what you and Holli went through. If I had heard about this back then, I would have come forward to tell the police I had seen you that night."

All Cook's bravado was gone, and Zoë felt bad for putting him through all this. "It's OK. Sorry for doing this to you."

"I don't blame you. I would have done the same if I were you. I just wish I knew something that could help the investigation."

"Are you sure you don't? Is it possible you remember some little thing that happened that night?"

He shook his head. "I was pretty buzzed. I just remember having fun."

She reached across and took one of his large hands in hers. His hand tensed, but for only a second, then he gave hers a light squeeze. "Please think. Someone roofied us, and I think it happened at the Smokehouse. Did anyone muscle in on you or get in our face? Or . . . was anyone a little too interested in us? Did you see anyone leave when we left?"

But Cook was shaking his head. "No. Nothing like that springs to mind. To be honest, we were so oblivious that Elvis could have made a surprise appearance and we wouldn't have noticed. I promise you that I'll talk to Andrew and people who were there that night, and if I get anything useful, I'll let these guys know. I really want them to get this asshole."

Craig Cook was a sweet guy. "Thanks."

Greening nodded for her to go. He shook hands with the chief, who promised to stay in touch if he got any leads. Then they found themselves back on the street.

"Is your car still at the Smokehouse?"

"Yes."

"I'll drive you back."

Bishop was so small, it was just a matter of minutes before Greening pulled up behind her rental car.

"So, I guess you being here means you're on a trip down memory lane."

Zoë wasn't in the mood for a lecture. "I know. I'm sorry."

"Nothing to be sorry for. I get it. So what's the plan?"

"To go home."

"Now?"

The dashboard clock said it was coming up on 3:00 a.m. If she left now, she'd get back to San Francisco by rush hour.

"Yes."

"Do you have to be back tomorrow?"

She looked at Greening. She didn't know what he was getting at. "I should be, but I don't have to. Why?"

"Well, we're both here trying to find out what happened to you and Holli, so let's do it together. Let's retrace your journey and see what else we discover."

*   *   *

Marshall Beck let himself into Urban Paws for his nightly visit with Brando. He enjoyed sharing his feelings with the dog. The fact Brando would never betray his confidence made it so much easier for him to disclose his innermost thoughts. Thoughts he even struggled to face himself. He'd never had a relationship with anyone like this before. There'd never been a friend or lover he'd been able to open up to the same way. This was new territory for him—and he liked it.

He let himself into the Assessment Annex. The former fight dogs stirred. Two of them barked but not for long. They were getting used to his late-hour visits. Naturally, Brando didn't react to Beck's arrival.

"Hey, Brando," he said. "Doing well?"

He spoke to the dog like a person and not like an infant. It'd be an insult to treat him as less than a human. He never understood why people used baby talk on their pets. No wonder there were so many animals in pounds.

He unlatched Brando's cage and opened the door. The dog remained inside his pen. That was OK. He'd come out of his own free will when he was ready. That day wasn't far off. Beck was sure of that. Today had been the first time he'd been allowed to work with Brando directly. Tom Fisher and he had worked on techniques to test Brando's temperament and to domesticate him. Brando being Brando had been cool and aloof. Tom had seen it as a problem, as it made it hard to read the dog. Beck had seen it as a display of Brando's self-control.

"I admire you, Brando. You have patience. Patience I wish I possessed, but I bet you're tired of sitting in there. I suppose you'd like to get out of here for a while, yes? I know I'd want to if I were you."

He reached for one of the slip leashes that hung on the wall. They were temporary tethers for the handlers to move the dogs from pen to pen or for prospective owners to walk the animals, before making a decision.

He knelt in front of Brando. The dog remained still.

Beck carefully slipped the leash around Brando's neck. He stood and took up the slack. The dog slowly padded out of the cage.

Beck smiled. "Good. Let's go."

They walked out into the night. It was late, the streets were deserted, and he was tired, but strolling with Brando invigorated him. He was a pleasure to walk. The dog kept to heel. No, heel wasn't right. Brando stayed alongside him the same way a friend or equal would. Yes, he could see Brando getting his reprieve. The dog was a remarkable creature. He wasn't sure he'd be so forgiving if he'd endured what Brando had.

They walked in silence. He wanted the dog to enjoy his freedom and take in the world around him, which he'd been denied for so long. *Get used to it, buddy,* he thought.

After twenty minutes, he started his conversation with his friend.

"Zoë wasn't home tonight. I'm afraid she might have skipped town on me. I don't think so, though. Most of her stuff is still at the apartment. She'll be back, even if it's to collect her things, but it makes me wonder what to do now. Do I stick with Zoë or move on?"

He paused for some reaction from Brando, but the dog kept going.

"Part of me says to move on. It might be all the sweeter to focus on someone else and let Zoë suffer with the uncertainty of whether I'll come for her or not."

A couple coming the other way gave them a wide berth. Their reactions disappointed him. Did they see him and Brando as a threat? They weren't, as long as the couple acted with honor and respect. Or maybe the couple recognized them as alpha males. He liked that.

"Time to get you home for the night," he said and circled the block to take the dog back to the center.

"I can afford to put Zoë Sutton on hold. If she wants to hide for a while, let her. I can wait. I need to focus on someone else. But whom?"

He'd been lucky with Laurie Hernandez. She'd fallen into his lap by displaying contempt for the animals where he worked. He had no one else on his radar. He'd do what he'd done for all the others. He'd fade into the background and observe the world. He'd hang out in the bars and clubs. He'd read the newspapers for evidence of the contemptuous. He'd hunt down the violators and teach them a lesson. Show them there was a price for bad behavior.

He looked to Brando for guidance and found it. They hurried back to the center, and he flicked on the computer in his office. He looked up the dog-fighting case and got the name Javier Muñoz. He was the alleged promoter of the dog-fighting ring. *Promoter* designated him as a professional organizer, as opposed to an amateur hobbyist. Latest reports said Muñoz was out on bail. That put the bastard in his hands. He smiled over at Brando.

After twenty minutes of revving a search engine, Beck had Muñoz's home address in Hayward along with a number of other vital statistics about the dog fight promoter. Beck loved how much of people's lives were readily available these days. It made his work very easy.

"C'mon, Brando. We've got somewhere to be."

He put Brando in his Honda. The dog sat up front as they drove out to Hayward.

Muñoz lived in a crowded and rundown neighborhood, which Beck found surprising. According to news reports, Muñoz made tens of thousands a year from running dog fights. He wondered if his home choice had something to do with image.

He stopped the SUV a half block from Muñoz's house. It was a small ranch-style dwelling with a flat roof. Except for music pouring from one home, Muñoz's, the street was quiet. Most residences were in darkness. The lights were on at the Muñoz home.

He would have liked to have gotten a close-up look inside, but he needed a better handle on these surroundings. He didn't like the close proximity of all the homes. It made it hard to walk up on someone unnoticed. With places that were always in motion, people were too preoccupied to focus on a single person. Quiet neighborhoods were different. Unfamiliar faces always stood out.

That wasn't a problem. A closer scrutiny of the house wasn't vital. He just needed to get a firm grasp of Muñoz's movements, look for an opening, and swoop in when he was at his most vulnerable. Right now, he had a starting point—Muñoz's home. Everything would develop from this place and point him forward.

A white Dodge Challenger roared past them and pulled into the driveway. A short, squat man in his late thirties climbed from the car. It was Muñoz. Beck recognized him from his picture in the news reports.

An ugly growl leaked from the seat next to Beck. He turned to Brando. The dog had been so cool and calm at the center, but here, face to face with his tormentor, he was a tense knot of anger. Beck smiled.

"Don't fret, my friend. You'll get your revenge. We just have to bide our time."

CHAPTER SEVENTEEN

Zoë and Greening stayed the rest of the night in Mammoth Lakes. Greening already had a motel room there, so she'd followed him from Bishop. When they'd arrived, she'd checked into a room of her own and had been asleep within minutes of stretching out on the bed. Greening woke her with a phone call at 9:00. She was up and out of the room in thirty minutes and found Greening waiting by her car. He was wearing a suit again. She guessed he was on the clock.

"You're riding with me today. You can leave your car here. I cleared it with the motel."

Zoë tossed her overnight bag in the trunk of the rental.

"You hungry?"

She nodded.

"Great. I found a good place yesterday."

They drove to a diner, where they got a booth with a view of Mammoth Mountain and ordered breakfasts. Zoë got the feeling that Greening had been working for a couple of hours before he roused her. He would have no doubt been reporting on last night's festivities.

"So you came out here to check up on me?" she asked.

"I'm looking into your case. It can help us with ours and, hopefully, vice versa."

"When did you come out here?"

"Yesterday."

"Have you learned anything?"

"Not much. I'm hoping for better luck today."

The waitress dropped by to refill their coffee cups before moving on to the next table.

"Why is it so important for you to come out here and torture yourself?"

She shrugged. "Because I have to remember what happened to me. That night is a blank. Everyone else can probably tell you more about it than I can, and that pisses me off. I've been meaning to come out and retrace my steps. I tried once before, but didn't have the courage to go through with it. I felt that if I came back and faced it all, I'd be facing what I did—or what I didn't do."

"Which was?"

"I ran when I should have stayed."

"You'd be dead if you had. You know that."

"It's not like my life has been all sunshine since. Dying in order to save Holli would have been the better option."

"Bullshit." Greening's remark came out with sharp edges and no sympathy. "Don't tell me Holli got the better deal. If she were here, she'd make you eat those words. If Laurie Hernandez is any reference, your friend died an ugly death that no one would wish on another person. You lived. Accept it. And love life because of it."

It was oh-so-simple to people like him who didn't understand what she had gone through. Their problem was they didn't comprehend shame's indelible mark and how deep it went. And why would they, unless they'd committed a reprehensible act? Even Jarocki didn't really get it. He'd lived a charmed life. All he knew about shame was what he'd learned in books or from the people he'd studied. Greening and Jarocki and everyone else saw it the same way—like it was a surface issue. *Oh, look—you have some shame on you. Don't worry, it'll come off with a little soap and water.* Shame was one of those things that had to be excised like a cancer, but it was a hard thing to remove when it was wrapped around your heart.

"Did you come out here hoping to run into him again?"

"No. I'm not on a suicide mission. I'm trying to help. Help Holli, Laurie Hernandez, and any other victims."

"And yourself?"

"Yes, and myself. I've hidden from that son of a bitch for too long. I was trying to repeat the trip from Vegas to home, to see if it could provide any clues."

"Like the Smokehouse."

"Yes. I don't remember the place at all, but they remembered me."

Greening shook his head. "And you apprehended Craig Cook, an innocent man. Do you see how dangerous that was? How that situation could have turned nasty on you?"

"But it didn't."

"You saying that concerns me, because that situation did get nasty, and you don't recognize that."

Greening sounded like Jarocki.

"You like to make waves, Zoë." He looked at his half-eaten meal and pushed it away. "Did you think Cook was the guy?"

"In that moment, I did. I saw him and I saw the possibility."

"Our man is in the city. Not out here."

"You don't know that. He could be commuting. Double identities and all that."

"Possible but unlikely. To have picked up Laurie Hernandez the way he did means he studied her. Trust me, he's in the city. Even if he isn't, you can't be so reactionary. It's going to get you hurt."

A lull followed, where they didn't say anything for several minutes.

"Look, I didn't mean to get overbearing or anything," Greening said. "Actually, you retracing your steps is a good thing. It's something I was trying to do, but it's a lot more helpful with you, so what I'd like to do is take you out to where the sheriffs found you and backtrack from there. Sound good?"

"Yes."

"Then let's get out of here."

Greening paid the check, and they hit the road in his car. She noticed him giving her sideways glances.

"What's wrong?" she asked.

"Your face. That bruise. You didn't pick that up last night, did you?"

She couldn't have done a very good cover-up job. "I got that at work. I was disarming a thief, and he clipped me."

"Disarming?"

She told him about the incident with the iPhone thief.

Greening shook his head. "How did you go from a PhD candidate to a mall cop?"

"After what happened, I couldn't go back to school. I needed to do something different, but I didn't have any other qualifications. Mall security was all I could get."

He frowned. "I think you're selling yourself short. You have a degree. I'm sure you could get something that pays better and is safer."

Her degree in environmental sciences gave her options, but none she wanted. "I could get something else, but I like mall security."

He smirked at her.

"Really, I do. I don't want to do a normal job. What the Tally Man did to me changed me. I can't do some nine-to-five gig. I have to do something that makes a difference, and I do that at the mall. I stop bag snatchers, pickpockets, shoplifters, and vandals. I help lost kids find their parents and pick people up when they fall down. I make the world a little better."

His smirk changed into a genuine smile. "You sound like a cop."

She said nothing.

"Did I say something wrong?"

"No. Dr. Jarocki says I should consider becoming a cop."

"Well, if you're serious about making a difference and helping people, give it serious consideration. It's a good career, far better than mall-security work."

"Do you really want someone with my baggage being a cop?"

"If by *baggage*, you mean someone who can empathize with a victim and is willing to do right by them—then absolutely."

Yeah, right, she thought. She studied him, looking for a sign of sarcasm and saw none. His faith in her surprised her.

They were approaching the on-ramp for US 395, the highway she'd been found on. He pulled over before reaching it.

"OK, I'm going to take you out to the spot where you were found. I know things are sketchy on what you remember, so we'll pace ourselves. If anything looks familiar or there's anything you want to see again, you tell me. We can take this as fast or as slow as you need. OK?"

The thought of doing this made her break out in a cold sweat, but she nodded.

They joined the highway, driving way under the speed limit. He drove with his light bar flashing so as not to piss off the other road users.

He told her what he'd read in the police report. It was surreal to listen to him relay events that had happened to her, that she had no memories of. She wanted to have a spark of inspiration, but nothing came.

He asked her to go over events as she remembered them, and he quizzed her on every detail. She slipped from reality back to that night. She didn't see the road. She saw herself, Holli, and the Tally Man. It was the same hazy and incomplete movie she'd played in her mind again and again. It was hard to watch, but for the first time, she wanted to see it all. Suddenly, he slowed the car.

"What's going on?"

"We're here." He stopped the car. "This is exactly where the sheriffs found you."

The revelation slammed into Zoë. Her reaction was immediate and ugly. She broke out in goose bumps, and the strength drained from her body. She struggled to unlatch the door and had to throw her weight behind it to fling it open.

Greening missed the change in her and strode over to a spot off the edge of the asphalt. He consulted the contents of a file folder before gesturing to the ground with both hands. "You ran off the road here, with your car pointing in this direction," he said, gesturing south.

She tottered over to Greening on unsteady legs. It was all too real for her, and her bravado shriveled. She had come here for the truth and to help catch a killer. Now she just wanted to run and hide.

Greening flipped open the file folder again. Reports were clipped to the right-hand side, while eight-by-ten photographs were pinned to the other. He tapped the one on the top of the pile. It showed her Beetle buried nose deep in the ditch, with a uniformed cop standing in the background, a look of disapproval on his face.

Memories of that night came back to her, but only in jump cuts: red-and-blue lights filling her vision, then a blinding light in her face. Silhouettes against the light. The creak of the car door opening. Someone saying, "Miss, miss, are you—? Christ, she's naked." Someone else saying, "This bitch is blitzed." Her screaming and striking out at hands touching her. Men shouting, yelling at her to calm down. Her saying a single word—*Holli*—again and again. Then nothing.

"You OK?" Greening asked.

Zoë wiped a hand over her face. "Yes. Fine."

The cop looked doubtful.

She took the folder from him, creasing the file back on itself to examine the photo. She oriented herself so that she stood in sync with the image.

"Remember anything?"

She shook her head. "Not really."

"The wreck shows that you were coming from the Mammoth Lakes direction and heading toward Bishop. That's the reverse of your trip. You were doubling back on yourself. Can you explain?"

She shook her head again.

"Did you want to get back to Bishop for some reason?"

"I think I was just driving to get away. The destination wasn't important. Sorry, I wish I knew."

Greening sighed. "That's OK. Let's look at it this way. You were heading south. Does that trigger anything?"

"I was so doped up that, for all I know, I could have been driving around in circles before I wiped out here. All I remember was getting in the car, driving, and praying he didn't follow me."

He nodded. Zoë felt Greening willing her to remember. She'd done the same herself, but had long ago given up on having sheer will step up to the plate. The lost memories would either come back or remain erased for all time.

"I believe the place you were taken is somewhere off this stretch of road. Considering the condition you were in, fear and adrenaline would have overcome some of the effects of the Rohypnol, but not all of them. You wouldn't have driven far before ending up in this ditch. I'm guessing ten miles at most in either direction. When you factor in the time you left Bishop, how long it would have taken him to drive you out here and get down to business—"

She winced at his use of the word *business*—a faceless euphemism for torture and murder.

"Sorry," he said.

"It's OK."

"I just want to say that we're close. Really close. Do you want to see if we can find this place together?" he asked with a smile.

"Yes, but the sheriffs did that. They checked out properties in the area and found nothing that matched."

"You couldn't tell them anything the last time. They based their search on where you ended up. They didn't know where you'd come from and where you were going. They had nothing to focus on. We do now. Everything that happened to you, happened to you between Bishop and the road to Mammoth Lakes. So I'll ask you again, do you want to see if we can find this place together?"

"I do."

He turned back to his car.

She remained on the shoulder, staring down the barrel of the road disappearing to the south. It narrowed to a point in the distance, the mountains and hills on both sides moving to swallow it up. This would have been her view that night. She wanted it to be familiar, to spark a memory or shine a spotlight on a feature of a featureless road. The road remained just a road, but it didn't change the fact that everything that had happened, had happened here.

"Zoë? You OK?"

She turned. "Yeah. I think we should go in this direction first."

His expression turned hopeful. "South it is."

They followed the road south, pulling off at every exit and exploring every side road until it dead-ended. They reached the end of the road—Bishop—without finding anything that matched her diluted memories.

Greening drove to the Smokehouse and stopped the car in their lot.

"I don't think they'll be too keen on having us for lunch."

"Most definitely." He was smiling, but his grin quickly fell away. "OK, I want to do things differently on the return sweep. I'm going to talk you through that night, and I want you to fill in the blanks."

She felt the hairs on the back of her neck bristle. "You know how to make me happy."

"I will be trying to push your buttons. I'm not going to apologize for it, because I think it's important and I think you know that too."

"As long as you're willing to pay for my therapy sessions afterwards."

"This is therapy. You should be paying me."

His smile was back. It was such a simple thing, but it gave her confidence. He gave her confidence. Doing this alone scared her, and she knew she might buckle if it got too painful. With Greening here, there was someone to protect her and push her forward.

"OK, let's get this show on the road," he said. "Where did you park that night?"

"I don't know."

Greening drove the car slowly through the lot. "You'd been kicked out of the Smokehouse. You and Holli walked back to your car. Were you alone? Did someone stop you or ask you for a ride? Was someone waiting by your car?"

A flashbulb flared in the recesses of her mind. Her and Holli arm in arm, in the dark, laughing. Then the image faded back into the shadows.

"Did anyone follow you? The roofie would have been in your system and working at this point. You would have been feeling drunker than you should have. Tired. Dazed."

Greening rejoined the road and headed north.

"You were in your car. Were you driving out of town—or was he? If he was, there would have been three of you in the car. Where were you sitting? In the driver's seat? Shotgun? Or in the back?"

The flashbulb went off in her head again. The glare was brief, but the image was clear.

"How about Holli? Where was she?"

"Wait a second. Stop talking."

He did, but kept driving.

"I was driving. Holli was next to me. He was in the back, bunched up because he was tall. Holli offered to swap places with him, but he said no. We were doing him a favor."

She was astounded that she remembered something with such clarity after so much ambiguity and confusion. But in spite of the sharp image that had just come to her, the fog continued to hide what came next.

"So you picked him up?" Greening said with excitement in his voice.

"I don't know. I guess so."

"Did he ask you to drop him somewhere?"

She shook her head.

They reached Bishop's city limits, and Greening kept on driving.

"OK, you're driving on US 395. Holli's sitting next to you. He's in back. The Rohypnol has its teeth into you. You're probably weaving on the road." For emphasis, Greening let his squad car wander across the road before overcorrecting too far the other way. "He probably suggested that he drive."

She clenched her mind tight, hoping for another flashbulb to go off. "Maybe."

"He's driving now. I think Holli is still in the front. You're in back. You and he simply swapped positions."

It sounded plausible, but it failed to ring true.

"You've been driving so long. It's late and dark. You're on roads you don't know. It's probably a relief to let him take over driving duties. Did you sit up or spread out across the backseat?"

Flashbulb, she thought, *please show yourself.* Greening was doing such a great job of re-creating that night with nothing, and she, who had been there, couldn't remember shit. She felt her heart rate gather speed and blood pressure rise with her increasing frustration. "I don't know. I don't remember. Damn it."

"It's OK, Zoë. Don't let it get to you. I don't need the whole picture. I just need enough pieces to assemble the puzzle. Help me find the corners."

He was quiet for the next five minutes. She was too, letting the frustration bleed from her. She kept her gaze fixed on the road, allowing its never-ending view to clear her mind.

As before, Greening pulled off at every turn to follow every secluded road to its end.

"Tell me about his place. What did it look like? Did you hear any strange noises? Did it have a smell? Tell me what you remember."

Abandoning Holli, she thought. *That's what I remember.* She bottled her guilt and pushed it to one side. She could always revisit it later. She always did.

"I woke up in a shack or a big toolshed with a tin roof. Ten feet by twenty, I think. It was full of junk and wasn't new. The floor was bowed with age and the weight of all the crap in there."

"Good. What else?"

She pictured herself naked, having just cut the cable ties binding her wrists and ankles. Reflexively, she rubbed her left wrist where the plastic had cut into her flesh. She was at the shed window, peering out, Holli's screams thick in the air.

"There's another crappy storage shed opposite the one I'm in. The workshop is to my right. That's where he's torturing Holli. It's just as weather-beaten. The lights are on, but the windows are so grimy that the light is dulled." She remembered looking through those small windows. "Stained glass."

"Stained glass?"

"All those little, dirt-covered panes. It was like unholy stained glass on the devil's church."

Greening didn't have an answer for that.

"OK, you escape from the shed. There's another in front of you. The workshop with Holli and him is to your right. You're naked. Hurt. Confused. It's night. What else do you see, smell, hear, and taste?"

"Stars. Lights, I think, way off in the distance. I hear nothing. No car or truck noise. No planes overhead. No voices. I smell the night air—dry and dusty. I smell flowers or trees or something, but I don't recognize them or see them. I don't taste anything."

"You're barefoot. What are you standing on?"

"Dirt."

"Just dirt. No concrete or asphalt?"

"No. Everything was dirt. The road was dirt. Just a track."

Greening stopped the car and pulled out a couple of maps. He marked a couple of places and rejoined the highway.

He changed his tack. Instead of following every paved cross street, he explored all the fire trails and unpaved roads. The Crown Victoria wasn't built for the loose and undulating surfaces. It struggled for grip and bottomed out on its suspension a number of times.

"OK, you've escaped from the shed, and you're standing in the dirt outside," Greening said.

She didn't see the road ahead. She was back in the past. The cool night had been drying the sweat on her body after she'd escaped the oppressive heat of the shed.

"Yes," she said.

"Do you see the mountains in front of you?"

"No," she said, then more confidently, "no. No mountains. Just the horizon."

"But the highway was in front of you."

"Yes. I think so."

He smiled at her. "That means you were on the west side of the highway."

He stopped the car again on the shoulder and pored over the maps, employing his highlighter again. "We're getting closer, Zoë."

They followed the next three dirt roads. They led to dead ends—physically and mentally. No light-bulb flashes and no tin-roofed sheds.

They were losing the light. The sun was over the mountains. She had thought they would be back in Mammoth Lakes before nightfall, but they hadn't even made it halfway.

Greening jammed on the brakes. The car slithered to a halt on the shoulder. An eighteen-wheeler leaned on its horn as it roared by.

Greening grabbed the map and spread it open. He ran his finger between places he'd marked and pointed across the road to a rough-looking track. A thick chain hung slack between a couple of rusted posts no more than a few feet high, preventing access. There was no signage advising anyone to keep out or indicating authorized access only. Anonymity was its only message.

"That track isn't on this map."

Zoë stared at the chain, then followed the trail with her gaze. "It doesn't look familiar."

"Let's make sure."

Their vehicle darted across the road and ground to a halt in front of the hanging chain. She jumped from the car to unhook it, but it was padlocked in place.

"It's locked," she called back to him.

"Take up the slack," he yelled.

She grabbed the chain and pulled it as taut as she could. He eased his cruiser forward until the push bars on the car stretched the chain tight across them. She let go, and he let the Crown Vic roll, putting pressure on the barrier. He gassed the engine, and one of the posts popped out, dropping the chain to the ground.

Zoë jumped back into the car. "Not much of a security system."

"It was never meant to be. Too much security draws attention. Not enough and everyone ignores it."

Greening's Crown Vic bounced and bumped over the rough road. It snaked left and right for a quarter of a mile before going into a gentle rise, which soon turned into a gentle descent. The trail kept going and going, running somewhat parallel to the mountains and the highway.

Zoë had an eerie feeling. There was no flashbulb this time, but the distance from the highway spooked her. It was the same feeling she'd had when she'd stepped from that shed. The feeling that she was isolated from the world. She looked over Greening's shoulder at the flat landscape stretching out to the horizon. *Is this it?*

They rounded another curve and Greening took his foot off the gas. "Zoë, look."

"Oh my God."

The outbuildings were no longer there. Just the flattened remnants of what had been three structures, first crushed by force, then left to the elements to corrode and be hidden with dirt.

Zoë jumped from the car, before Greening brought it to a halt, and ran up to the remains. There were the tin roofs and the shattered windowpanes. The orientation was as she remembered it. It was possible these could be three other buildings, but the panicked way her heart was beating told her she wasn't wrong. She turned to see Greening rushing toward her. She pointed to the ground she'd once been forced to stand on barefoot. "This is the place."

CHAPTER EIGHTEEN

"I think we've got something" was all Greening had said to bring in the cavalry.

Over a dozen Inyo sheriff deputies, detectives, and crime-scene officers covered the remains of the Tally Man's kill site. Greg Solis from Mono County Sheriff's Department was there. Zoë hadn't seen him since her abduction. He didn't look pleased to see her again. She knew why—jurisdictions. She might have been found in Mono County, but the Tally Man had done his work in Inyo County. No wonder they hadn't found this place. Nobody was looking over the county line. She could play the blame game, but she was interested in only one thing: Were Holli and the other victims buried here?

In the failing light, the cops were staking out a perimeter around the remains of the three buildings and hurriedly erecting lights. Greening was deep in conversation with the sheriff and two other men no one had bothered to introduce her to. He had dumped her in his car like an inconvenient child, while he did his grown-up cop thing.

Watching them work, she wondered what they would find under the rubble. She hoped she wouldn't get to see.

Greening broke away from his meeting and slipped into the driver's seat. "OK, I'm going to have one of the deputies drive you back to the motel. I'm probably going to be here for another day, maybe two, but you're free to go home."

"Why are you sidelining me?"

"Zoë, please. You know you can't be involved. You're a witness."

And a suspect, she thought. More than a couple of the deputies had given her sideways looks. After all, these were the guys who'd first blown her off as a wasted party girl, then someone who'd offed her friend.

"Look, I don't get to decide. It's their jurisdiction. Their crime scene. I'm just an observer."

"But you're staying."

"Just because there's crossover between our cases. That's all. They're probably going to kick me out of here in a little while. If you're going to stick around tonight, I'll catch up with you in a couple of hours, and I'll update you with what I can."

She wouldn't stay. She had a long drive ahead of her, but if she left now, she'd be home before midnight. Besides, Greening was putting up the big blue wall that kept noncops out.

"I think I'll go home. Can you at least tell me what's going on?"

"Procedure. They're going to button the scene down tonight and start picking this place apart tomorrow. They're bringing in some special equipment to help examine the area."

"For what?"

Greening's expression turned guarded. She knew what they'd be looking for. She looked over at the deputies working the scene.

"Do you think she's buried out there? That maybe they're all buried out there?"

"I don't know. They'll search the area with ground-penetrating radar and bring out the dogs."

She appreciated his omission of the term *cadaver dogs*. "I hope you find them."

Greening said nothing for a long moment. "I do too. I'll get you that ride."

He climbed out of the car and rustled up a uniform to drive her back to Mammoth Lakes. When he approached with the officer in tow, she got out to meet them.

"Deputy Beatty here will drive you back to the motel. I'll be in touch tomorrow. The Mono Sheriff's may need another statement from you, but they'll probably have you give it back in San Francisco."

She listened to the blah-blah-blah and pat-on-the-head talk. Greening must have picked up on her mood, because he took her hand.

"Zoë, don't feel you're being excluded. You helped today. We're one step closer to finding this guy because of you."

*   *   *

Interdepartmental help went as far as a "thanks, and don't let the door hit your ass on the way out" for Greening. Now he knew how Zoë felt when he'd brushed her off. If he removed his stung emotions from the equation, it wasn't that bad. The Mono sheriff and Deputy Solis were cordial and grateful, but they planned to stick to the jurisdictional rule book. They were keeping him in the loop, even if they wouldn't let him play in the sandbox. All niceties aside, he did detect a little irritation from them for discovering the crime scene. No one likes having their professional abilities shown up by someone else.

He couldn't complain too much. They'd be the ones working the scene all night, while he got to write up his report at a reasonable hour. Shown the door, he drove back to Mammoth Lakes. Zoë Sutton's car was gone from the motel lot when he arrived. It was a shame she'd left. He would have liked to have smoothed things over with her. She was the key to this case.

He let himself into his room with his cop-on-the-go dinner: burger, fries, and a Coke from Carl's Jr. He could have gone out for a sit-down meal with his per diem, but he never liked eating alone.

He dumped the food on the room's desk, slipped off his jacket, and kicked off his shoes. He took a bite out of the burger. It tasted pretty damn good. He couldn't decide if it was because of the altitude or the fact he hadn't eaten since breakfast.

He waited until he was halfway through his meal before calling Ogawa to fill him in. Ogawa wasn't impressed that he'd spent the entire day with Zoë, but he'd told him to get close to her, so he couldn't really complain. Keeping her close was the way to go. Her history said she was volatile, and she was no good to the investigation if she was in a combative mood.

"She found the site." He held off saying *the kill site*. At this point, there were no bodies.

"After all this time, she suddenly remembered where it happened?" Ogawa said.

His skepticism was hard to miss. Zoë still had a ways to go before winning him over.

"It was more the process of elimination. We hit every road until we came across this one. I didn't need her to tell me this was the place. It matched the one from her statement from last year."

"I don't like that she was out there."

"She wants answers."

"Or she's covering her ass."

Greening returned to his food and picked up a fry. "So, you don't trust her."

"There are too many unanswered questions. She's far from being cleared from our investigation."

Greening smiled. He liked working with Ogawa for this reason— he didn't trust a single soul. "So what's your assessment of her?"

"I don't have one because there are too many possibilities," Ogawa said.

"Something happened to this girl fifteen months ago. There's been a distinct personality and life change. But I can't find a connection with Laurie Hernandez."

"Ms. Sutton is far too interested in throwing herself into our investigation for my liking."

"OK, but why is she interested in our investigation? If she killed Holli Buckner and wanted to stay off our radar, she simply had to keep her mouth shut. We wouldn't have made any connections between Laurie Hernandez and her, or any other potential victims."

"And that's what I don't like. We've been led on a merry dance since this woman busted into our crime scene. You are only where you are because of her."

Ogawa had a point.

"When do you think you'll be back?"

"I'll check in with the sheriff in the morning and then head out."

"How are the mountain boys in blue treating you?"

"Like a distant cousin."

"Another reason for you to get your ass back here. Look, I don't have anything against this Sutton woman, per se. At this point, I can't implicate her and I can't dismiss her, so she's a problem that needs cleaning up. Now, to do that, I suggest you go through the case and her accounts and look for inconsistencies."

Greening hung up on his partner. Ogawa was a son of a bitch. A healthy mistrust of people was a handy weapon for every cop, but Ogawa took it another step. Greening wasn't quite sure of Zoë, but he'd been pretty sure she was the victim and not the perpetrator. Now Ogawa had him thinking his way. Plenty of things pointed toward her innocence, but Zoë's situation was so vague in places, he didn't really know what he had.

He threw out the rest of the fast food and brought out his maps. He marked the location of the Tally Man site with a Sharpie, then traced with a green highlighter the roads from the Smokehouse in Bishop to the site. Lastly, he indicated in orange highlights Zoë's escape route, to where she'd crashed. He sat back, trying to make sense of what he'd charted.

Zoë had followed the winding track back to US 95, driven north to Mammoth Lakes, and somewhere along the way, had pulled a U-turn in order to crash in the southbound lane of the highway. Yes, Zoë had been in no condition to drive, and it wasn't surprising she'd ended up turning around and running off the road. However, it was odd that after she'd escaped the Tally Man, she'd crashed less than five miles from his lair. If Greening squinted at this picture through Ogawa's jaded eye, it looked as if she'd been driving back to the scene of the crime.

*   *   *

Crossing the Bay Bridge into San Francisco, Zoë was reminded of how overpopulated and impatient the Bay Area was. Even at this late hour, everyone was driving too close and going too fast. In the two days she'd been away, she'd adjusted to the isolation outside California's big cities and had been able to be alone with her thoughts. Squeezed onto the bridge with hundreds of others, all she could think of was not being hit by cars weaving in and out in front of her.

The drive back had been good for her. The solitude had helped her decompress and lose the resentment she'd felt when Greening had kicked her to the curb. He was right. It was out of her hands. She'd done her part. She'd been the sniffer dog and rooted out a clue. It was down to the cops to do something with it. She'd hold Greening to his word and pressure him for updates.

The solitude had also given her an opportunity to mourn for herself and Holli. That night had always straddled the line between reality and nightmare. Had she really been abducted? Had she actually seen Holli dangling from a hook? Had she really escaped a killer? She'd known how the Mono Sheriff's Department felt about her—that she'd made the whole thing up while in a drunken stupor. Finding those outbuildings meant it was real. It had happened. It also meant she truly had abandoned Holli.

That single thought preoccupied her through most of her drive and took the urgency and aggression out of her driving. She let the other cars swarm around her. They could have their extra foot of real estate. She would get home when she got home.

She came up on the entrance to her apartment complex and hit the remote. The gate slid back, and she squeezed through. It was too late to return the rental tonight. She parked next to her motorcycle and carried her bag up to her apartment, then let herself in and flicked the lights on. Dulled by the long drive and the emotional rollercoaster she'd been on, it took her a moment to realize something about her place was off. She couldn't put her finger on it. She walked into the living room and stopped. Nothing was out of order, but nothing felt right, as if everything had been moved, then put back in the exact same spot. Then she realized what was wrong—she could smell the faint odor of cologne.

It took her only a matter of seconds to realize her mistake, but the damage was done. The door had closed behind her, cutting off her escape. One hand was still holding the handle of her roller bag, and her mind wasn't in a defensive mode. She'd handed her intruder all the edge he needed. He came at her from her bedroom, entirely in her blind spot.

"Shit."

She had enough time to drop the bag and spin around to see a large black-clad-and-gloved figure, wearing a ski mask. She didn't know why he'd bothered with the ninja disguise. She knew exactly who was hiding under the mask. The Tally Man had caught up with her at last. He charged at her with a Taser outstretched. She chopped her hand across his forearm, sending it flying across the room.

It landed far from both of them. She sorely wanted it, but she wouldn't rely on it.

She might have disarmed him, but it didn't stop his momentum. He slammed into her, wrapping his arms around her and driving her forward into the armchair. The chair back chopped her across the stomach, exploding the breath from her, but it also stopped her from crashing to the ground, which would have given him all the advantage he needed.

The impact drove the armchair forward a few inches on the carpet. With his weight on top of her, she was forced onto her toes—but so was he. He was off balance. She pounced on her good fortune and smashed her foot down on his. Her running shoes deformed over a steel toecap. He'd come prepared. She was in real trouble.

He laughed.

His arrogance would be his downfall. She fired an elbow into his gut. His laugh turned into a groan, and he staggered back a step.

The pressure was off her body. Air rushed into her lungs, dulling the pain across her stomach. With no time to rest, she spun around to drive the heel of her hand into the underside of his chin. Instead, she met his backhand. With his size and weight advantage, he whipped her head violently to one side, sending her flying and crashing to the floor.

She didn't stand a chance on the ground. She was done if he got to her. She scrambled to rise, but only managed to get to all fours before he kicked her in the stomach. Starlight exploded in her vision as air was vacuumed from her lungs. Recovery moves and defense strategies filled her brain, but her body betrayed her, and she deflated under the punishment.

Come on, Zoë, she thought. *You're better than this.* It was a rallying cry she believed but that her body did not.

He staggered toward her, rubbing his stomach.

Keep on coming, she thought. *Let him think he's won.* That was the key. She still had options. Her strength was returning one ragged breath at a time, but she feigned serious injury. She raised her legs, bending them at the knee, and moaned. It looked good. It looked real. She was ready for him.

He reached into his pocket and brought out a wadded rag. She didn't have to be told what was on it and what it was for.

When he got within range, she shot out a leg, smashing him in the groin. She felt her foot connect with a cup. She didn't hurt him, but it did repel him.

He was way too prepared. Way too practiced. Way too frightening.

She scrabbled away on her back using the armchair as a barrier between them.

He was moving in when someone banged on the door.

"What the fuck is going on in there? People are trying to sleep."

Her assailant turned toward the door. Zoë saw her opportunity, rolled over, and lunged across the carpet for the Taser. "Help! Call 911," she yelled.

The door opened and in the doorway stood her neighbor from downstairs. She didn't know his name. His appearance created an awkward dilemma for her attacker—who to disable first, Zoë or her neighbor?

He chose Zoë. It was obvious her neighbor was no match for him. He charged at her, and she snatched up the Taser. Before she could get to her feet, he kicked it from her outstretched arm.

"Hey," came a feeble cry from her neighbor.

The intruder dropped on top of her, pinning her arms to the ground with his knees. She peppered his back with knee blows but just didn't have the power or reach to have a real impact.

He smashed her with a right hook that took the fight out of her. "You've done so much better this time around, Zoë," he said with real admiration in his voice.

He put his hands around her throat and squeezed. He was applying pressure to all the right spots. She knew she'd black out soon if she didn't break his grip. She wrenched at his hands, then clawed at his face but couldn't reach. She felt a buzzing in her head and the world collapse in.

"This isn't over. I still need to cross you off my to-do list."

CHAPTER NINETEEN

Zoë exploded back into life to the sound of voices around her and hands upon her. An intense light was in her face, obscuring everything and everyone. She screamed and struck out in all directions, occasionally making a connection.

"It's OK," a voice bellowed over her screams. "You're safe."

She paused for a second. Her hands remained balled into fists, ready to lash out at the hint of a wrong move from any of them.

"Get that damn light out of my face."

"Sorry," a voice said, and the light was extinguished.

Her eyes adjusted and faces came into focus. Two EMTs and two uniformed cops surrounded her.

The female EMT said, "We need to examine you. OK?"

Zoë nodded.

While the EMTs worked on her, the cops questioned her. She had only one question for them. "Did you catch him?"

"No," was the crushing yet simple answer.

"Did you know your attacker?"

Yeah, I know him, just not his name. "It was the Tally Man. You need to contact Inspector Ryan Greening."

"The Tally Man. You're sure about that?" the cop said.

"Look, we need to get her to the hospital," the male EMT said.

"Wait a second," the cop instructed.

"Of course I'm sure. Get Inspector Greening. He knows me."

"OK, I'm coming with you to the hospital."

The EMTs put her on a gurney despite her protests and wheeled her out. There'd been a cop on the door to keep her neighbors away. He was forced to clear a path for the EMTs. She hated the stares and questions.

"Vultures," the female EMT murmured when they got clear of the onlookers. They rolled her to one of the two ambulances.

"I don't need two ambulances."

"The other one is for your neighbor," the male EMT said. "That asshole tipped him over the railing."

She closed her eyes and shook her head. She couldn't have another death on her conscience. "Is he . . . ?"

"He's OK. He has a broken leg, but he'll be fine."

They bundled her into the ambulance with the cop who'd done the questioning. They took her to San Francisco General, and a doctor checked her out in the ER. She found bruising and minor abrasions but no broken bones or concussion. Once the doctor gave her the all clear, she was put in a private room with the officer.

Just as he was finishing taking her statement, two inspectors and an evidence tech arrived. The cop and the inspectors talked in the hallway while the tech went over her the way a gorilla grooms one of its own. He took nail scrapings, examined wounds, and took her clothes. She knew the process was a waste of time. The Tally Man was too good at his craft. She hadn't gotten a piece of him and he hadn't left a piece of himself on her.

The inspectors reentered her hospital room.

"I'm Inspector Sean Dwyer, and this is Inspector Joel Arnold," Dwyer said. "Could you tell us about tonight?"

She wasn't in the mood for another round of pointless questions. "I want to speak to Inspector Ryan Greening."

She got Ogawa instead. It was an hour before he arrived, forcing her to suffer through small talk with Dwyer and Arnold. He took a seat next to her bed, while Dwyer and Arnold leaned against the walls.

"Was it really him?" he asked. His tone was cool and calm, but she felt little warmth and compassion.

"Yes."

"You sure?"

"Of course I am. He called me by name and said I put up a better fight than last time. Who else would it be, for Christ's sake? I don't believe in coincidence. Do you?"

Someone knocked at the door. Dwyer opened it, and David Jarocki appeared.

The sight of Jarocki in the doorway confused Zoë. "Dr. Jarocki, why are you here?"

Dwyer looked to Ogawa, and Ogawa nodded. Dwyer held the door open for Jarocki, and the psychologist walked in. Then the pieces fell into place, and she glared at Ogawa.

"I asked Dr. Jarocki to come by. I thought you could use his help."

She saw through Ogawa's lie. It was for his benefit that he'd brought in Jarocki. He was there to calm down the crazy girl if she got out of hand.

"Do you want me to stay, Zoë?" Jarocki asked.

She nodded.

He smiled, then pulled up the remaining chair in the room and sat down on the side of the bed, opposite Ogawa.

He looked her over. She felt his gaze land on her ever-growing collection of injuries. She'd become the universe's punching bag of late.

"Are you OK?"

"Yes. I fought back."

He smiled a pained smile and took her hand. "I'm glad, but I wish you hadn't needed to."

Ogawa cleared his throat. "I have a few more questions."

Jarocki released her hand.

"You say it was *him*, but how did he find out where you lived? Are you living in the same place you were when he abducted you before?"

She shook her head. Moving had been one of her first priorities after the abduction. She'd moved to hide from him. She'd moved to hide from everyone. "I was still in school at Davis when he abducted us, and I've been very careful about what public information is out there about me."

"So how did he find you?" Arnold asked.

It was the one thought that kept replaying over in her head. He knew who she was, and he knew where to find her. Her hand went to the scar where he'd marked her. In his mind, she belonged to him, and he would take what was his.

"I don't know."

"Probably the same way I did—the TV," Jarocki said. "We all saw Zoë gate-crash Laurie Hernandez's crime scene on the news. He probably did too and recognized her, then went from there to track her down."

"We never gave out Zoë's name to the press."

She remembered some Ben Franklin quote about secrets and that they could be kept only if everyone was dead. There was no such thing as an airtight seal when it came to secrets.

"You have some housekeeping to do, Inspector," she said.

Ogawa frowned.

"I do have to correct you, Inspector," Jarocki said. "You have a much bigger issue than how the Tally Man found Zoë tonight."

Ogawa winced. "I'd prefer you didn't use that name."

"Catch him, and I won't have to," Jarocki said with a smirk.

"What's the bigger issue, Doctor?"

"Keeping Zoë safe from him."

Zoë didn't know if that was possible. He'd proved he could get to her at any time.

"The doctors want to keep you in for observation tonight," Ogawa said to Zoë. "You'll have a police guard at all times."

"And after that?" Jarocki asked.

Ogawa looked embarrassed. She guessed what was coming.

"You can't protect me, can you?"

"The harsh reality is the SFPD isn't in a position to offer around-the-clock protection. We can do something short term, but long term . . . "

It isn't like the movies, she thought. She made eye contact with each of the police officers. To their credit, none of them looked away. All they offered her was their condolences.

"So what do I do? Let him take another swing?"

Ogawa frowned. "No. You have to take precautions."

"Precautions," Jarocki blurted. "You're the police. You're supposed to be the precautions. Protect and serve. That's your job, for Christ's sake."

Zoë liked seeing Jarocki lose his temper. She hadn't been sure he was capable. It was nice to see he was human, after all.

Ogawa raised his hands in surrender. "I know it's not good enough, but that's the limit of our power. It doesn't mean we won't help you."

"So what do I do?"

"Naturally, you can't go home. Like you say, he knows where you live, and he's proved he can pick a lock. We'll put you up in a motel for the short term."

"What's the short term?"

"A couple of days."

"A couple of days? Jesus," Jarocki said.

"There are charities and private groups that specialize in providing support in these situations, and they can probably cover a week in a motel."

"That sounds great, because you'll have this guy in jail in a week, right?" she said.

No answer.

"Don't do me any favors, guys. You know this guy is hell-bent on killing me, yeah?"

"Zoë, please. I understand your frustration."

He didn't, but she kept from telling him so. As Jarocki had drummed into her, lashing out solved nothing. Ogawa knew the situation sucked, and their powers were pitiful. She would eat her rage for now and use it when it was more practical.

"What do you suggest then?"

"Get out of town. Do you have family or friends you can stay with?"

"That's the best you can come up with? Stay with someone and put them in danger?"

"You'd be surprised how effective it is," Arnold said.

She doubted that. "So, I leave town. What about my job?"

"If he knows where you live, there's a good chance he knows where you work too," Ogawa said. "I would suggest you take a leave of absence."

"You know where I work. It's not the kind of job that comes with a leave-of-absence option."

"I can talk to the mall and smooth things over. I'm sure they'll be understanding."

"You don't know how mall security works."

"So, you lose your job. It's better than losing your life," Dwyer said.

He was right, but it didn't stop her from wanting to hit him with a palm drive to the sternum. Asshole.

"So, the upshot of all this is leave town, lose my job, and start over, while he gets to carry on doing his thing. That's just what every victim wants to hear."

Ogawa sighed. "I'm sorry, but that's the way it is sometimes. It won't be that way forever. You can come back after we catch him."

"*If* you catch him. He's been doing this shit for a long time. That means he's good at it, and I could be living the rest of my life always looking over my shoulder."

"Maybe. I won't promise you anything. I can only focus on the achievable at this point—and for now, that's finding you a safe house. Could you stay with family—your folks or siblings, maybe?"

The mention of her family took the sting out of her. She'd pushed them away since her abduction. Maybe this was the time to reach out, but she wasn't about to put them in danger. He'd found her. He'd find her again. She wouldn't do that to her parents.

"We aren't in contact."

She saw Ogawa about to say something but change his mind. "That's fine. What about friends?"

A wave of embarrassment swept over her. There were no friends. Not anymore. Just like with her parents, she'd thrust them aside. It was just her against the world. She knew she'd done this to herself, and she suddenly felt sad for her pathetic little life. The Tally Man hadn't been the only person who'd damaged her life. Suddenly she was the one who couldn't make eye contact with anyone in the room.

"No, there's no one."

Ogawa sighed. "OK, let me talk to the groups that help us in these sorts of situations. I'm sure they'll have someplace that you can use."

"There's no need," Jarocki said. "I have a family place in Napa that Zoë can use for the duration."

She turned to him and thanked him with real gratitude.

"It's not much, but it'll be safe. No one will think to look for you there."

"That's very generous," Ogawa said. "We'll keep you here tonight and move you in the morning. I know it might not seem like it, Zoë, but we will keep you safe."

*   *   *

Marshall Beck let himself into Urban Paws. After his failed abduction of Zoë, he craved the quiet and stillness of the center. He went into the Assessment Annex, unlatched Brando's cage door, and sat against the wall in his usual spot opposite the dog. Brando remained sitting, strong and stoic.

"I didn't get her," he said to the dog. "She's a different woman. Far more accomplished than before. I had the upper hand, though—the element of surprise, superior strength, and skill. A neighbor ruined it for me tonight. It's those little things you can't control that ruin everything. That's the problem with cities. Too many people. Too many variables. That's why rural areas are better. I have control over the environment."

He looked to Brando for a reaction. The dog gave him nothing. Or was he wrong about that? Did he see a flicker of disappointment in his eyes? Had Brando smelled the stink of failure on him? He knew he smelled it on himself.

"Yes, I'm making excuses. I'll do better next time. And yes, there will be a next time."

Brando gave him no encouragement. No wag of the tail. No whimper or bark. Beck liked that. The dog was a stern friend. No commiserations. Just silent faith.

He pushed himself to his feet. "Shall we go for our walk?"

He grabbed a slip leash off the wall. Brando padded over to him in anticipation, and he looped it over the dog's neck. He walked the dog out of the center and onto the streets. There was a smattering of people. They gave the large pit bull a wide berth. They needn't have bothered. Brando wasn't dangerous. He just wasn't intimidated by his environment. The dog trotted alongside him—so much so that the leash hung slack in his grasp to the point of being unnecessary. Brando was dominant but not aggressive. He wouldn't lash out unless provoked, and only a fool would provoke him.

He walked Brando down to Union Square, then over to Chinatown and up to Nob Hill before returning to the center. It was a good walk. Brando behaved well and was a pleasure, as always. Yet, as Beck stood with the key out to slide into the center's lock, he paused. He was unsatisfied. He'd set out to do something, and it had fallen apart. He wasn't ready to call it a night. He couldn't take a second run at Zoë right now. She'd be at the mercy of the doctors, then the cops. She was off-limits for the short term. Still, he wasn't satisfied. He needed to end his day with an achievement.

He looked down at Brando and realized where they needed to go.

* * *

Beck put Brando in his Honda Pilot and drove out to Javier Muñoz's home in Hayward. The lights were on in the house, but Muñoz's Challenger wasn't outside. He continued on to Muñoz's other haunts—a couple of houses in Hayward, a bar in Union City, and a strip club in San Francisco—but struck out at each one. He finally found the Challenger parked in Fremont, outside the warehouse that was the front for his dog-fighting operation.

He couldn't believe Muñoz had returned to the scene of the crime. He supposed once an asshole, always an asshole.

There were no other cars around, so this wasn't a fight night. He wondered why the promoter was here. He turned the SUV around and parked a few blocks from the entrance to the warehouse.

"Stay here a minute," he said and patted Brando on the neck. He felt knotted muscle and tension. "You remember this place, don't you, boy? Plenty of bad memories. I know. I get it. Don't worry. No one is sending you back."

He climbed from the SUV and walked toward the Challenger. The area was dead. The occasional derelict vehicle sat silent, but there was little else. The streets were so quiet he could hear the hum of the streetlights. The seclusion was the reason the area worked so well for Muñoz and his dog-fighting ring. And seclusion would be the reason tonight would work so well for him.

He stopped by Muñoz's car. He listened for a moment, then smeared the contents of a dog-poop bag over the driver's door handle. The shit had been happily provided by Brando during their walk.

Tying off and repocketing the bag, he went in search of Muñoz. He gained entry into the building through a boarded-over door. The place had been a factory of some kind in a past life. He found himself in the office area, judging by the rotted partitioning and open studs. It stunk of piss. He guessed he was standing in the holding area where Muñoz had kept the dogs. He waved a penlight at the ground. There were no signs of previous pens or cages. No doubt the cops would have taken everything as evidence, leaving only the smell.

He listened for noise and heard faint movement deep inside the building. He threaded his way through it until he reached the factory floor. Over fifty thousand square feet of open space stretched out in front of him, punctuated only by steel support columns. This would have been where they trained the dogs and held the fights. Nothing provided any indication of that now. The place was bare except for trash and rubble on the cracked floor.

He spotted Muñoz waving a flashlight over the debris. It lit up what was left of his business—namely nothing. He rooted around in the mess and muttered to himself in Spanish.

Beck couldn't decide whether Muñoz was searching for something or examining the wreckage of his enterprise for a possible reboot. It was academic. There'd be no do-overs or restarts. It all came to an end tonight.

He'd seen enough. He'd learned what he wanted to learn. Muñoz was alone and isolated. He backtracked his steps to the entrance of the factory, used a concrete pillar to conceal himself, and waited for Muñoz to appear.

Twenty minutes later, he emerged. He had a funny gait. He pressed forward with his head down and his arms swinging. His thick build and squat size reminded Beck of a fire hydrant.

Muñoz reached his car and grabbed his shit-covered door handle. He jerked his hand away and examined it under the glare of his flashlight.

"*Que la chingada,*" he snarled.

Beck laughed.

Muñoz swept the flashlight in his direction. He stepped out into the beam's path.

Muñoz held up his hand. "You think this is funny, asshole?"

Beck laughed again. "Very."

"Will you be laughing when I make you lick it off?"

Beck backed up a step, then broke into a run, retreating in the direction of his waiting Honda. He turned back when he heard the patter of Muñoz's feet. The piece of filth ran with a stunted and clumsy gait, which was no match for his longer and more developed stride, from years of being a runner. He knew that he had the measure of Muñoz in a footrace. It was why he'd parked the vehicle four blocks away.

"Don't think you can get away, fucker."

"I have no intention of getting away," he said to himself with a grin as he reached his car.

"I've got you now."

Muñoz didn't. He was still over a block behind, beating a flat-footed tattoo on the asphalt.

"No, I've got you," Beck said. He yanked open the passenger door and said simply, "Take him down."

Brando burst out and pounded the pavement with his powerful legs. His acceleration as he zeroed in on Muñoz was a thing of beauty to observe.

Muñoz stuttered to a halt before turning tail. Beck grinned. He wondered if the dog promoter knew he'd been played. Did he realize he'd been drawn out into the open, far from the safety of his car, so that Brando could have his revenge? Beck doubted it. Deductive reasoning probably wasn't in his skill set.

Brando caught his tormentor before he'd gotten sixty feet. The dog slammed into the man's back, driving him to the ground. The second he was down, Brando lunged on his prey.

Muñoz screamed out for help. He raised his arms to protect himself, but Brando simply bit the hands that had previously forced him to fight to the death. The night was filled with more howls and pleas, which would go unanswered.

Beck reached inside the glove compartment and removed his marking knife. He grabbed Brando's leash before casually walking toward the very one-sided fight.

By the time he caught up to the carnage, Muñoz's arms were a never-ending series of lacerations. He was no longer able to keep them raised to protect himself, and Brando had latched on to his throat. Blood was jetting from a wound in his neck and had spattered the street where the dog had dragged him.

Muñoz looked at Beck with dread and fear. But Beck felt no sympathy.

"It's not so entertaining to see two animals fight to the death when you're the other animal, is it?"

Muñoz said nothing. He was beyond speech. He was beyond saving.

Brando finally released his quarry when Muñoz was long dead. The dog simply stepped back from his handiwork, and Beck slipped the leash around his neck. Brando let him do it without a fuss.

He pulled out his marking knife to add Muñoz to the score, but then stopped. It wouldn't be right—this was Brando's claim, not his.

He looked down at the dog and stroked its head. "I know this doesn't make up for what he did to you, but at least he paid the price for his crimes."

CHAPTER TWENTY

Zoë was having a hospital breakfast the following morning when her protection arrived. Her dynamic duo consisted of Officer Martinez, out of uniform for once, and Ryan Greening. Greening looked how she felt. He must have driven through the night from Bishop to get back here. She swore he was wearing the same clothes she'd seen him in yesterday when they'd searched for the Tally Man's compound. A wave of shame washed over her at the sight of Martinez. He'd been good to her, but he'd rescued her from too many drinking binges over the last year. She guessed they were meant to be her feel-good detail—people she knew and trusted.

"How're you feeling, Zoë?" Martinez asked.

Wrecked was the simple answer. With her adrenaline supplies depleted, her body was letting her know how much of a fight she'd put up and amplified the message. She felt every bruise, scrape, and torn muscle fiber. It took extra effort to move this morning.

"I think I'm doing a little better than him," she said, nodding at Greening.

"Forget appearances. I'm good. I just need a change of clothes," he said. "And speaking of clothes, I've got these for you."

He held up her roller bag. "One of our female officers packed you a few things to last you for the next couple of days. She was flying blind, so if there's something specific she missed, let us know and we'll get it over to you."

She was glad someone had thought about clothes, seeing as Ogawa's forensic people had taken everything but her underwear last night.

"So, what's the plan?"

"We leave for Dr. Jarocki's place in Napa as soon as you're ready."

"Where is he?"

"He's at the house already," Martinez said.

"You didn't catch the Tally Man yet?"

Greening frowned and shook his head. "Sorry, no."

So, hiding from the world it was. "OK, let me get changed then."

Greening and Martinez saw themselves out. They stood guard with the assigned officer outside her room. She would have loved a shower before changing into fresh clothes, but she wanted out of the hospital more.

She hopped out of bed and went through the bag that had been packed for her. It looked as if the cop had been thoughtful about it. In addition to the basics, the officer had been considerate enough to include a dress, heels, her shampoo, a hairdryer, and makeup. These things would help make her feel like herself instead of like a frightened animal in hiding.

She changed into yoga pants and a T-shirt and put on running shoes. If she needed to run or fight, her outfit wouldn't hinder her. She also pulled on a baseball cap for anonymity.

She checked herself in the mirror. She was a roadmap of violence. She examined her jawline. There was no swelling, just one big, purple bruise that clambered up the side of her face where the Tally Man had socked her. It blended nicely with the handprint bruises around her throat where he'd choked her. She lifted her T-shirt and sighed at the bruising that mottled her stomach where she'd been kicked and slammed into her sofa. She let go of the fabric, and it covered the worst of the injuries.

"Well, you're still here," she said to her reflection.

She opened the door to the room, and Greening and Martinez turned to face her.

"Ready to go?" Martinez asked with a smile.

She wasn't sure she liked the smile. It smacked of forced optimism. After last night, there was no room for optimism, but for nicety's sake, she said, "Yeah."

"This way," Greening said.

He took the bag from her, and she followed the policemen down a corridor to a staff elevator.

"We have a car waiting outside," Greening said. "I don't expect there to be any issues, but should anything happen, just follow our instructions. OK?"

"OK."

Despite Greening and Martinez's casual attire, they stood out to Zoë and probably to anyone else who was paying attention. Their jackets bulged awkwardly where their weapons hung. They both moved with a cagey gait, not like visitors unfamiliar with the layout. They looked like what they were—a conspicuous security team trying not to be conspicuous. Zoë didn't let it bother her too much. She had numbers this time. Three of them to his one.

They took an elevator to the street level and emerged on the back side of the hospital, away from the main entrance. They headed toward a green Ford Expedition parked in a red zone, beyond another cop standing idly by.

"We good?" Greening asked as they passed.

"No one went near it."

Martinez went ahead, unlocked the SUV, dumped her bag in the trunk, and opened a rear passenger door for her. She climbed in while Greening and Martinez got into the front, Martinez taking the driver's seat.

As soon as they got moving, Greening and Martinez talked in cop speak, cutting her off from the conversation. Greening kept his gaze centered on the vehicles around them. Martinez made a number of circular maneuvers and doubled back on himself twice before pronouncing, "We don't have a tail."

"OK, let's get out of here," Greening said.

Martinez picked up US 101 and headed toward the Golden Gate Bridge. Despite his pronouncement, Greening kept a lookout until they were across the bridge, then he relaxed.

It didn't take long to reach Napa. When Jarocki had said he had a family home there, Zoë had pictured someplace surrounded by vineyards. Instead, they ended up in a residential neighborhood backing on to a park. Martinez turned into the driveway and stopped the car in front of a large, ranch-style dwelling.

Jarocki emerged from the house with a smile and a wave. He hugged Zoë and shook Greening's hand. The street was quiet with no one passing by, but he said, "Let's get inside. I don't want to make a spectacle."

The house was cool with the air-conditioning churning. Zoë guessed Jarocki was around fifty, but the place seemed furnished by someone much older. There were lots of floral prints and furniture that predated IKEA by a few decades.

"I'll show you to your room," Jarocki said, and led them to the master bedroom. "You've got your own bath, so you'll have total privacy."

"I don't want to take yours. Any one will do for me."

"This isn't mine," he said. "It was my parents'. Now it's the guest room."

Martinez put Zoë's bag on the bed.

"Dr. Jarocki, Officer Martinez needs to go over some security precautions for the property, and I need to go over some things with Zoë."

Jarocki nodded, and Martinez led him out of the room. Zoë followed Greening inside. He perched himself on the window ledge, looking out at a secluded backyard.

"OK, this isn't witness protection, and you're free to do as you want, but here are some ground rules," he said. "Stay inside. Don't answer the door. If you need anything, ask Dr. Jarocki to get it for you or text me—you have my number. If you take precautions, you won't come to any harm."

Zoë sighed. "It doesn't sound like fun."

"It's not meant to be. Look, I know this sucks and it's going to drive you crazy, but please be sensible. I don't want you getting hurt."

She dropped down onto the corner of the bed. "Are you or Officer Martinez staying here?"

He shook his head. "You aren't in protective custody."

"I'm just hiding out."

He frowned. "Yes. I wish I could have someone here with you at all times, but to be honest, you're better served having every possible officer working the case. I've asked the local PD to drop by every couple of hours, and I'll be checking in with you throughout the day to make sure you're OK."

"How long do you honestly expect me to stay here?"

"I can't give you a realistic answer at the moment. There are too many unknowns. Let's give it two weeks, then we can reassess."

Zoë looked around the room filled with other people's possessions. This was her new home. Her new prison. She wanted none of it. Maybe she should do what Ogawa had suggested the night before and start over someplace else.

"Look, I know this is for my own good, but I need something to keep me going," she said. "Did the sheriffs find anything useful out at the Tally Man's place?"

"He shook his head. They're still combing the area for evidence, but they didn't find any bodies."

"Do you think they'll find her?" She couldn't bring herself to say Holli's name.

"My gut feeling is no."

"So he buried her somewhere else?"

"Or she got away, like you did."

"Don't you do that," she barked at him. "Don't bullshit me. If Holli was alive, she would have come home. She's dead, and that sick bastard did something with her body—don't pretend any different."

Greening raised his hands. "Sorry. Sorry."

Jarocki and Martinez appeared in the doorway.

"Something wrong?" Jarocki asked, his eyebrows raised.

"No. We're good," Greening said.

"Zoë?" Jarocki asked.

"We're fine."

"I'm done with the doctor," Martinez said.

Greening pushed himself off the window ledge. "Then we'll let you settle in. Do you have everything you need for now?"

"There's a few things I could use."

"Make a list, get it to me, and I'll have someone bring them by later. I'll call you tonight."

Jarocki saw them out, while Zoë remained in the bedroom. Jarocki's home probably held a special meaning for him, but to her, the place seemed cold and uninviting. She felt tired and alone. The Tally Man was tearing her life apart again. Maybe she should just let him finish the job and kill her. At least it would be over.

Jarocki reappeared in the doorway. "I was going to make some coffee—want some?"

"Sure."

She followed him into the kitchen. He put a pan of water on to boil and tossed coffee grounds into a large French press.

"So, this is the family estate."

He looked around the place and smiled. "Not quite. It's the family home. My parents left it to my two brothers and me. We never had the heart to sell the place because it held so many memories, like family Christmases and Dad pointlessly trying to teach us how to pitch, so we hung on to it. We let friends stay here, my brothers use it when they visit, and I sometimes come out here to work when I need a little seclusion."

She imagined his childhood. From the way he talked and the house's '50s-throwback look, it sounded Norman Rockwell idyllic. She didn't resent his upbringing. It sounded no different than hers—until the Tally Man. There was a home like this waiting for her, with parents who cared, but she'd turned her back on them. She pushed the image from her thoughts.

Jarocki made the coffee and showed her into the living room. She stretched out on the sofa, feeling every one of her injuries again. The doctor had sent her home with pain meds, but she wasn't taking them. She wanted her full wits about her. Jarocki sat kitty-corner to her in a lounger, with his back to the window.

"What happens now?" she asked.

"Whatever you want. I'm here at your disposal."

"I don't need a babysitter."

"That's fine. If you want to be alone, this house is yours for as long as you need it, but if you prefer company, I can stick around. I've canceled my appointments for today, and I can work from here. I will have to go into my office to see patients, but I can be here the rest of the time. Would you like me to stay?"

She didn't know. She wasn't sure what she wanted, so she remained silent.

"Don't decide now. Think about it."

"Why are you going to this trouble?"

He put down his coffee mug and clasped his hands together. "You're my patient. You need help and support, and I'm in a position to provide that."

She should have said thank you, but she didn't. She hated being indebted to people, relying on their help. It was probably why she didn't like this house. It was a big reminder that she couldn't do this alone.

"How are you feeling?"

"Sore." The stiffness she felt from the pummeling she'd taken wasn't much different from the morning-after feeling she had after a tough self-defense class. Her throat was a different matter. When she touched her neck, she could feel the ghost of the Tally Man's fingers deep under the surface of her skin, as deep as her soul.

"Do you want to talk about what happened last night?"

The question sounded as if it came without strings, but she felt them dangling in the air. This wasn't just a general inquiry. "You want to turn this into a session?"

Jarocki raised his hands and smiled. "We're here, aren't we?"

*   *   *

Marshall Beck returned to the scene of the crime—Zoë's apartment building. Was it a crime? It was more like the scene of a public service. His only crime was his failure to capture her. This was the second time she'd gotten away from him. He needed to get it right next time. She had to be punished.

He'd come back here on his way into the office, the morning following the scuffle, and found cops still milling around. They were still there at lunchtime, when he dropped by again, though their presence had been reduced to a single squad car parked on the street. Now it was after five, and there was no squad car, although his instincts told him the old Intrepid parked in the spot where the cop car had sat was a plant.

He made a casual pass by the sedan, noting that the guy sitting in the passenger seat looked bored. Could he really just be waiting for someone? The big test was time. How long does someone sit in the passenger seat of a parked car? Thirty minutes? An hour? Two? No, if you're waiting for a friend, you don't hang out in your car for more than thirty minutes. Any longer than that, and you go looking for your friend.

He could be patient. Precision work like his made you patient. After ninety minutes, the man in the Intrepid remained where he was.

"You're a cop, my friend," he murmured to himself from the quiet of his Honda.

So, they were watching Zoë's place. It made sense. Her Chicken Little act had exposed him. It made it essential that he snatch her the next time around.

He felt his blood pressure build up in his veins and stared at his white-knuckle grip on the steering wheel. A hot head wouldn't help him here. He had to be calm and relaxed if he was to get to Zoë again. He let his tension bleed from him.

He wondered how long the cops would stake out Zoë's apartment. A day? A week? Longer? He was ruing his failure to grab her last night. It was forcing his hand. With all the police interest surrounding Zoë now, he needed to adjust his plans. He was still a ghost when it came to law enforcement. They had a dumb name for him, and that was about it. He could back off and just keep tabs on Zoë for now. He could always take her after the police had lost interest.

But there was something about walking away from unfinished business that didn't sit well with him. Running away was failure. Failure was cowardice. And one thing he wasn't was a coward.

Besides, if he left town, what stopped her from doing the same? He'd hate to come back and find that she'd upped and run too. Yes, he knew her name, but there was nothing stopping her from changing it.

It was all very frustrating, but it illustrated to him that he needed to be on his game in the future. No more mistakes. No more failures. He couldn't allow himself to be caught.

He climbed from his SUV again. Even though the cops were there, he needed to check on Zoë herself. If there was a cop on the outside, was there also one with her in the apartment?

Since the cops didn't have a good description of him, he could stroll up to the apartment gates, but the cop who was watching the place might be logging everyone who went in and out of the building. Luckily, he didn't need to go into the complex to observe Zoë's place. He simply needed to get to a neighboring rooftop.

He crossed the street and walked into the building next to Zoë's complex. A security door prevented him getting access to the stairwell, but it didn't stop him from getting to the fire escape in the back. He climbed the stairs to the rooftop, pulled out a pocket set of binoculars, and peered over at Zoë's apartment. The drapes were drawn, and the lights were off.

Was she in there? If she wasn't, why were the cops staking out her place? If they weren't watching out for her, then they had to be waiting for him. He needed to see how far the cops had taken this.

He descended the fire escape and rejoined the street, then circled the block before deciding his next move. He needed an up-close look at Zoë's apartment to know if she was in there. It meant crossing in front of the stakeout cop. So be it.

He bided his time and waited for someone to drive in and open the security gate. As the gate slid open, he slid in. He crossed the parking lot to Zoë's building. He didn't bother climbing the stairs to the second floor. He didn't have to. From the street level, he could see the police tape sealing off her front door.

That was interesting. If Zoë's apartment was considered a crime scene, where was she? Was she staying with a friend? It was possible, but he hadn't seen her with anybody. She seemed to be a loner. Had Zoë skipped town without the cops' knowledge? Maybe the police hadn't staked out the place, looking for him. Maybe they were waiting to see if and when she would return.

He scanned the parking lot, and there was Zoë's motorcycle. Now, she might have skipped town without taking her bike, but it was unlikely. Zoë was somewhere and somewhere close.

It was time to leave. He'd learned all that he could tonight.

A young woman with long, curly hair pulled her Honda Civic into the driveway, activating the security gate. He walked out as the car swept in.

Averting his gaze from the stakeout cop, he crossed the street and headed back to his SUV before casting a glance over his shoulder. The woman who had been driving the Honda was now on the second floor of Zoë's building. She stopped in front of Zoë's apartment.

He watched her from his vantage point across the street. *Who are you, young lady—friend, nosy neighbor, or something more?*

The woman ignored the police seal and let herself into Zoë's apartment.

Well, what do you know? Zoë does have a friend. He smiled.

He returned to his Honda and got behind the wheel. It was a half hour before the woman reemerged, carrying a bulging gym bag.

"Well, Zoë can't be expected to live without her essentials," he said to himself.

He gunned his engine and waited for the Honda Civic to emerge. When it did, he tailed the small sedan. The stakeout cop didn't react, so he obviously knew about Zoë's little helper.

He followed the Honda through the city to US 101 and across the Golden Gate Bridge into Marin, keeping a discreet distance from the Civic. The driver didn't show any signs that she'd spotted him. Neither did she drive like someone who expected to be followed.

"What kind of friend are you, Miss Civic?" he asked. "How far are you willing to go to help your friend Zoë?"

He hoped it wasn't to the ends of the earth. He had only a half tank of gas. He needn't have worried. They went only as far as Napa.

He stopped his SUV when Miss Civic halted in front of a house farther down the block. She walked up the walk, carrying the gym bag, rung the bell, then went inside.

He didn't see her, but he didn't have to. He knew he'd found Zoë's hideout.

CHAPTER TWENTY-ONE

The doorbell rang. Instinctively, Zoë got up off the sofa to answer it. Jarocki came flying out of his office.

"I answer the door, remember?" he said.

She did, but enforced captivity was proving to be a difficult adjustment. Coming and going as she pleased was so natural to her that suddenly trying to remember she couldn't leave the house was like trying to remember how not to breathe.

"Go to your room," the therapist said.

Despite the situation, the parentlike instruction brought a smile. She did as she was told and went to her room. Getting out of sight was a protocol set by Greening.

A moment later, Jarocki called out, "It's OK. It's Inspector Greening."

Returning to the living room, she found Greening manhandling half a dozen grocery bags and a pasta-making machine through the door. Jarocki relieved him of the equipment and a couple of the sacks and led him into the kitchen.

"Glad to see you're sticking to our rules," Greening said.

The afternoon heat was spilling into the house. She went over and closed the door. "Dr. Jarocki is keeping me honest."

Greening dumped his bags on the countertop. "I think I got everything you requested. That should keep you busy."

Keeping busy was the name of the game. It had taken her only twenty-four hours to discover that witness protection sucked. No leaving the house meant no self-defense classes, no gym, no jogging, no shopping, no working, and no barhopping. Mothballing everything that defined her and kept her busy was driving her crazy. Even prison inmates got an hour of yard time. She'd always thought her life was empty until she'd been forced to stay confined. That was why she'd decided to throw herself into a pursuit like cooking, which would fill the hours.

"Do you have a few minutes to discuss some issues?" Greening asked.

"I have more than a few minutes," Zoë answered.

"Do you need privacy?" Jarocki asked.

"If you don't mind, Doctor."

"No problem."

When the therapist returned to his room, Greening took a seat across from Zoë on the sofa.

"How are you doing?" he asked.

"I've discovered there are only so many DVDs one person can watch back-to-back."

The inspector smiled and jerked a thumb in the direction of the groceries. "Hence the shopping list."

She smiled back. "Hence the shopping list."

"Look, I know it's tough, but it goes with the territory, I'm afraid. Just hang in there. Stick to the rules, don't do anything reckless, and you'll be fine."

The bruising to her throat, which she felt every time she swallowed, guaranteed she wouldn't be doing anything reckless. As long as Greening and the SFPD did their part and caught the Tally Man.

"Do you have everything you need for now?"

"Yes, your officer brought over the rest of my things last night. What's the latest on the investigation?" she asked.

Greening's smile fell away and she knew the direction of this conversation before it started.

"We have your place staked out should he return. Our people have been through your apartment looking for forensic and trace evidence but haven't found anything useful."

"I could have told you that. He's careful. He doesn't make mistakes."

"He does—or you wouldn't be here now."

His answer took the sting out of her. "What about the investigation in Mono?"

"Sadly, that's at a standstill. Whatever he used those sheds for, it wasn't to bury bodies. The dogs found no trace. The forensic team did find some possible blood evidence, but it's so degraded, it won't be of much use. The detectives there are working with the people at the Smokehouse to see what customers were there the night you and Holli were. If he ate there, we could have a credit card record, which could lead us to him. Also, they might be able to track down a witness who saw something."

It was maddening to hear. Everything was so tenuous, built on *maybes* and *possiblys*. She could feel her anger building up inside.

"None of this sounds like you're any closer to finding him."

"I know it's hard, but this is how police work goes. If you ever get into it yourself, you'll see this is the harsh reality of how it works. You don't kick down doors every five minutes. There's no instant gratification. It's about long, hard, diligent work. We're doing all that we can, but it's going to be slow."

If that was how law enforcement worked, then maybe being a cop wasn't for her. It was why she liked her mall job. Something happened or it didn't. When it did, the culprit was dealt with at that moment. The crime was solved as quickly as it occurred.

"So, do you have anything positive to tell me?"

"Yes, and it's the main reason I came by to talk to you. I think we've found a connection between you, Holli, and Laurie Hernandez. Or at least the reason behind why the Tally Man targeted you."

A chill ran through her. It served to cool her growing frustration with Greening.

"I'm sorry to say this, and I don't mean any disrespect, but it looks as if he targets women behaving badly."

Zoë flushed.

"Sorry, it's just our working theory."

She waved off his apology. "What do you mean by 'behaving badly'?"

"Checking into Laurie Hernandez's background, we found that she had a string of petty offenses to her name—theft, disturbing the peace, public drunkenness. And according to the witnesses I interviewed, she was hard to get along with. Things of that nature."

Laurie Hernandez's résumé sounded eerily familiar, but she saw one problem with it. "That wasn't true of Holli and not of me, really. I had a clean record before the Tally Man."

"Yes, but think about your night at the Smokehouse. You were being loud and raucous. The two of you were playing up to Craig Cook. The Tally Man would have witnessed this and found your behavior distasteful. You were breaking his rules."

She sagged under the weight of shame, embarrassment, and guilt. They'd gone to Vegas only to let off a little steam. Yes, they'd been a pain in the ass with their antics at the Smokehouse, but they didn't deserve to die for it.

"We were only passing through Bishop that night. How would he have targeted us?"

"He could have been in Vegas, but I don't think so, seeing as he had an established place where he took you two. My feeling is that it was an impulsive move on his part. He was at the Smokehouse, and he acted."

Impulse control. It seemed it wasn't a problem confined to people suffering with traumatic-stress disorders. The what-ifs started building in her head. If she and Holli had behaved themselves, would the Tally Man have ignored them? If they'd taken a different route or driven at a different time, would they have avoided him altogether? If they'd driven at a different time . . . If they'd flown . . . If they'd stopped somewhere other than the Smokehouse . . . One what-if was harder to swallow than the others.

"If the Tally Man selected us based on our behavior at the Smokehouse, a few hours difference either way, and we would have never run into each other. None of this would have happened."

She looked at her life over the past fifteen months and the shift it had taken from PhD student to mall cop, from content to miserable, from sociable to lonely. All of it was due to a random encounter. Tragic didn't begin to describe it.

"Unfortunately, that's how these things happen," Greening said. "'Wrong time, wrong place' describes a lot of victims of violence and crime. It's not right. It just is."

"Do you think that's how he got Laurie Hernandez?"

"Possibly. It looks as if he grabbed Laurie on her way home from work. There wasn't an incident at her work that day involving her, which leads us to believe he selected her, then studied her before abducting her. The theory is that he encountered Laurie at some point, didn't like what he saw, then decided she was next. I'm guessing when you escaped, he learned that he couldn't be so impulsive."

"Glad to have been of help."

"Well, predators like these aren't created perfect. They develop their methods from their errors."

"What does this big discovery mean?"

"Obviously, we know there are other victims, and we have a victim profile we can use. We'll search for missing women who have a history of petty crimes and poor social behavior and connect some dots to a suspect."

"Sounds like a vague search."

"It is and a wide one. The Tally Man isn't confined to one location, as evidenced by the fact that he abducted you in Bishop and Laurie Hernandez here in the city. We don't know if he's California-based or national. So we are up against it. But again, this is how police work goes."

"What I can't wrap my head around is how petty this all is," Zoë said.

"Petty—yes. Surprising—no. Name one psychopath who has a noble, cogent, or understandable reason for killing people. They're damaged people inflicting more damage on innocent bystanders. We'll never be able to understand it."

Nothing Greening told her filled her with confidence. The Tally Man looked to be holding the SFPD and everyone else at bay. She asked the one question that mattered to her most. "How long am I going to be stuck here?"

"A week. A month. I can't say."

She shook her head.

"You're here for the duration, until something breaks."

"Let's hope it breaks soon."

CHAPTER TWENTY-TWO

Marshall Beck let himself into Urban Paws for what was probably the last time. There was no coming back from what he was about to do. He'd miss it. Of all the jobs he'd worked, this was the most enjoyable. The charity performed a selfless service for the betterment of creatures that couldn't help themselves. But for all his love of this place, it had broken his heart today.

That morning, Kristi Thomas had entered his office with a pensive look on her face and closed the door behind her.

"I need to have a word with you, Marshall."

She took the seat across from his desk. Her hands were clasped tightly enough for the whites of her knuckles to show.

"I've got bad news. We conducted the last of our behavioral testing on the fighting dogs."

He knew what was coming before she said it.

"Only three of the twelve dogs passed. Brando wasn't one of them. Tom and Judy said you and Brando worked well together during the rehabilitation sessions, but Brando didn't show a safe temperament during socialization testing. I know you really bonded with the dog, and you were hoping to take him, but that won't be possible. I'm really sorry, Marshall."

He knew this outcome was a possibility, but he'd expected Brando to keep his composure. He guessed the dog was too proud to play by the rules. He understood and respected him for it.

"What does this mean?" he asked.

"Brando and the other dogs will be euthanized at the end of the week, in accordance with the court order."

"Can the test be done again? Can I conduct it? Can I appeal the decision?"

"No, the dogs can't be retested. You can appeal the decision, but I don't think it'll do you any good."

"I see."

"I know you had your heart set on Brando, but there are the other dogs. They'll need loving homes with dedicated owners. I hope you'll consider one of them."

"I'll think about it," he said without any intention of doing so. "Can I still work with Brando until his time comes?"

Kristi smiled. "Of course."

Although he wanted to, he couldn't be angry with Kristi. She was following the rules. This was the fault of the recently deceased Javier Muñoz and a shortsighted judge. "Thank you for letting me know."

"I know it's of little comfort, but just know you gave Brando a taste of humanity in his final days."

The conversation had stuck with him all day. Brando's final days were a long way off. He would make sure of that. He let himself into the Assessment Annex. The dogs stared at him through the moonlit room. Were they aware that this was their last week of existence?

"I wish I could save you all," he said.

He unlatched Brando's pen, and the dog stepped out. He looped the slip leash over the animal's head and walked out to his Honda Pilot.

Loading Brando into his vehicle, he said, "You're safe. We just have one more person to collect before we can leave."

*   *   *

Dr. Jarocki's Napa house backed on to Alston Park, which was a nice feature for a homeowner but a terrible one for home security. It left the doctor's residence open to a simple breach from the rear. Marshall Beck had scouted out his approach the night before.

He left his Honda parked in front of the house, with Brando inside. He'd be going in through the rear, but coming out through the front. Zoë was small enough to carry the half mile through the park, but getting her over the fence would be problematic. Audacity worked best. Just toss a blanket over her, carry her out to the SUV, and toss her in the back, the same way someone would handle a bundle of athletic gear. If he acted as though everything was normal, people would behave accordingly.

He'd been forced to wait for an hour before making his move. A Napa Police Department squad car was sitting outside the house when he drew up. He didn't get the feeling it was a permanent fixture. The guy made no contact with the house and was more preoccupied with doing paperwork. This was for show. The cops hadn't bothered with full protection, just periodic drive-by checks and drop-ins. He was proved right when the officer drove away.

He waited another twenty minutes to see if the sentry would be replaced. When there was no changing of the guard, he slipped from the SUV, leaving Brando inside, and circled around to the park.

He cut through the freshly trimmed grass. When he reached the fence, he searched for the X he'd spray painted on his first reconnaissance to mark the backyard. The last thing he wanted to do in the dark was leap into the wrong yard.

He found the *X* and pressed himself to the fence. It was six feet high and easy for him, with his height, to peer over. He surveyed the neighboring residences. Both were dark. He had to look three houses down to his left before he saw light spilling from the interior. It looked to be an early-to-bed crowd around here, for which he was grateful.

Jarocki's place was more active. Zoë was in the kitchen, cooking from the look of things. Windows glowed in one of the bedrooms, but the drapes were drawn. Zoë's activity in the kitchen meant he had to keep to the right side of the house to remain hidden.

He didn't have to worry about security lighting. He'd checked out that situation during his recon. The man staying with Zoë had none on his property, although his neighbors did. Beck had tested the range by waving a branch at various points along the rear fence until he found the limits of the sensors. As long as he kept within a specific zone, he wouldn't trip them.

He edged over to the right side of the fence where it intersected with the neighbor's property, and climbed over in a single, deft move. He dropped to a crouch and paused, watching Zoë work. She was at the sink overlooking the backyard. If she looked up or caught movement, it would be game over for him. He waited until she turned away, then dashed forward.

He went to his entry point—a sliding door—and dropped to his knees. It opened into the master bedroom, from the looks of it. He loved sliding doors. They used lock technology a half step up from a filing cabinet. He brought out his pick and worked the catch, which yielded to him in a matter of moments. He allowed himself a smile before slipping inside.

CHAPTER TWENTY-THREE

Cooking wasn't one of Zoë's things. It wasn't that she was bad at it, she just didn't have the inclination. Meals for her had always been simple affairs—salads and things she could buy premade. This was a byproduct of college life, where there had been little to no time between classes and internships to invest in meal preparation, nor any once she'd started the long shifts at the mall after she'd taken the security job. Her enforced detention meant she had a lot of time on her hands. Since Jarocki was putting a roof over her head, the least she could do was make him a decent meal.

She was making beef-and-pork raviolis in a vodka sauce. It wasn't particularly adventurous, but she was making it all from scratch. She'd looked up a recipe on the Food Network and had gotten Greening to bring the ingredients. She'd thought making pasta was going to be a fast and straightforward affair, but it wasn't proving to be as simple as the recipe implied. Her first attempts at making the dough, let alone constructing the raviolis themselves, hadn't passed muster, but she persevered until she had something that bordered on competent. However, competence had taken time. It was close to midnight. She had the salad and the vodka sauce done. All she needed to do was put the raviolis on to boil.

She left the vodka sauce on simmer and went to Jarocki's bedroom office. It was the smallest of the rooms in the house. He could have had any one he pleased, but he stuck to his childhood room. She found him at work on his laptop.

She leaned against the doorway. "Dinner will be ready in about five minutes."

Jarocki checked his watch. "More like a midnight feast."

"I'm sorry. I didn't think making pasta from scratch would take so long."

"It's OK. I had work to do. I'm just finishing up now, so perfect timing."

She returned to the kitchen and put the raviolis in the boiling water. They sank to the bottom of the pan. When they were done, they'd all float to the top. She liked this communication method between food and chef.

This was nice. She found cooking relaxing. Her world was in turmoil and still she could find peace among it all. Jarocki had been telling her for months to find hobbies and interests that brought her pleasure and emotional nourishment, but she'd resisted because she hadn't seen the point. If she was being honest, she'd never taken the time to find leisure pursuits. Her self-defense classes provided her with a sense of accomplishment but offered no relaxation. She'd always claimed that hitting the clubs and bars, getting wrecked, and seeing who'd pick her up was her release valve. It wasn't. She put herself out there with no idea how the night would end, which was its own form of stress.

She smiled as the raviolis, good to their word, all rose to the top of the water. Maybe cooking would become her next thing.

"Two minutes," she called out and received a grunt in reply.

She drained the raviolis and dumped them in the vodka sauce, letting them soak it up for a minute or two before dishing them up.

"C'mon, Doctor. It's going on the table."

She heard the bang of what sounded like a drawer closing. *At least he's finishing up*, she thought as she took their plates over to the dining table.

Another thump followed. It sounded like something hitting the ground. Then a choking sound came up the hallway from the bedrooms.

Zoë froze for a moment as her instincts kicked in, then went into motion before she even knew the conclusion her brain had reached.

She dropped the plates on the table, the pink sauce splattering the surface and her T-shirt, then lunged for the kitchen and snatched up a butcher knife from the block. It was heavy in her hand, which was good for momentum, but bad for agility. There was no time to change her selection.

From the corner of her eye, she caught movement in the dark hallway. A figure, large and black, held a struggling Jarocki in a one-armed headlock, dragging him toward her. In his free hand, he held a Bowie knife to Jarocki's throat. She'd seen that knife before.

The Tally Man stopped at the threshold of the living room and watched her. He was dressed the same way as when he'd attacked her a few days ago—in black with a ski mask to hide his identity.

Thirty feet of living room separated them, but Zoë was less than twenty from the front door. She had more than a ten-foot head start, and she wasn't encumbered by Jarocki. She could make it to the street before the Tally Man and wake the neighborhood, which would force him into a decision—kill her and be caught, or run and hide.

Jarocki was the flaw in her simple plan. If she ran, the Tally Man would kill him in a second. She'd abandoned Holli, and living with the shame had destroyed her life. There'd be no coming back from the guilt if Jarocki died because of her.

She felt the psychologist's gaze on her, terror shining in his eyes. It had to be hard for him. He always dealt with other people's fears. He never experienced them. She couldn't abandon him. She wouldn't abandon him.

"Don't hurt him."

"Drop the knife, Zoë." The Tally Man waited for her to comply. He had over six inches in height on Jarocki, and he hoisted the shrink onto his toes, cutting off his breath. "I will kill him."

As usual, the Tally Man thought he held all the cards, but he didn't. The fact she'd already escaped him twice proved that. Having Jarocki as a hostage was an advantage, but it was also a hindrance. He couldn't attack her and lug Jarocki around at the same time. He could kill Jarocki, but that would take time, and it was time she could use to attack him. Where the Tally Man really fell down in odds was that this fight was two against one. That was, if she could get Jarocki to join the battle.

"You're going to kill us both. Why pretend?" she said.

A grunt of acknowledgement came from behind the ski mask.

She shared a quick glance with Jarocki. She hoped he got the message she was trying to transmit. He needed to watch for a distraction.

She sidled over to the dining table, then grabbed one of the dinner plates and hurled it Frisbee-like at the Tally Man. Instinctively, he raised his knife arm to protect himself.

In that moment, Jarocki yanked on the arm the Tally Man had around his neck. Off balance, the Tally Man staggered forward, losing his grip on the doctor. Suddenly free of his captor, Jarocki scrabbled toward Zoë as the plate of food hit the Tally Man in the chest.

Zoë charged at the Tally Man as soon as she released the plate. With so many things happening to him at once, he was vulnerable. Zoë wouldn't get another chance like this. She hurled herself forward.

She slammed into him, but the Tally Man had turned his body to reduce the impact. Instead of hitting full on, it was only a glancing blow, and she went flying over the top of him. She crashed down on her back in the hallway, losing her grip on the knife.

She flipped over and jumped to her feet. She expected to see the Tally Man bearing down on her, but he was running the other way, chasing after Jarocki, who was making a beeline for the front door. He didn't make it. The Tally Man dropped a shoulder, slammed into Jarocki, and drove him into the closed door. Jarocki yelled out, then slumped to the ground.

Zoë raced across the living room, but not before the Tally Man hauled Jarocki to his knees. The therapist gasped when the Tally Man jammed the knife back under his neck.

"You shouldn't have done that."

Zoë stopped dead and raised her hands in surrender. Any thought she had that the Tally Man wouldn't harm Jarocki evaporated. The Bowie's blade was tight against the doctor's throat. Before, the Tally Man had just held it close. He wasn't toying with her anymore.

"I have to kill him now."

"No. Stop. Please."

The Tally Man froze. "Give me a reason why."

"It's not right."

"What do you know about right and wrong?" he said with disgust.

She needed to save Jarocki, for her sake as well as his. Her only chance was to fight the Tally Man on his own terms. "It's not about my right and wrong. It's about yours. You chose Laurie Hernandez, Holli, and me for a reason."

"Don't do this, Zoë," Jarocki said before the Tally Man pressed the blade even deeper.

"We broke the rules, your rules, and we paid the price. Dr. Jarocki hasn't broken your rules. He's a good man who helps people, and he doesn't deserve to die. If you kill him, everything you've ever done will be tainted. You'll be just as bad as me and all the others."

The Tally Man paused. It was impossible to tell what he was thinking behind that mask, while Jarocki had no mask to hide his emotions. His expression was clearly one of stunned amazement.

"What do you want?" the Tally Man asked.

"I want to make a bargain. You let him go, and I'll go with you. No questions. No games. No more fighting. It's about time we finished this thing. I'm tired of looking over my shoulder. Tired of you hounding me. I just want an end to this."

Her proclamation had started as a line she was selling the Tally Man, but there was a lot of truth in it by the time she finished saying it. Her life was a train wreck and had been for over a year. She'd escaped a horrible situation only to live in another, one which had intensified since the Tally Man had rediscovered her. How much longer was she expected to exist like this, not knowing when he was going to pop up next, not knowing if the police would track him down so she could stop looking over her shoulder? At least if she surrendered herself to him now, it might sate his desire to add another woman to his tally for a while. Her sacrifice might be the thing that would get him caught, which would at least bring him to justice. Something bordering on a sense of relief washed through her.

"OK," the Tally Man said, "but betray me and he'll pay the price."

She wouldn't have another death on her conscience. "I won't."

"Zoë, no."

The Tally Man reached into his pocket and tossed her a Ziploc bag with a cloth inside. She picked it up. Drops of moisture clung to the inside of the bag.

"It's chloroform. Take the rag out and hold it to your nose and mouth."

"Let him go first."

"There's no negotiation here, Zoë. We play by my rules."

"I need to know you won't hurt him."

"Like you said, he hasn't broken any rules, so I won't hurt him, but I can't very well have him running down the street, screaming for help. We need to finish our business."

She wanted to believe him. As bizarre as it seemed, she did believe him. He had a code, a twisted code, but a code all the same. Jarocki was outside it. The doctor was safe as long as she gave the Tally Man what he wanted.

"Please don't do this, Zoë. Not for me," Jarocki pleaded.

The Tally Man jerked the knife back and smacked the butt of it across Jarocki's temple. He released the doctor. He fell to all fours, sucking in ragged breaths.

"OK, OK. I'm doing it," Zoë said, opening the bag and pulling the damp cloth free.

She stared at the rag in her hand, her heart thumping in her chest. Was she really about to do this? She wasn't ready, but she never would be, so she raised the cloth to her face and inhaled.

She expected a sharp, chemical smell like bleach, but the chloroform smelled very sweet, floral even. The smell reminded her of dryer sheets, until she realized her hands and feet were going numb.

She kept breathing in. The numbness traveled up her arms and the strength left her legs as the peculiar feeling spread to her core.

The Tally Man pulled off his mask and smiled at her.

She recognized the Tally Man instantly, and she couldn't believe it. It was Brad Ellis, the man from the mall. She'd gotten his iPhone back and disarmed a knife-wielding thief to do it. She'd been face-to-face with him, and she hadn't recognized him. *How could I have been so stupid?* She tried to confront him but could barely string together her thoughts. All she managed was, "You. Mall. Phone thief."

As his grinning face melted into a blur, her hand holding the cloth dropped. Then she was falling.

CHAPTER TWENTY-FOUR

Greening slewed to a halt a half block from David Jarocki's house. Napa police cars and an ambulance prevented him from getting closer. The report from Napa PD had been brief. Jarocki had phoned in a 911 call forty minutes earlier. The Tally Man had broken in, clubbed him, and snatched Zoë. Greening couldn't believe it had all gone sideways and couldn't imagine the fallout they'd be facing if Zoë turned up dead. Should that happen, they deserved any backlash they got. They should have done more to ensure her safety. That was what the cops were there for. Bounding across Jarocki's front yard, he bottled the self-recriminations. Zoë needed him on the ball. He flashed his creds to get past the uniform on the door.

Inside the house, paramedics had Jarocki propped up on the sofa. Two Napa PD detectives were hovering around him, asking questions.

"Dr. Jarocki," he said.

Greening introduced himself to the Napa detectives but that was as far as interagency protocols would go tonight. He didn't have time for niceties. The Tally Man had a head start on them.

Jarocki pushed aside the paramedic who was working on an ugly gash at his temple. "Inspector, I need to talk to you."

The psychologist pushed himself up from his seat, and Greening guided him back down. Greening dropped to his knees in front of Jarocki, giving the paramedics the room to carry on with their work.

"Tell me what happened."

"The Tally Man broke into the house. He was going to kill me, but Zoë stopped him."

"How?"

"She traded herself—her life for mine."

"Why am I not surprised? That girl seems to have a death wish. Look, Doctor, it's important we get details from you. When did this happen? What time? The clock is running."

"I don't know exactly."

"The 911 call came in fifty-two minutes ago," one of the Napa detectives said.

"He made Zoë chloroform herself, then he knocked me out cold. I don't know how long I've been out, but I had just closed a file on my laptop. It'll be time stamped."

"Where's the laptop?" the other detective said.

"In my room," Jarocki said, pointing to the rear of the house. The detective dashed off.

"Did you see a vehicle or anything?" Greening asked.

"No. He came in through the back of the house."

The detective returned with Jarocki's laptop. He fired up the computer and read off the time stamp on the file. Greening checked his watch. The Tally Man had up to an eighty-five-minute head start. That meant the prick could be halfway to Tahoe or in San Jose by now.

Would he travel that far? He hadn't with Laurie Hernandez. He'd grabbed her and killed her in San Francisco. The first time he'd snatched Zoë, he'd driven her and Holli less than an hour from the grab site. It was more than likely that wherever he was taking Zoë, he'd gotten there by now.

"This guy likes to work close to home," Greening said to the detectives. "There's a good chance he's in the area. We need to canvas commercial districts, farms, rail yards, anywhere secluded and with low security. He likes room to work and areas where no one can hear the noise."

The detective who'd retrieved the laptop jumped on his cell and walked into another room.

Greening pulled out one of Ogawa's business cards and handed it to the other detective. "Call him, please. Tell him the Tally Man could be bringing her back home, and they should be looking for a probable kill site there."

"Sure thing," the detective said and followed his colleague.

"What else can you tell me?" Greening asked Jarocki. "What did he look like?"

"I didn't see much of him. He was wearing a ski mask, so I didn't really see his face, but he was big—six-one or six-two. He was also strong. Not Muscle Beach big, but just strong. Something weird happened though that didn't make sense to me."

"What was that?"

"After she made the bargain to go with him quietly in exchange for my life, he tossed her a chloroformed rag to knock herself out with. Just as she raised it to her face, he pulled off his mask."

"Did you see what he looked like?"

"No, he kept me on his blind side, but he wanted Zoë to see him. She recognized him, Inspector Greening. I saw it in her expression, and it's the only thing that explains her last words. She said, 'You. Mall. Phone Thief.'"

Greening's heart skipped a beat. She was talking about the perp she'd taken down at the mall. The son of a bitch must have stolen a phone to put himself face-to-face with Zoë to see if she remembered him from Bishop. The balls on the bastard.

"Thank you, Doctor. You've been very helpful."

He pushed himself to his feet and waved the paramedics back, then tore through the house to find the detective on the phone to Ogawa. He took the phone from the guy.

"Edward, she saw his face. It's a phone thief she took down at the Golden Gate Mall. I'm going over there now. Make some noise for me with their security."

"I'll meet you there."

"This is our break. I think we've got him."

CHAPTER TWENTY-FIVE

Zoë came to. It had happened again. Her past was her present. She was trussed up in a confined space in the dark, her hands and feet both bound together, this time with her arms behind her. A blanket covered her.

She was in his hands—again. Surrendering to the Tally Man to save Jarocki had seemed like the right option at the time. Now it seemed like a dumb, impulsive one. She could only imagine what Jarocki would say to her if she ever saw him again. "Control your impulses, control your life." She hadn't and now the Tally Man controlled her. Flashes of Holli hanging from a hook in that workshop filled her mind, and closing her eyes couldn't shut them out. She'd gotten away then, but not this time. She would end up like Holli and Laurie Hernandez and all the other women. A scream rose in her throat, looking for escape.

Keep it together, she thought. *You aren't the person you were then. Twice he's tried to kill you, and twice he's failed. You're a two-time survivor of the Tally Man. You'll survive this.*

The scream sank back down inside her, but not the fear. Nothing was assured. She was a long way from safety. Yes, he'd failed on his previous attempts, but this could be the time he succeeded. If she wanted to survive, she had to keep her shit together. If she stayed strong, stayed determined, and believed in herself, she'd make it through. If she lost her grip on any one of those, she'd likely be killed.

Her breathing had been fast and shallow, but with effort, it was returning to normal. She helped it with long, slow mouthfuls. Each inhale sucked oxygen into her brain. It would make her sharper and mentally agile.

When she was calm, she told herself, "Time to see how bad it is."

She flicked her head around until it was free of the blanket.

Two things were different from before. She was in the back of a moving vehicle, instead of a shed, and this time, she wasn't drugged. The chloroform had knocked her out, but it hadn't doped her up. She still had her wits. She still had a chance.

How long had she been out? Minutes? Hours? She pulled herself up as best as possible to peer through the windows. They were tinted, but it was obvious it was still night.

We can't have gotten very far, she thought—and hoped.

She heard a snarl, and a pit bull peered over the backseat at her. She recoiled from the dog.

"It's OK, Brando," the Tally Man called in a soothing tone. "Hey, you awake back there?"

She felt like saying nothing in some hope of maintaining an advantage but saw none. "Yes."

"OK then. Brando won't hurt you if you behave."

The dog leered at her.

Has anyone told the dog that?

"We've still got a ways to go, so try to settle in for the duration."

Settle in? Zoë thought. He'd abducted her in order to kill her, and he was making it sound like they were on a cross-country jaunt. Maybe this was how he saw it—that there was nothing wrong with what he did. *How do you fight that type of crazy?*

The dog dropped down from sight.

She wasn't about to sit back and enjoy the ride. She needed to use this time to plan her escape. She needed information.

"Is Dr. Jarocki OK, Brad?" She used his name, thinking that using his name would create some bond between them.

"Don't call me that. That's not my name."

"You want me to call you the Tally Man?"

He snorted. "That's a damn fool label the media invented. Morons. I have no dumb identity to hide behind. I am who I am and nothing else."

"What do I call you? What's your name?"

"Marshall Beck. Now, no talking please."

"I need to know. Is he OK, Marshall?"

"Dr. Jarocki?"

"The man who was protecting me. You said you wouldn't hurt him."

"Him? Yes, he's fine."

She hoped he wasn't lying. She'd have no way of knowing.

As if reading her thoughts, he said, "I said I wouldn't hurt him, and I didn't. I am a man of my word."

The honorable killer, she thought. *How pathetic.*

"I don't harm good people."

The remark puzzled her. *So, he harms only the bad?* Did that mean she and Holli were bad? How had that been determined? This confirmed Greening's belief that the Tally Man operated to some warped moral code, punishing those who didn't meet his standards. There might be something in that she could use against him or to buy her more time.

"Does that mean you think I'm not good?"

"Zoë, this isn't a topic for discussion."

"You're going to kill me, and I don't know why."

"That's disappointing. I thought you had changed. I've seen how you live your life now, and how you traded your life for your friend. It looked promising, but if you don't know why you're here, maybe you haven't changed after all," he said with seemingly genuine regret. "Now, quiet please."

Yes, quiet was good. She needed the time to formulate an attack and defense.

She hoped Beck was telling the truth about Jarocki. His survival meant he could raise the alarm. It would be the slender thread that connected her to the SFPD. They'd be searching for her, which was a start. She needed to pile more things in her favor.

She didn't know how far he was taking her, but she needed to keep him on the road. Wherever he had his torture chamber, it was bound to be secluded. Once he got her there, it was game over for her. But if she could keep him traveling for longer than he intended, it increased the chances of them running into a patrol car or roadblock. She knew only one way of doing that.

"Marshall."

"I said quiet."

"I know, but I want to make a bargain with you," she said.

"We've done that. I didn't kill your friend, the doctor."

"I know, but I want to make another. Remember, killing Dr. Jarocki would have gone against your code. I saved you from that mistake. That has to be worth something."

"You have nothing to offer me, Zoë."

"Then call it a request. Just hear me out. It's important."

Beck was silent for a long moment. "What is it?"

"Is Holli dead?"

A longer silence came from him this time. "Yes."

The confirmation hurt. She felt it twist up inside her. Her friend was really dead. She closed her eyes, and tears leaked out.

"I'd like you to take me to where you buried her."

"What makes you think I buried her?"

"I don't know what you did with her. I don't care what you did. I just need to go to her final resting place."

"Watch your tone, Zoë."

"Sorry. It's just that it's important."

The engine note dropped, and Zoë felt the SUV slow. He pulled off the road and stopped. She didn't know whether to take this as a good sign or not.

Without the road noise underneath her, the world was eerily quiet. She listened for vehicles and heard only the sound of the SUV's idling engine. The scenic route they were taking would be the death of her.

She heard him move in his seat. "Why is it important?"

"I let down my friend when I escaped, and I let down myself when I didn't try to save her. Those things have been eating me up ever since. They've poisoned me and destroyed my life. Nothing brings me pleasure. I can't remember the last time I was happy. You'll finish what you started, and that's OK. I'm not sure I can ever come to terms with what I did, but the one thing I have to do is visit my friend's grave so I can apologize. I have to atone."

It wasn't just a line she was using on Beck to buy time. She meant every word. Yes, she was hoping to delay his plans long enough for a rescue, but all this would end one of two ways. Either Beck killed her, or the cops killed him. However it happened, it would rob her of her chance to apologize to Holli—and that just wasn't acceptable.

"I applaud you, Zoë. I am very conflicted about you. You show great honor, but it won't save you from your punishment. What it does do is buy you a favor. Your friend is buried, and yes, I can take you there."

"Thank you," she said.

"It does mean a much longer journey."

That was just fine with her.

*   *   *

The shopping center was in darkness. Greening stopped his car on the sidewalk in front of the north entrance. A mall cop was waiting for him.

"Inspector Greening?" the guy called.

"Yes."

"I'm Jared Mills. Your colleague told me to expect you."

Ogawa had done his job. He was a real door kicker. It didn't matter what it was—red tape, an obstinate witness, or another law enforcement agency—his bark always forced people to bend to his will. Before Greening had reached the Carquinez Bridge, Ogawa had called him to let him know he'd find someone waiting for him.

He slipped through the door, and Jared locked it behind him.

"This way. I've got everything set up for you," Jared said and led Greening through the mall. "This is about Zoë, right? She's a friend. Is she OK?"

"It's about the phone thief from a week or so ago. Do you know anything about it?"

"I know everything about it. The guy cut me." He touched his chest. "Until I'm healed up, I'm working the graveyard shift."

"So you know who this guy is?"

"Oh yeah, we've got his name and address. I gave your partner the information. I also have our security feed teed up for you."

Jared took Greening into a cramped security booth on the upper level. A dozen screens displayed various live shots of the mall. With the mall closed and no movement on the concourses, the feeds looked as if they were on freeze frame. Greening took a seat next to Jared, who handed him an arrest report. His gaze went straight to the arrestee's box, which listed the guy's name as Leroy Porter. Finally, the Tally Man had a name.

Jared pointed at the screen in front of him. "This is Zoë taking this guy down."

Jared hit play. The camera's angle wasn't the best. It was close enough to pick up the action, but too far away to make out faces. Zoë's takedown was fast, efficient, and reckless.

"Damn," Greening said.

Jared laughed. "I know, right? That self-defense shit she does really works."

Greening looked at the report, then at the figure on the screen. He might not have been able to make out Porter's face, but he could make out his size. He was skinny and wasn't much bigger than Zoë. That didn't jive with Jarocki's six-foot-plus estimate.

"How big was this guy?"

"Not big. Five-eight at the most."

"Shit."

"What's wrong?"

"This isn't our guy. He's too small. Fuck it!" Greening tossed the report away.

"What's going on?"

"The Tally Man has taken Zoë."

"Oh my God," Jared said. "I can't believe it."

"We have a witness. He said the Tally Man is a strong guy that's six-one or six-two. He also said Zoë's last words before he took her were, 'You. Mall. Phone Thief.'"

Jared snatched up the report. He scanned it, then pounded a line with his finger. "This guy. The victim. He was over six feet."

Greening took the report back. It said that Brad Ellis had been the victim, complete with a Walnut Creek address.

Jared forwarded through the feed. He stopped at the post-melee footage and tapped the screen. "That guy. That's Brad Ellis."

"Can you improve that image, or do you have another shot of him? A close-up or something?"

"I can't do much with the feeds, but I may have him on another camera. You should also talk to the local news. They were here. ABC, I think. They did a piece on it."

Greening pulled out his cell and called Ogawa. "Forget Porter. He's the wrong guy. It's not the phone thief. It's the victim. His name is Brad Ellis, and I have his address."

*   *   *

Zoë had gotten what she wanted—a stay of execution. She estimated they'd been on the road for a couple hours now. Each extra minute on the road was a minute in her favor. It was all good news, but she was relying entirely on luck. Luck that a passing cop would come their way. Luck that they'd run into another motorist or trucker. Luck that he'd pick up a flat and someone would see her while he changed a wheel. Luck wasn't proving to be a reliable friend.

She'd listened for passing cars and trucks and heard very few. It was in the early hours of the morning, after all, which just went to show that luck couldn't be depended on. She'd considered screaming when a vehicle passed but thought better of it. The chances were the motorist wouldn't hear her from their vehicle, considering engine noises, two sets of windows, and the speed they would be passing each other. Screaming was a one-shot deal. She could use it only when she knew for sure that it would bring help. Squander that chance, and Beck would either chloroform her again or renege on his promise to take her to Holli's grave. Neither outcome was acceptable.

She'd love for luck to take a hand in her rescue, but she knew it was down to her to save herself. Luck would step in only when she did something to invite it.

Beck slowed down the SUV. A spike of adrenaline went through her. This was either the opportunity she'd been waiting for or they'd reached their final destination and she'd blown her chance.

"Have we arrived?"

"No." He stopped the SUV, came to the rear, and opened the tailgate.

The sudden rush of night air excited her. She looked past him at the world behind him. They were in a town. Streetlights lit sidewalks and storefronts. She looked for people and saw none.

"I need gas, and I need you to be quiet."

He held his chloroform rag in one hand. She kicked and bucked. Brando barked and snarled.

Yeah, bark, you son of a bitch, she thought. *Wake the neighbors.*

He pinned her in place with one hand to her chest. She opened her mouth to scream, and he smothered it with the rag. She inhaled in reflex and blacked out.

When she came to, the SUV was on the road again. She kicked out in frustration at having missed her chance.

"Zoë, don't be stupid. Not now that we have an understanding."

Screw you, she thought. She hated that he had all the angles covered. Then again, maybe he didn't. Finally, luck had presented itself. The edge of the blanket he'd covered her with was trapped in the latch of the tailgate, keeping it from fully closing. It shuddered with each bump in the road.

Carefully, she rolled over so she faced the tailgate. Could she get it open? Yes. With a bit of contortionism, she could pop it and roll out onto the road. It would probably cost her a couple of broken bones and a concussion at the very least, but it would be worth it if it stopped traffic.

Would it work, though? They were on a fast road, judging by their speed and the lack of stops for lights, but it wasn't a freeway or she'd hear more noise from other traffic. When she really thought about it, she hadn't heard the sound of another vehicle since she'd woken up. If she jumped out, he'd simply stop and put her back in.

She tried not to let the despair creep in. She'd bide her time and simply wait for traffic to build up. She spent twenty minutes repositioning herself without alerting Beck or his dog. When the chance came, she'd be ready.

The miles went by. Beck never reduced speed or stopped. Zoë had the dreadful feeling that he'd never slow down. Her fate was to ride in the back of his damn car until the end of time.

Then her body lurched forward under the weight of the SUV braking. This was her chance. She inched her way up to the tailgate. She grabbed the blanket with her bound hands and pulled. She felt it slip through the lock, which meant the latch wasn't quite engaged. Just as she felt the SUV turn, she tugged on the blanket and slammed her back into the door, causing it to pop open.

Please, please, can I have a soft landing? she thought, closed her eyes, prayed, and rolled out. She hit the road hard, crashing down on her shoulder. The momentum carried her forward faster than she'd expected. She balled herself up as best she could to protect her head but managed to bang every square inch of her body.

Stunned, she lay sprawled in the road, her hands and feet still bound. She'd hoped her fall would break the cable ties, but luck wasn't with her again. If she needed any more evidence of that, instead of finding a slew of motorists on hand that had witnessed her tumbling from a moving vehicle, she was alone on a tree-lined, two-lane highway. Alone, except for the Tally Man.

He stopped the SUV in the middle of the turn, hopped out, and pounded toward her. She didn't bother making a run for it. There was no escape while she was still bound. She resigned herself to her recapture and waited for him, taking in the clear sky and fresh night air. It was probably the last night sky she'd ever see.

"That was very stupid, Zoë." He gathered her up in his arms and carried her back to the SUV. "How long have you been planning that little stunt? Just as I think I can trust you, you prove me wrong."

He dropped her in the back of the SUV, to the backdrop of Brando's earsplitting barking.

"You've insulted me for the last time."

All Zoë could think about was how she'd screwed up. "I'm sorry. I'm sorry. You're still taking me to see Holli, right? Please."

"Oh yes, I wouldn't deny either of us of that."

He brought out a hypodermic needle and jammed it in her shoulder. The effect was immediate. She tried looking at him, but she couldn't stop her eyes from rolling back in her head.

"Time to sleep, Zoë."

CHAPTER TWENTY-SIX

Greening stood in front of the Walnut Creek house, while SWAT and Walnut Creek PD officers teemed all over the place. It had all been a bust. They'd woken up a whole neighborhood for nothing.

Ogawa emerged from the house with the SWAT commander. He left the commander behind and crossed the front lawn over to Greening.

"The place is a short sale. It's been vacant for months," Ogawa said.

Greening shook his head. He should have seen this coming as soon as the cell phone proved to be a burner with no ownership record. Even the guy's name, Brad Ellis, was bogus. No such person existed in the Bay Area, at least not matching his description.

Ogawa held up a couple of letters. "These were inside."

Greening took the letters. They were both from the Richmond Police Department. They were follow-ups on the Tally Man's cell phone–theft case. They were the icing on the cake.

"He choreographed this stunt to get to Zoë," Greening said.

"And it's costing him. Until now, we've learned almost nothing about him because he works so anonymously, but going after Zoë has exposed him. Now we have a description and an alias. They will lead somewhere. It may not feel like it, but we're closing in. We *are* going to catch this guy."

It was a good pep talk. Ogawa was right. After weeks of shining a flashlight into the dark, they finally knew who they were going after. Under normal circumstances, he'd be excited, but not this time.

"But are we going to get to him before he kills Zoë?" Greening said.

Ogawa didn't have an answer.

Greening's cell rang. It was ABC7.

"Inspector Greening, this is Thom Futrell. We spoke earlier. We went through the tape for that news piece, and we do have a headshot of the person who had their phone stolen. We didn't have much on him as he didn't want to be interviewed, but we did catch him on camera. I'm texting it to you now."

Greening needed some hope, and this was it. His phone beeped a few seconds later, and he opened the attached screen capture. It wasn't the perfect photo. The man had turned his head away from the camera, but it was still a three-quarter face shot of him. If anyone knew him, they'd recognize him. He appeared to be in his late thirties, with a good head of blond hair. His face was blocky with a weak chin. So, this was the face of the Tally Man.

"Who do I have to talk to to get this broadcast?" he asked.

*   *   *

A sudden jolt awoke Zoë. The SUV was bouncing over an uneven surface. She forced herself upright. Out the back window, she saw the main highway. Ahead was an unpaved dirt road.

"You've come around at the right time," Marshall Beck said. "We've arrived."

Beck hadn't lied. They had arrived. He drove down a dirt road for a couple of minutes at a slow speed. She estimated that at the speed he was doing, they traveled a quarter mile before he stopped. Zoë bookmarked the distance in her mind. She wasn't far from the real world, if she managed to make a break for it.

He popped the tailgate and hoisted her over his shoulder. Dawn was showing itself, and the sky was turning blue. It meant they had been driving for hours. They had to be way outside the Bay Area. How far could he have gotten in a night—Oregon, Nevada, Southern California? She scanned the horizon, hoping to see a feature, a hill or mountain she'd recognize. It was all alien to her.

She'd asked to be brought here, but this wasn't the place she'd imagined. The morning light illuminated a stable of some kind. There were also two paddocks and a house. It was easy to see the place was no longer active. It wasn't derelict by any means, just ignored. The grass in the paddocks was high, and the stable was empty. It had probably been pretty once and could be again, with a little work. It was idyllic and seemed a million miles from the real world. Her thoughts soured. Holli was buried here.

Brando bounded from the SUV and ran in an excited circle.

"Where is this place?"

"This is where I grew up and learned the difference between right and wrong. Where I learned respect."

Beck carried her toward the stable. Zoë's heart quickened. She knew how this story ended. There were numerals carved into her flesh to prove it. She bucked in his grasp.

"Enough, Zoë," he barked and continued walking. "You knew this was happening. You made this bargain."

"Yes, and you need to hold up your end of it."

He stopped and lowered her to her feet. He had over a foot in height on her. Brando padded around them in slow circles.

"I have. We're here."

"You said you'd take me to where you buried Holli."

"She's buried here."

"Where?"

He threw an arm back in the direction of the larger of the two paddocks. Vagaries weren't good enough.

"I have to see where."

Beck examined her with a penetrating stare. She hoped he'd see why it was important.

"Please."

He shook his head. "If this is a delay tactic, it changes nothing."

"It's not."

"Wait here."

Beck jogged back to the SUV, while Brando stood guard over her. She eyed the dog. This was no pet. It was a killer. Scars marred its muzzle and crisscrossed its body. The dead-eyed stare it gave her said it would pounce at the first inkling of provocation. Beck returned with a handful of cable ties and his knife.

Zoë couldn't take her eyes off the knife. It was old but honed from years of hand sharpening. It was *the* knife. The knife he marked all his victims with.

"I'm trusting you, so please don't betray my faith in you," he said. "Now sit down."

Beck guided her to the ground. The dog sat a few inches too close to her for comfort. Beck took half a dozen of the cable ties and formed a daisy chain with them. She didn't know what he was doing until he slipped the outer two loops around her ankles and cinched them tight. He'd made a makeshift set of shackles.

He cut the original cable tie he'd bound her ankles with and helped her up.

"Now you've got a little movement."

A little movement was right. He'd sized the shackles to give her about half of a normal stride. There was no chance of running. Just more chance of falling.

"C'mon, this way."

He led her to a gap in the paddock fencing. She found it hard to walk through the long grass. Progress was slow and tiring. It was waist high on her, and the shackles dragged across every blade. Even the dog was having trouble, forced to bound over the grass instead of through it. Even without the shackles, it would have been hard going. Her knees and back had taken the brunt of the impact when she'd rolled from the SUV, and they protested when she walked. She wondered if he was doing this to her on purpose. Maybe he thought the long hike through the grass would wear her out and make her more malleable.

"Is Holli the only one buried here?"

"No."

"So all your victims are here?"

"Not all. Not Laurie Hernandez. Not you."

Zoë swallowed.

"But they're not victims," he said. "Society is the victim. They, you, are the perpetrators."

She'd struck a nerve, and it exposed his warped view of the world. "Perpetrators of what?"

"Bad behavior. You think it's OK to take shortcuts, walk over people, make a mess, and expect others to clean up after you."

Was that it? The crime she, Holli, Laurie Hernandez, and the others were guilty of—bad behavior? Did he have any idea how crazy that sounded?

"Bad behavior? I still don't know what Holli did to you. I don't even know you."

"That's your problem. Your kind never know what you do wrong, but I will teach you. You will know what you've done and the price you have to pay."

The veiled threat forced her to shudder, which knocked her off balance. She stumbled, then fell to the ground. He helped her up and waited for her to get moving again. She remained where she was.

"Why bring them here?"

"Because," he said, then trailed off, leaving the answer unfinished.

Another nerve touched, she thought. *This place means something to him. Does he think of it as sacred ground?*

He clamped his hand on the back of her neck and shoved. "Keep moving. We're nearly there."

When they reached the far side of the paddock, he lifted her over the fence, then pointed to a small stand of trees.

"There."

They walked to a spot under the trees. The grass was shorter here, ankle deep, stunted by the shade depriving it of enough light to grow. Nothing indicated to her that this was a grave. There was no sign of previously disturbed ground. This could be anything.

She shuffled around the spot, careful not to step directly on it, just in case it was the real thing. "Where?"

Then she saw the grave marker. It was understated, but fitting for a killer. The Tally Man couldn't build monuments to what he did, or it might draw attention. The stone was large and smooth, a river rock polished by centuries of fast-moving current. A Roman numeral *III* painted onto its surface identified it as Holli's grave.

Her heart broke at the sight of it. Until this moment, she'd held a microscopic belief that Holli was still alive, hiding somewhere under an assumed name to protect herself from him. There was no more proof required. Holli was dead.

The revelation broke Zoë. She'd lived with the knowledge for over a year that she'd abandoned her friend. Worse, she believed that she'd let Holli die. But the ambiguity of never knowing for sure whether Holli was dead or not had given Zoë hope. There was always an element of possibility, a slim chance that Holli had escaped, just like her. It was a dumb thought, a salve to keep the pain at bay, a delusion to keep her from this moment—true confirmation and the guilt that came along with it. Truth—Holli was dead and it was her fault. She couldn't keep herself upright any longer, and she collapsed on top of Holli's grave.

"I'm so, so sorry, Holli. I never should have left you. I should have tried harder to save you. I let you down."

She pressed her cheek into the ground, feeling the dew-sodden earth on her face. She sobbed long and hard. Her chest felt as though it would implode with each gasping breath.

The Tally Man came up behind her and lifted her to her knees. "That's enough. You got what you wanted."

A sudden realization struck her. If Holli's stone was here, then the others' would be also. As if a veil had been lifted, all the stones revealed themselves to her. Similar river rocks formed a curve around the tree to her right and left. There were five of them. Each one was marked with its numerals. Her gaze stopped at *IV*—her stone.

"Oh God," she murmured.

"Your place has been waiting for you for a long time," the Tally Man said. He walked up behind her and pressed the chloroformed rag to her mouth. "I've held up my end of the bargain. Now it's your turn."

CHAPTER TWENTY-SEVEN

It was 6:00 a.m., and the Investigation Unit's office was quiet. Only Greening and Ogawa were at their desks. Neither of them had left since returning from the raid in Walnut Creek. Everyone else who'd been working through the night had gone home for a shower and a change of clothes. The team had pursued every lead, but it had been hard going with so little to act upon. They didn't have a print or an ID to direct them. Everything boiled down to a screenshot of a man calling himself Brad Ellis.

The two of them worked the Tally Man's picture. They got it, along with a photo of Zoë, out to every media channel. Every law-enforcement agency in California, Oregon, and Nevada was on the lookout. Cops from more than a dozen Bay Area cities were combing every vacant building as a possible nest for the Tally Man. Everyone was looking, but no one knew where to look. Greening remembered Ogawa's remark about cases turning ugly. This investigation couldn't have gotten any uglier. He'd never felt so impotent as a police officer.

While they'd done everything possible to get the Tally Man's face out to the world, the lateness of the hour had worked against them. By the time press releases had gone out to the media outlets, it was three in the morning, when the viewer pool was at its lowest, reduced to night workers and truckers. They were forced to wait for the West Coast to wake up and catch their morning news over breakfast or on their commute into work.

"We've lost her," Greening conceded. "That fucker finally gets to close accounts on number four."

"Hey, you don't know that," Ogawa said.

"I don't, but the odds say it's so. The bastard likes to kill close to home. He did it with Laurie Hernandez here, he did it with Holli in Bishop, and he probably did wherever he rubbed out victims one, two, and five."

"She isn't dead until we find her."

"What the fuck is that—the Schrödinger's-cat defense?"

"No," he barked. "It's called being a professional. That woman is out there, in trouble, fearing for her life, and we treat her like she's alive until it's proven otherwise. Now grow up and be a cop."

They glowered at each other, but Greening couldn't maintain his anger. Ogawa was right. Zoë needed him on point, but he couldn't ignore his faltering sense of hope. The Tally Man now had a six-hour head start. He could be hundreds of miles away and hard at work, flogging the life out of Zoë. It was hard to be optimistic when he thought about their chances of finding her alive.

"I warned you that if this was a serial case, it would get ugly," Ogawa said without rancor.

"I know, but I screwed up. I didn't do enough. We knew this guy was gunning for her, and what did I do? Let her shrink protect her. I should have been there or had a cop there at all times."

"And if that shrink were here now, he'd be all over you."

"What?"

"Listen to yourself. 'I didn't do enough.' 'I should have been there.' Those are all pretty big statements beginning with I. You don't work for an *I* organization. You work for a collective body.

We did what we could within the limits of our role. *We* as a body will do everything we can to find Zoë. *We* will take any and all blame should anything go wrong. Got it?"

It was easy to put it in those terms if they tracked down Zoë in time, but he wasn't so sure how it would hold up if they didn't. He couldn't have her death on his conscience. For the first time, he truly understood how Zoë felt about leaving her friend to die. The past few hours were killing him. He couldn't imagine suffering through fifteen months of this.

"I'll take it under advisement. I'm going to dunk my head in a sink and change this shirt. It's starting to crawl."

"No, it is crawling. You've been curling the blinds with your stench for some time."

Greening smiled and grabbed a spare shirt, which he kept for situations like this, from his desk. He walked into the men's room and stripped off his soiled garment and tie, tossing them on the counter next to the sinks. Since there were no stoppers, he plugged one with paper towels, filled it with cold water, and dunked his face. He let the chill seep into flesh and spread through him. He felt his body temperature drop and his equilibrium return. He was running on empty, physically and emotionally. The chill helped restore him. He was a cop again. As a cop, he could help Zoë. He raised his head and dried it with a fistful of paper towels.

He drained the sink and refilled it with hot water. With soap from the hand dispenser, he washed his face, chest, and under his arms. He felt human again. He was astounded that the simple act of bathing could do so much for his well-being. He dried himself off, pulled on his clean shirt, and retied his tie. He checked himself out in the mirror. Yeah, he was a cop again, a tired one, but a cop.

"Hang in there, Zoë. We're coming."

As he carried his dirty shirt into the Investigations Unit, Ogawa tossed him his jacket.

"We've got an ID. Someone just phoned it in. His name is Marshall Beck."

Minutes later, Greening was holding on to the handle of the passenger door as Ogawa sliced through traffic, lights and sirens blaring. Ogawa blew through a red light and stopped their Crown Vic in front of the Urban Paws Animal Rescue Center in a no-parking zone. A slim, middle-aged woman who'd been standing outside the entrance to the shelter rushed toward them.

"Kristi Thomas?" Ogawa asked.

"Yes. Call me Kristi."

"I'm Inspector Ogawa, and this is Inspector Greening. Now, you're sure the person we're looking for is your employee?"

"Yes, I can show you."

Kristi pushed the door open. Greening and Ogawa followed her in. She stopped in the lobby and pointed at a wall that held nearly two dozen individually framed photos.

"This is our staff, and this is Marshall." She pointed at a photo on the second row.

Greening didn't have to compare the photo with the one on his phone. He'd burnt the image of the Tally Man into his head, and Marshall Beck was the guy.

"What does he do here?" Greening asked.

"He's our financial officer. He takes care of our accounts and writes grants. I don't understand this. Marshall is a nice guy, a bit stiff and awkward, but a good guy. Has he really abducted this woman?"

"Do you have Marshall Beck's contact information, address, phone numbers, things like that?" Ogawa asked.

"Yes, of course. In my office."

"Which office is Beck's?" Ogawa asked.

"His is across from mine."

"Do I have your permission to search it and check out his computer?"

"Yes. I give you permission."

"Thank you," Ogawa said. "I'm calling this in. Greening, you go with Kristi."

Kristi took him into her office. She went to her computer and pulled up Beck's details. Greening scribbled down the San Francisco address.

"Edward, I've got his address."

Ogawa came rushing in with his phone to his ear. He snatched the paper with Beck's info on it and left the office, requesting a SWAT team.

Shock spread across Kristi's face. She turned to Greening. "Is SWAT really necessary?"

"You think you know Mr. Beck, but you only know a version of him. We know another. Have you called him? If you've warned him, I need to know."

Kristi frowned. "I have called him, but not about this. Something happened here yesterday."

"What?"

"A few weeks ago, Fremont Police busted a professional dog-fighting ring. We took in those dogs for assessment. Marshall took a liking to one of them. He wanted to adopt it, but it failed the assessment, so we were ordered to destroy it, by the court. Marshall didn't take the news well, and I think he stole the dog. I called him and even went to his place, but he wasn't there. I don't know where he is."

Loves dogs, hates people, Greening thought. There was no figuring some people.

He looked at the address on Kristi's screen. It was a residential address in Noe Valley, not the kind of place for torturing people without being heard.

"Besides this address, is there anywhere else he would hang out or go? We're looking for somewhere quiet or private."

"I believe he owns some other property—a farm or something. He's mentioned it before. Up past Redding, I think. I don't know where, though."

Public records would, he thought. He really needed to work the databases on this guy. Beck wouldn't be at his home, and he'd know the SFPD and just about every other law enforcement agency would be on to him by now. He'd go farther afield if he was looking to disappear.

"Thank you for your help. I'd like to talk to your staff about Mr. Beck. When do they come in?"

"Some in the next half hour."

"I appreciate your cooperation. Again, please have no more contact with Mr. Beck."

Kristi was eerily quiet.

"Is there something else?"

"Laurie Hernandez. The news mentioned a connection."

"Yes. Did you know her?"

"She came here. We had to throw her out a couple of times for being cruel to the animals. She was here the day before she died. Marshall escorted her from the building. He couldn't have killed her, could he?"

"Edward," Greening called out. "We have possible motive on Laurie Hernandez."

Within an hour, the SFPD had taken over the animal rescue center. Greening and a handful of officers interviewed staff. Ogawa supervised crime techs, who were crawling through Marshall's office and computer. Now that they had a name, social security number, and a bank account his salary was deposited into, the Investigations Unit had a paper trail to follow. Who Marshall Beck was and had ever been was a database away. Thanks to the DMV, a BOLO was out on his Honda Pilot. Beck would be caught. It was just a matter of time. And that was the problem for Greening. The investigation was moving fast, but not fast enough for Zoë.

Greening checked his notes and thanked one of the animal techs for her time. He was conducting his interviews in the adoption office. He'd gotten from her what he'd gotten from all of Beck's coworkers—he was quiet, socially awkward, and kept to himself.

As the animal tech saw herself out, Ogawa walked in. "SWAT just went in. No one there."

Greening had guessed as much.

"They're combing the place now. It sounds clean. Nothing connecting him to Zoë or Laurie Hernandez."

Greening hated Marshall Beck. The son of a bitch was reckless, but he was careful too. He hid himself so well. "What now?"

"The battleship approach. We comb every square inch of this city until we find him. That's how it's done."

The problem was it was slow.

Greening's cell rang. It was Rogerson from Investigations, so he put it on speaker. "Check your email. I've just sent you Marshall Beck's background."

Greening opened his laptop. He'd had it brought over after he and Ogawa had occupied the rescue center. "Have you found the location on a second property?"

"Yes, I think we have it. It's near Burnt Ranch. It's a ranch or stable or something, but it used to be a foster home. He bought the place at auction five years ago, essentially covering the back taxes. He put it in a trust, which is why we didn't find it at first."

After Rogerson read them off the property's address, Greening hung up and opened his email. Ogawa came around the desk to peer over Greening's shoulder. The attachments made for interesting reading. Beck had never been arrested. In fact, he'd never even gotten a speeding ticket. His DMV address history put him in Bishop, Stockton, Redding, and Sacramento.

"When this is over, it'll be interesting to see if there are any accounts of missing women in those areas who meet Beck's profile," Ogawa said.

Yes, but that can wait, Greening thought.

He clicked a link that came with the intro: *You're going to want to look at this.* The link went to an *LA Times* piece from the late '80s. It told of the Palomino Ranch, a foster home in Trinity County. More than a dozen kids had been removed from the care of Jessica Wagner, who'd been arrested on charges of child abuse. Wagner had regimented a policy of corporal punishment on the children, flogging them with a switch until they were bloody. The practice had been going on for over a decade before the authorities got involved. Forty-seven of an estimated eighty children had come forward to testify. The only reason the horror had been exposed was that one of the children had escaped after a brutal beating.

"What are the chances that Beck was one of these kids?" Greening said.

Ogawa shook his head. "Christ, no wonder he's fucked-up."

This is how monsters are made, Greening thought.

Another link took him to a follow-up piece in which Jessica Wagner killed herself upon being released on bail.

"The bitch got off easy," Ogawa said.

One question was on Greening's mind—had Beck taken Zoë there? It was possible. He was finished in San Francisco. He had two choices—kill Zoë quick and run, or cart her somewhere where he could hole up and take his time with her. Greening hoped it was the latter. Trinity County was a six-hour drive from Napa. Given that distance, Zoë was more than likely alive.

"Do you think he's taken her there?"

"It's a long shot. That's a long way to travel when you're on the run. My money is that he's got her somewhere closer, but I'll call the Trinity Sheriff's and have them run out there to get some eyes on the place."

CHAPTER TWENTY-EIGHT

Zoë awoke suspended by her wrists, naked. The chloroform hit she'd taken had left her a little woozy, but its effect was fading fast. She slowly took in her surroundings. She was in the stable, hanging from a hook driven into a wooden support column. She hung a clear two feet above the ground, but a stool supported her. He'd secured her wrists with bondage-style cuffs that had a sheepskin lining. That suggested that he intended on hanging her here for a long while.

Her clothes lay on the dirt floor in shreds. The thought of Beck cutting her clothes off her forced a shiver from her. She doubted the act was sexual. She never got the feeling from him that any of this was about sex. Still, him seeing her naked was another violation.

He appeared in front of her, causing her to flinch. He had the one thing she'd feared seeing—that damn Bowie knife in a scabbard on his hip. The whip was coiled, and he held it in both hands low against his hips. Her heart quickened. The whip meant she was near the end. She'd never reached this point before. He'd abducted her and stripped her naked before, but she'd never gotten as far as the flogging. Holli, Laurie Hernandez, and the other women had been lashed, but she'd managed to escape this fate, until now.

He saw her staring at the whip. He held it up and examined it. "I made this myself. It took me over a year to make it work. I followed the techniques used by the ancient mariners for keeping their crews in line. It's an effective tool in the right hands . . . in my hands."

"Why are you doing this?" she asked.

"That's the wrong question. You should be asking, what did I do to deserve this?"

Nothing, she thought and let out a sob. She hated herself for it. When she'd surrendered to him, she'd promised herself she wouldn't show him any weakness so she could deny him his satisfaction. Now, demeaned and scared, she felt her resolve crumple.

"Your failure to recognize your failings is the reason you're here."

"My failings?" she barked at him. "What exactly am I guilty of—being loud in a restaurant? What were the other women's failings? Being noisy in a library? Jaywalking? Christ, how can you be so damn petty?"

She expected a tirade in return, but her scorn bounced off him.

He sighed. "I thought you, above all others, would have changed. You had the advantage of time, which was something your friend and the others were denied. They had to work it out as they received their punishment. You had a chance to reflect on the situation. I thought you'd come to understand."

Understand, no. Change, yes. She'd changed the entire course of her life after escaping him. Jarocki had spent a year trying to understand that course and why she was on it. All she knew was that the Tally Man had altered her for good—she was broken.

"Over these past weeks," he went on, "I've been watching you live your life. You are not the woman I first encountered. You've grown, and you know your place in the world. The way you put the recovery of my cell phone before your personal safety amazed me. I almost absolved you of your past transgressions and gave you your freedom right there."

Dangling liberty in front of her was cruel. The thought that she might have been free of him was worse than knowing he'd been tracking her. "Why didn't you?"

"I saw that you hadn't really changed. I spoke to Rick Sobona. Do you remember him? You nearly broke his nose after you led him on. Despite what happened to you and the chance you were given, you still choose to act like a slut. Now you see."

She didn't and never would. His manifesto made sense to him and him alone. She shook her head.

"You and all the others were guilty of the same thing—a lack of respect for your fellow citizens."

"Is that it? My crime is disrespect? Do I really deserve to die for displaying bad manners?"

"Yes."

His answer was so matter-of-fact that it stunned her. "Why aren't you going after killers, rapists, and drug dealers? Those people do real damage to society."

"Because there are laws for them," he said. "Unfortunately, bad behavior isn't a crime, and disrespect isn't punished. People do it without consequence while the rest of us have to accept it."

She shook her head. It was so juvenile. His logic was beyond comprehension. He abducted women, marked them with a number, then flogged them as some sort of punishment for their bad behavior. How was his solution in any way justified?

"Do you know how Chinese water torture works? It doesn't involve nearly drowning a person. It's a single drop of water striking the person between the eyes, again and again, until it drives them insane. That's what you and all the others are—drops of water splashing off society's forehead. By yourselves, you are meaningless, your effect minimal, but combined and repeated a thousand times a day, you are a detriment. You upset people, then they act badly toward others, propagating the cycle of disrespect. Now do you see? Now do you understand?"

She did see. She understood that he was crazy and there was no reasoning with him. "Who did this to you?"

"No one did this to me. A good woman once taught me the difference between right and wrong. A good woman who paid the price for her beliefs. No more talking."

He tugged the stool from under her feet. She dropped just a few inches but the effect was immediate. Suddenly, all her weight was on her wrists and shoulders. The cuffs might have been lined, but they couldn't insulate her from the intense pressure on her wrists, which burned. Her shoulder sockets took the full brunt too. Gravity seemed to grab a hold of her legs and pull. Her arms felt as if they were being separated from their joints. He didn't need to flog her; this was suffering enough. How had Holli and the others endured this for more than a moment?

"Time for your punishment, Zoë."

No, she thought. She didn't want to die. She didn't want to go through what Holli had. She'd seen her friend's face in that workshop. It was like the expression of the living dead. She didn't want to end up like that. She bucked and half twirled in her shackles. The steel ring holding the cuffs together was looped over the hook. "No, please. You don't have to do this. You don't have to kill me. I've learned my lesson."

She struck out at him with her legs. He dropped the whip and bear-hugged her legs with both arms until she stopped thrashing.

"Zoë, this is beneath you. It's time to suffer the consequences of your actions."

"I don't want to die." She'd never said anything so sincere.

He looked up at her. "You may not, but you have to take your punishment."

His answer sounded just as sincere. She couldn't tell if he was lying to her to give her false hope. She wanted to believe there was an out, but who was she kidding? This was her final day on earth if she let him continue.

He released her legs and dropped to one knee to pick up the whip. His head was within striking distance. She lashed out hard with her foot. She missed his head, but connected squarely with his shoulder, her bare toes ringing out in pain from the blow. Suspended, it was hard for her to put any real force behind the kick, but he hadn't been expecting it, so the strike was enough to knock him off his feet.

He looked up at her with disgust and shook his head. "There's no saving you, is there?"

She'd had her one shot and she'd blown it. She didn't bother with pleading. They were past that.

He stood with the whip in his hand. The dirt floor was damp, and his shirt was soaked where he'd landed on it. He examined the soiled garment and crossed the stable to where a duffel hung off a hook between a couple of stalls. He removed a clean polo.

Cleanliness is next to godliness, she thought.

He turned his back to her and removed his shirt. His back was all lean muscle, covered in a crisscross of scars. He'd said a woman had taught him about right and wrong and paid the price. Seeing his bare skin, all of her questions were answered. Who he was and who he'd become was all there in the damaged flesh. He pulled on the polo.

He returned to the bag and pulled out something small. He walked up to her and held it up for her to see.

"You'll need this."

It was a rubber bit. Teeth marks from previous users marred the surface.

Tears ran down her face as she took it into her mouth.

He walked behind her. She heard the whip unfurl and hit the dirt, then he swished it a couple of times. The sound of it cutting through the air and ending its arc with its trademark crack caused her to flinch.

Not seeing him was so much worse than seeing him. Not knowing what he was doing added an additional element of fear. She couldn't make out if he was getting pleasure from his work. She wouldn't know when the whip was about to strike her. Did he know how much worse he was making this? She didn't think so. He wasn't sadistic, just self-absorbed, too wrapped up in his agenda to consider anyone else.

"I'm going to begin now, Zoë. It's best that you brace yourself physically and mentally for the pain."

This was really happening. There was no escaping it. She tried to prepare herself for what was about to happen, but she couldn't. Her mind couldn't wrap itself around the concept. Her breaths came fast and shallow, and sweat broke out all over her body.

"Remember, you brought this upon yourself."

She clamped down on the bit, balled her hands into fists, and wrapped her legs together at the ankles.

The swish of the whip slicing through the air was the only sound she could hear beyond that of her pounding heart.

"One."

A swish, a crack, then pain. It happened so fast she wasn't ready, and it took her a confused second that lasted a lifetime before she realized she'd been hit. The impact was brutal. How could something that was as inherently flexible as a whip feel like a steel rod? The agony was searing and explosive. At first, it was a thin blaze across her back but it quickly ignited, spreading down the length of her back and to the center of her body.

She tensed every muscle to deal with the sensory overload she was experiencing. Her body turned to rock.

"Two."

Swish-crack-fire.

Her brain filled with the noise of her pain. It deafened her. If she screamed, she didn't hear it.

"Three."

This lash felt as though it had crossed a previous one. She wasn't so sure a moment later. The nerve endings in her back could be deceiving her. All of them were firing at once.

"Four."

Swish-crack-fire.

Her body swung back and forth. The soft breeze failed to cool her; it only heightened the temperature across her flesh. The sweat sprang from every pore, leaking into her wounds and ramping up the pain another notch.

"Five."

Something slow and thick trickled down her spine. A new wave of panic lit her up. *Am I bleeding?* her mind screamed. She couldn't tell if it was real or a delusion.

Far off, someone was calling her name. She opened her eyes. The Tally Man was standing before her. He reached up to remove the bit from her mouth and placed the stool under her feet. She sagged under its support.

"That's just the beginning," he said. "We have a long way to go. I want you absorb what has just happened before we continue."

An image of Holli hanging in the workshop filled her mind. Her body had been slack, streaked with sweat, dirt, and blood. She'd looked so bad that Zoë had thought she was dead. How many lashes had her friend endured by the time she had peered through the grime-encrusted windows? A low number was just as frightening as a high one. A low one meant the whip possessed devastating power. A high one meant she had much further to go.

"Are you sorry, Zoë?"

"Yes." The word took all her effort to utter.

"Really? Your carelessness has brought people pain and frustration. Do you understand that?"

What people? she wanted to ask. *Who exactly did I hurt?* But the questions weren't worth asking. There were no answers. There was no making amends. None of it made any difference to him. He was making a statement, and nothing she did would change his mind.

He hopped up onto the stool with a bottle of water. He uncapped the bottle and put it to her mouth. She drank greedily, spilling as much as she swallowed. It didn't matter. The water cooled the fire inside her, dulled the pain, and damped down the white noise in her brain.

"I'm sorry," she said.

He smiled sympathetically. "That's good. Let's continue."

He put the bit back in her mouth and removed the stool from under her feet again.

She closed her eyes in resignation, then snapped them open. She'd just heard the sound of a vehicle drawing up outside.

CHAPTER TWENTY-NINE

"Trinity County Sheriff's Department," the officer called. "Anyone here?"

Shit, Marshall Beck thought. Zoë screamed, but with the bit in her mouth, it was reduced to a growl. He spun around and drove a fist into her stomach. The scream died in her throat as she fought to get her breath back.

"You need to be quiet, Zoë. I can't have you spoiling this."

"Hello?" the officer yelled and followed it up with a blast from his car horn.

Beck jumped down from the stool, snatched up the chloroform rag, and gave it a fresh dousing before hopping back up. "I apologize for the interruption, but this shouldn't take too long."

She screamed again through her bit, but he smothered it with the rag. He watched the chloroform take effect and Zoë's body go limp.

Beck slid off the stool and tossed the rag on his bench. "Yeah, I'm here."

He had to be careful with this deputy. Confrontation wasn't the answer. He had no beef with the officer. The man was only doing his job. But more importantly, his dispatch would know he was here, although the bigger question was why. This place was under the radar, so nobody should have any reason to be here unless they thought he was a suspect—and that would be problematic. He picked up his Bowie knife and slid it into his pants at the small of his back.

"Coming," he called.

He strode out of the barn with Brando at his side. A broad-shouldered deputy in his forties was standing next to his cruiser, looking toward the house. He took the sight of a lone deputy as a good sign. This was a fishing expedition. If it had been truly serious, there'd be a whole SWAT team here.

"Hi there," Beck said brightly. "Anything I can help you with?"

The officer spun around. His hand went to his right hip, and he drew his gun.

Beck knew in that moment his secret hideaway was no longer a secret. It wasn't the end of things; it just meant he would be starting over again. He could easily disappear and reemerge under a different identity. He knew this day might come. He just had to lose this officer.

He stopped moving and raised his hands. "Whoa, what's going on?"

"I need you to stop right there."

"You've got a gun on me. I'm stopped. Just tell me what the problem is."

"Are you the property owner?"

"Yes."

"Are you Marshall Beck?"

"Yes."

"Are you alone?" the deputy asked.

An edge crept into the deputy's tone, but Beck didn't detect fear. The man was a professional in a high-pressure situation.

"Yes, it's just me and the dog. I'm here working on restoring this place."

"Sir, I have to take you into custody."

"Custody? Why?"

"It's in conjunction with a San Francisco Police Department matter."

"What matter?"

"You'll have to take it up with them. I just have to take you into custody. Now I need you to lie facedown on the ground with your fingers interlaced behind your head."

Despite the situation, Beck wasn't worried. This deputy didn't know who he was dealing with. He could be talked down.

"Oh, this is crazy. You don't have to do this. If you need me to come with you, I'll come with you. There's no need for the *America's Most Wanted* act."

"Sir, I just need to you to follow procedure."

The deputy reached for the radio mic clipped to his shoulder. Beck couldn't let the deputy spoil his plans by making contact with his department and having them storm the place. He had to finish up here first. Had to finish with Zoë. He strode toward the deputy.

The deputy took his hand off the radio. "Hold it right there, sir."

"OK, OK. I get it," Beck said and stopped.

He might have gotten it, but Brando hadn't. The dog breezed past him and kept on approaching the deputy.

"Sir, I need you to secure the dog."

"I thought you wanted me to lie down. I can't do both."

"Sir, please."

Beck detected the hint of fear in the deputy's voice. He made no move for Brando and let the dog continue edging toward the cop. "It's OK. You're a stranger, and he just wants to check you out. I can make this a lot simpler. Let him come over there and sniff you and then he'll be as good as gold."

The deputy swung the gun to aim at Brando. Beck liked that the gun was off him, but not at Brando's expense.

"Just secure your dog. I don't want to be forced to shoot it."

Beck bottled his sudden flare of rage. "There's no need for that."

"Then secure your dog, sir."

Brando had covered half of the forty yards between him and the deputy.

Beck held out his hands. "His leash is in the car, so I need to come over there to get it." He took an exploratory step closer to the deputy. "Is it OK if I come over there?"

The deputy swung the gun back to Beck. "Hold it right there."

Beck did. He watched the deputy play through his options. He didn't have any. It was two against one. No solution worked to his benefit.

"I'll get the leash and throw it to you. Just tell me where it is."

"Backseat or passenger seat. You should see it. It's not locked."

"Don't move."

Beck raised his hands again in confirmation.

The deputy went to the side of Beck's Honda, his gaze and aim vacillating between Brando and Beck. Brando was less than ten yards from the squad car now.

"Tell the dog to stop moving."

"Brando, stop."

Brando ignored Beck, as he'd hoped.

"Like I told you, he's curious."

The deputy had to take his gaze off them to search for the leash. The moment he turned his head to open the door, Brando bolted for him.

Beck grinned. The dog was a true friend. The truest he'd ever known.

Brando moved with speed and stealth. The deputy had his head in the SUV and was totally unaware the dog was closing in on him until the animal was upon him. He had about a second's notice before Brando slammed him into the side of the vehicle. He crumpled under the dog's charging eighty-pound weight. The deputy yelled out when the dog bit down on his gun arm.

Beck took the yell as his cue and ran at the downed deputy. Brando had him pinned against the side of the SUV. The dog continued to chew on the deputy's arm, thrusting him forward and slamming him into the side of the vehicle. The deputy smashed Brando again and again with his free arm with little effect. He tried kicking, but it was also pointless. The deputy was fighting an animal that knew one thing—killing.

Brando changed tactics and yanked at the deputy, dragging him away from the vehicle and out into the open. He was also hauling him away from his weapon. The deputy lunged for his dropped gun, but it was out of reach. The cop had lost this one.

Then the deputy reached for his belt and pulled out his Taser. He pressed it to Brando's neck and pulled the trigger. The dog recoiled from the electric shock with a yelp, confusion and pain on his face. He stopped, appraising the deputy. That was all the edge the deputy needed.

Beck saw how it would all play out before it happened. "No," he screamed.

The deputy rolled toward his gun. He snagged it, aimed it at Brando, and fired twice into the pit bull's chest. The two rounds dropped the dog where he stood.

Seeing the dog go down, the deputy let the strength go out of his body and lay on his back, trying to catch his breath.

Still running, Beck yanked his knife free from his waistband. "You bastard."

The deputy popped back up with his gun aimed, but Beck loomed over him and kicked the pistol from his hand before dropping on top of him. The deputy yelled something at him that he didn't register. All he could hear was the rush of blood in his ears, fueled by his rage and hate. He rammed the knife into the cop's stomach, where the bulletproof vest didn't cover it, and jerked it up in the search for vital organs.

The deputy screamed out. Shock overwhelmed his expression, then froze it. His body stiffened, his back arching. Beck intensified his pressure on the knife, twisting and turning, forcing it that little bit deeper, letting it do that extra bit of damage.

"You shouldn't have shot my dog," he said, then yanked the knife out. Blood poured from the devastating wound, but the deputy did nothing to stanch it and neither did Beck.

He clambered to his feet and went to Brando's side. The dog was still. He dropped to his knees and put his ear to the pit bull's chest. There was no heartbeat.

He wept, the sobs racking his body. He couldn't remember the last time he had cried for anyone. He hadn't even done that for himself in his worst moment.

He wanted to hold his friend longer, but his priorities kicked in. He didn't have much time to finish things here. When this deputy didn't report in, they'd send others. He estimated he had an hour before anyone else came by. Trinity County was big, and the police force was small. He had time.

"I'm sorry, Brando. You deserved better."

He pushed himself to his feet, looked down at the dog, gone but not forgotten, then over at the deputy. He wasn't conscious, but his chest rose and fell shallowly. An ever-expanding pool of blood circled him. There was no saving him. It was just a matter of time.

There was just one more thing left to do before he could go. He strode back to the stable. What had happened here wasn't Zoë's fault, but she would pay the price for it.

When he reached the stable, Zoë was nowhere to be found.

CHAPTER THIRTY

The gunshots had jerked Zoë awake from her chloroformed daze. Gunshots were a good sign. Beck didn't have a gun. It had to be the cops.

I'm safe, she thought, but the screaming that followed made her thought fleeting. She couldn't see anyone outside the stable, but she knew, just knew, it was the policeman who'd screamed.

She'd almost lost hope, but the arrival of the cop had changed things. People would know he was here and follow up when he didn't report in. How long before that would happen? Twenty minutes? An hour? It wasn't worth speculating on. She needed to focus on staying one step ahead of Beck, and he'd given her the opportunity.

He'd been sloppy when dealing with the cop's arrival. He'd left the stool in front of her. It wasn't underneath her, but it was within reach. Arms and shoulders screaming in pain, she stretched her leg out, hooked her big toe under the seat, and pulled it back. She had to be careful. The dirt floor was soft and uneven. If it toppled, it was over. She was dead. She inched the stool toward her and its feet cut into the soft dirt, making it list to one side. She froze, keeping it upright with her other foot.

"Please don't fall," she murmured.

The stool listened, staying upright until it was under her. It was a small victory. While she could get her feet flat on the stool, it wasn't tall enough to help her clear the top of the hook. She stood on tiptoes and was an inch too short.

Just a small jump to freedom, she told herself.

She jumped up with everything she had, swinging her leaden arms forward, and swung free of the hook. She landed awkwardly and toppled forward, hitting the ground with a thud.

The sudden rush of blood back into her arms was both exhilarating and excruciating, far outweighing the sensation of hitting the ground. She wanted to revel in the moment, but there was no time. Hands still shackled together, she pushed herself to her feet and darted over to the stable door.

She peered out. She'd heard gunshots, so she expected to see Beck dead. Not this. The cop lay on his back, blood everywhere and not moving, while Beck slumped over his damn dog, sobbing. Her rescue was in tatters. It was all down to her now.

Beck had screwed up by killing a cop. That screwup might have just saved her life. They'd sent the cop for a reason. When he didn't report back, they'd send more. With any luck, they'd be here soon. She just had to stay out of Beck's clutches until then.

That wasn't going to be easy. She was naked, alone, and unarmed, but she had one thing going for her—hope. A rescue had to be a half hour away at most. She could survive that long.

"You can do this," she murmured. "You won't die today."

She looked past the scene at the dirt road to freedom. A straight run for it was the simplest answer, but she'd never make it. Escape wasn't the answer, hiding until the cops arrived was. One thing this place had in spades was places to hide.

Beck climbed to his feet, wiping tears from his face. She had to act now, or her reprieve would be over. She backed away from the door, tore through the stable, and out the back entrance. Tall grass covered everything except for a horse trail leading to the tree line on the far side of the property. If she kept to the path, he'd spot her, but she could hide in the grass.

She took off left toward the paddock Beck had marched her through earlier. She ran with her shackled hands pressed to her chest. It helped her balance and protected her naked body from the sharp, dry blades of grass.

"Zoë," came Beck's bellow from inside the stable.

She stopped running and dropped to her knees, letting the foliage conceal her. She looked back at the stable. Beck emerged, knife in hand.

"Don't think you can escape me again, Zoë." He paused as if waiting for an answer.

Sweat ran down her back into the open wounds. She winced but bottled a moan.

He scanned the landscape for her. Her breath was fast and ragged, but she remained as still as she could. The grass was her greatest friend and her worst enemy. Any movement, and it would give her away.

His gaze passed over her position and kept going. He didn't have a clue where she was. That was good. All she had to do was stay a step ahead of him until the cavalry came.

He retreated back inside the stable. The second he was gone, she ran again. She kept low, below the level of the grass, to remain unseen. She kept zigging and zagging to hide her path but always headed in a direction that put more and more distance between herself and the stable.

"Oh, Zoë," he yelled.

Again, she dropped to her knees and held fast. He reemerged from the stable, carrying something in his hand. He strode back toward the dead cop.

"Do you know how you find a needle in a haystack?"

The randomness of the question confused her.

"No? Well, I'll tell you. You set fire to the hay."

Fear knifed through her. He was going to burn her out. She peered at the thing in his hand. It was a gas can with a hose. He stopped next to the patrol car. He was going to siphon the tank.

He wouldn't need much fuel to get a fire started. Once it took hold, the bone-dry vegetation would do the rest. She needed a new hiding spot. The house looked like the best bet. She was closer to it than he was. It might have things she needed—a phone, clothes, water—and it was shelter. She could barricade herself in, at the very least, and rely on the house's ability to survive a fire in the short term. Short-term solutions were her primary drive. She just had to stay alive long enough for the police to arrive.

She looked over at Beck. He was funneling the tube into the gas tank, not watching for her. She broke into a run, aiming straight for the house.

The grass stopped short of the dwelling, and she dropped to her belly when she reached the edge of her cover. She looked the place over. The last thing she needed was it to be some sort of trap. It looked like what it was—an abandoned house. She wouldn't know if there was anything wrong with it until she got inside.

She pushed herself up and looked back at Beck. He was still busy siphoning the patrol car's tank. Staying low, she darted over to the building and kept going until she reached the back porch. She dropped to her butt and leaned against the wall with her shoulder.

It was time to lose the shackles. If he'd shackled her with the cable ties he'd used earlier, she would have needed a knife to get through them, but he'd used the leather cuffs, held together with a steel ring. A strap with a buckle cinched the restraints tight. She worked the band free with her teeth, then bit down on it, pulling it tight to release the prong. With her newly liberated hand, she undid the other.

Getting to her feet, she gingerly massaged her bruised wrists and went to the back entrance. She tried the knob. It was locked. It wouldn't take much to break one of the door panes but she needed something to deaden the noise. She found an ancient feed sack and put it up to the glass. She'd been taught that the elbow was the strongest bone structure in the body in her defense classes, so she put it to the test. She drove it into the center of the pane. The impact sent a crackle of fire through her arm, all the way to her fingers, but the move worked. The pane fractured into three shards, tumbling into the house. She grabbed the knob and let herself in.

The kitchen smelled stale, the air bottled. It had to be years, if not decades, since someone had opened up this place. A thick layer of dust covered every surface. Her feet were the first in a long while to disturb its abandonment. The stable might have been Beck's special place, but the house wasn't.

She went to the living room. It was furnished but had been left to rot. She lifted the receiver of a rotary dial phone. She wasn't surprised that she didn't get a dial tone.

"Don't worry, the cops are coming," she said to herself.

If this place had been left exactly how it had been years ago, there'd be clothes. She cut back through the kitchen and toward the bedrooms. She opened the first door on her left and her breath caught in her throat.

Unlike the kitchen and the living room, this room was bare—no furniture, no possessions, nothing. There wasn't even carpeting or hardwood, just bare boards. The room contained only two things—graffiti on the walls, and something she could only describe as a pillory.

The pillory was crude and obviously homemade. It was T-shaped, with straps at the ends of the crossbeam for the hands and a chin rest where the crossbeam and the post met. It was low to the ground, meaning a person would have to kneel when strapped into it. Then, in horror, she realized it wasn't just low to the ground—it was child-size. The sight of it sickened her and in the cloying, stale air of the house, she wretched.

If she thought this was where Beck had plied his trade, the graffiti daubed across the walls proved his innocence. In big, clumsy letters, someone had written: THIS IS WHERE DISRESPECTFUL CHILDREN LEARN RESPECT. It had been painted haphazardly, almost like a person signing a cast on someone's arm. There were dozens of names written on the walls, as well. Beck's name was among them. Next to each, there was one other detail. If she hadn't been scarred by him, she would have mistaken the markings as meaningless gibberish, but she knew better. They were Roman numerals. Every child had them. Next to Marshall Beck's name was *XX*.

That didn't signify his number in the order of punishment. She could see where the numerals had been painted over and repainted many times. Beck wasn't the twentieth child. He'd been punished in this room twenty times.

In this room, a monster had spawned a monster. In this room, the Tally Man had been created.

"Zoë!" Beck yelled again, his voice muffled by distance and glass. "It's time to burn."

CHAPTER THIRTY-ONE

Marshall Beck touched the lighter to the small trail of gasoline. It ignited immediately, and an orange flame chased along the ground and into the grass. The tinder-dry vegetation caught without effort. The blades withered and turned black in seconds. As each one burned, it ignited the ones around it. The fire moved with a speed he found satisfying.

He knew he was being reckless. He should be running, not lighting fires, but he had too much invested in Zoë to give up now. He couldn't let her escape punishment again. It was her time to die, today, now, even if it cost him everything.

He laid the fuel trails every ten yards or so, to either side of the dirt road. He went to each one and lit them to create an ever-expanding avenue of fire.

"No hiding from this, Zoë," he murmured.

Once the fire took hold, he tossed the gas can, with the remaining fuel inside, into the training paddock. When the flames caught up with it, it would serve as an additional booster to keep the blaze going.

The fire moved swiftly, reaching both paddocks in minutes. The heat radiating off the pastures forced him to the center of the road.

He didn't fear the inferno. Grass was a weak fuel for a sustained blaze. There'd be only superficial damage, and it would burn itself out quickly enough. But destruction wasn't the point of this exercise. The fire just needed to last long enough to flush Zoë out. She'd been smart to hide in the grass. He could have spent all day hunting her and gotten nowhere. The flames would speed up their reunion. He just hoped they didn't trap her and kill her—that wasn't in the plan. She needed to die on his terms, after paying for her transgressions.

He jogged up and down the dirt road, from the stable to his Honda and back. He watched for movement and listened for cries, but found it hard to detect anything through the flames and towering smoke. It was providing her with unintended cover.

Then he realized a bigger mistake. He'd miscalculated. Instead of the fire driving Zoë toward him, it would drive her away from him. Worse still, it would push her into the protective cover of the tree line. He should have started the fire from the periphery to force her to the middle. He took solace in the fact that if she wanted to reach civilization, she'd have to come back to the dirt road. As long as he remained here, she couldn't escape. If she wanted out, she had to come through him.

*　　　*　　　*

Beck disappeared behind a wall of smoke and shimmering flame, unnerving Zoë. She wanted him in full view, but took comfort in the knowledge that if she couldn't see him, he couldn't see her either. That meant she could move with the same freedom that he did.

The blaze chased across the paddock toward her. She guessed that it would be twenty minutes before the surrounding pastures would be totally engulfed.

C'mon, cops. You're taking too damn long.

She could wait it out here. The house was quite a ways from the main fire and solidly built, so she'd probably be safe from the flames for a while. But she didn't think Beck would be so patient.

She couldn't wait for the cops. They could be around the corner or fifty miles away. She needed to get to Beck's SUV and bust out of here. But Beck wasn't dumb. He'd be expecting her to try something, so she'd have to distract him. There had to be something in this house she could use.

The house was vast, with six bedrooms and several bathrooms. She went from room to room, searching for something, anything to divert his attention. After experiencing the punishment room, she feared what she'd find in the other bedrooms. She wouldn't have been surprised to find Norman Bates's mummified corpse in a rocking chair, and if she had, she would have taken it. It would have made a great body double. But there was just cheerless bedroom after cheerless bedroom. Each housed two to three mattresses, all without box springs. Bare walls greeted her where teen-idol posters should have given the rooms personality and life. Clothes and possessions were absent. Whether they were taken or they never existed, it was impossible to tell. One bedroom was different—the master. That room was a real room, fit for a person—a queen bed, complete with linens, a nightstand, dressers, photographs, paintings, and drapes. Only one thing marred the perfect room—a spray of rust-colored stains covering one wall and the ceiling. Zoë didn't have to check to know someone had eaten a shotgun at some point in the past. What the hell had gone on in this place?

Desperately hoping that the shotgun was still there, she ignored the carnage and ran to the closet. Inside she found ladies' clothing but no gun. It confirmed her feeling that this was a woman's house. Despite its sparseness, the place felt feminine. She didn't detect a male's influence in any way. She pulled a dress off a hanger and threw it on. It was floral and three sizes too big, but she'd wear anything to cover her nakedness.

Finding the dress was a nice bonus, but she still hadn't found anything to cause a distraction. There was nothing here. The place was a damn shrine. It was all so useless. But that wasn't true. Her mind shifted gears. Yes, this place was a shrine. She didn't know why, and God only knew the damage it had done to Beck. But for some reason, he'd left it for posterity. Destroying his shrine would bring him running.

She ran back to one of the bedrooms and peered out of the window. A propane tank sat just outside. She'd seen it when she'd first reached the house. She just hoped it had some gas inside. She didn't need much, just enough to start a fire.

She cut back to the kitchen and turned the knob on a burner. Gas leaked from it.

"Thank you, Jesus," she said and turned it off.

She picked up a wooden chair and smashed it down on the floor. It buckled under the force. She smashed it down again, and it shattered. She tore one of the legs free. From the living room, she grabbed a doily and wrapped it around the leg. Her torch was complete. Now she just needed a flame.

She left the house with her torch and ran headlong back into the grass toward the blaze. The heat was intense. She felt every drop of moisture on her face evaporate and her skin turn brittle as she approached the oncoming fire. She jammed the torch into the flames. The doily blackened but didn't ignite. The fire's heat ate into her hand, but she kept it steady. The need for this to work outweighed any pain she had to endure.

"Burn, goddamn you."

And her blasphemy was rewarded. The torch ignited.

She raced back to the house, shielding the flame with her hand. The makeshift torch was burning, but the flare was meager.

She reached the house just as the torch was going out. She took it into the living room and touched it to the sofa. The cheap, synthetic fabric ignited on contact and a blaze began. She tossed the torch on a lounger and darted into the kitchen, where she turned on all the burners on the range. On her way out of the house, she closed the door, leaving the marriage of propane and a naked flame to occur.

She hid in the grass again for cover. She ran parallel to the oncoming fire but away from the house and the all-important path back to the dirt road. That couldn't be helped. She didn't want to be anywhere close when the house went up. She had no idea how large a propane explosion would be, so the farther away from it she was, the better. She just hoped the blast was big enough to bring the cops running.

She saw her best bet for getting back to the road was retracing her steps from the stable. The exact route she'd taken was in flames, but for all the fire's swiftness, it hadn't claimed every avenue. The pasture behind the stable was virtually untouched. There was a portion that connected to a small horse trail, which would take her back to the stable, as long as she was quick. The shortest line to freedom was a straight line, but that would bring her close to the fire. It didn't matter. Couldn't matter. She had to go now.

She moved fast, using a combination of a crouched run and scampering along on all fours. Technique didn't matter. Speed did. She stayed close to the fire line. Only the intensity of the heat and choking smoke kept her back.

Just as she was nearing the horse trail, an earsplitting explosion threw her to the ground. It was a huge shock, even at over a hundred yards away. The blast sounded like it was right by her head.

She gathered herself up and moved faster. She had only one shot at distracting the Tally Man, and this was it.

*   *   *

Marshall Beck had his back to the explosion. He'd been watching the south paddock for Zoë. He whirled to see glass and splintered wood shooting in all directions. He knew there was a risk that the fire might take out the house, but it hadn't even reached it yet.

"Zoë," he murmured. This was her doing. "Clever girl, but not that clever."

Her blowing up the house told him exactly where to find her.

He raced back to his SUV, fired the engine, then rocketed the vehicle along the path to the house. Flames poured from the blown windows on the ground floor. Drapes fluttered in the breeze, burning tatters flying off in all directions. He couldn't believe Zoë had the audacity to blow up Jessica's house.

Had she gone inside and seen the rooms? He hoped so. That way she would finally understand what he was trying to do and why it was so important. He realized now that he should have taken her to Jessica's house before taking her to the stable. Then all this mess could have been avoided.

He slid to a halt and leapt from his SUV, then raced up to the door and stopped in front of it as the heat blistered paint. A mix of emotions rooted him to the spot. The house wasn't that special. It was just wood. It shouldn't have meant anything to him, but it did. With Jessica's teachings and punishments, this place had made him into the man he was. It was a symbol of what he'd become.

"Good-bye," he said to the home.

Respects paid, he circled the house searching for Zoë. He half expected to find her laid out by the explosion, but she was nowhere to be seen. He scanned the tree line and the pasture for her, with no success.

"Where are you?" he said to the absent Zoë. She was nowhere close. She'd played him, drawn him away from the entrance road. She'd come so far since their first encounter. She was no longer the drunken slut. She was smart and resourceful—a born survivor. She had him to thank for that, if she had the courage to recognize it.

He scanned the dirt road for her and finally found his prey. She was on her knees next to the deputy.

"He can't help you, Zoë. No one can," he said and sprinted back to his SUV.

*   *   *

Just as Zoë reached the horse trail, she heard a car engine burst to life. It was Beck's SUV. The tires churned in the dirt before the vehicle tore along the foot path to the house.

The distraction had worked, but not perfectly. She'd hoped to take the Honda. She'd have to make do with the cop car and prayed it had some gas left in the tank. She sprinted up the trail, through the corridor of fire lining it on both sides. She ignored every stone and rock her bare feet struck. Once, she stumbled and fell, but clambered back up. She sucked in the scorched and smoke-ridden air and coughed it out. It all hurt, but she told herself it was temporary. One way or another, it would end soon.

As she raced up to the cop on the ground, she looked toward the house. Beck was out of the SUV, looking at it.

"Stay there, you bastard," she murmured.

She dropped down at the cop's side. She didn't have to check whether he was dead or not. He stared blankly up at the sky.

"I'm sorry," she said.

The radio on his shoulder crackled. A female voice asked for a status update.

Zoë tore it free and keyed the mic. "Hello. Hello. I'm at a place that has a stable. I don't know where. A man called Marshall Beck abducted me and killed the officer you sent here. Hello?"

"Did you say our officer is down?"

"Yes, I'm looking at his dead body."

"Ma'am, what's your name?"

"Zoë Sutton. None of that matters. He's burning the place down. He's going to kill me."

"Ma'am, I need you to be calm."

"Fuck calm. Do you know where I am? Are you coming?"

"Yes. We know your position. I'm dispatching units now. Get somewhere safe."

Is anywhere safe? she thought.

A roar of an engine jerked her attention away from the dispatcher. Her distraction had run its course. Beck was on his way back.

"You'd better get someone here now. He's coming."

She dropped the radio and snatched up the pistol the cop had dropped. She looked at the weapon. It was an automatic. She had no idea how it worked. Her self-defense training went only as far as hand-to-hand combat. She'd never bothered with weapons. Point and shoot, she hoped.

She looked up. Beck wasn't bothering to stick to the path from the house. He made a straight line for her, barreling across the paddock, straight into the fire. The vehicle bumped and crashed over the rolling surface. Flames licked at it, but none took their toll.

She jumped behind the wheel of the police cruiser. The key was in the ignition. She twisted it and the engine turned over but didn't catch. The gas gauge registered just above empty.

"Start, damn it." She deserved for something to go her way, and it finally did when the engine fired.

She pulled on her seatbelt, then jerked the shifter into reverse. She looked over her shoulder at the dirt road that would take her to freedom. Was it freedom? She'd run before and escaped nothing. If she escaped, he'd just hunt her down again. She was his obsession. Fleeing would be just another stay of execution. Even if the cops put him in jail, there was always the chance he'd get out. She couldn't have that. It was time to end this one way or another. She shifted into drive and stamped on the gas.

The cruiser leapt forward into the blaze. She plowed through the paddock's fire-ravaged fence, heading toward Beck. Flames and embers flew up over the hood and windshield as it gathered speed. The needle on the speedometer passed forty miles per hour. She fought to keep the car on course. It bottomed out on the dips, and the rear end went airborne on the rises.

Beck was doing better at riding the bumps. His SUV kept coming at her. She wanted to meet him head-on, but she was struggling to keep her car on course and the distance between them was running out. They were so close now she could see him through the flames. His expression was simple—total focus. He hadn't let emotion take over. He had a job to do, and he was going to do it. The simplicity of his drive scared her. How could she compete?

She hit a dip, which wrenched the steering wheel from her hands. The car slewed right, teeing her up for Beck. He slammed the SUV into the rear passenger-side corner of the police cruiser, sending it into a spin. The cruiser threw up dirt and mowed down burning grass. The world was lost to her in an explosion of sound and a blur of flying dirt and embers. The car came to a sudden halt at a right angle to Beck's SUV.

His vehicle was a wreck. The crash had collapsed the front end. He wasn't going anywhere. But was she? The cruiser's engine was dead. She jammed the shifter back into park and tried the ignition—nothing. She tried again and again. Each time the engine turned over but failed to fire up. So many things could be wrong—heat vaporizing the gas or smoke being sucked into the intake or luck just running out on her.

Then movement caught her eye. Beck swung open his SUV's door. Zoë's mouth gaped as he stepped into the fire with his fist wrapped around the knife. The flames here were only knee deep, but the heat had to be intense. She marveled at his twisted desire. "Zoë, there's no escaping your punishment," he said, staggering toward her.

She couldn't believe the sight, the insanity of it all. But it was coming to an end. Sirens filled the air. Authority figures were en route. But she couldn't let it end their way. Their way left room for error. It had to end now, between victim and victimizer. The engine fired on the third attempt. It sounded rough, but if it was running, it was the sweetest sound in the world. She jammed it into drive and a terrible racket came from the car's rear as it lumbered forward. Something was broken back there, but it wasn't enough to stop its momentum.

She aimed the car straight at Beck and smashed into him. The force pinned him to the hood of the cruiser. Zoë kept her foot down. She plowed into her tormentor's SUV, pinning him between both vehicles. He yelled out in pain and thrust his knife into the cruiser's hood, as if stabbing the car would help him. His display reminded her of a toddler's temper tantrum. He was lashing out at the world because it didn't do the things he wanted it to do. It was sad and pathetic. Just like him.

She reveled in his pain. It was what he deserved. Despite the trauma he'd suffered, it was fair payback for what he'd done, but it wasn't enough. Not yet.

She picked up the dead cop's pistol and pointed it at him through the windshield. He was still flailing in pain, oblivious of her. That wasn't good enough. She wanted him to see this coming.

"Tally Man," she yelled.

He stopped flailing and looked directly at her, then the gun.

Good. She wanted to see fear and terror in his eyes, the same fear and terror that she and all his other victims had suffered at his hands. She wanted him to know the misery he'd put her through.

"How does this feel? Are you scared? I hope this hurts as much as you hurt us."

"You still don't get it, do you? I was right. I changed you. I made you better. Admit it."

He'd love to believe that. It disgusted her that he could even think that. "I changed me."

He grinned. "Zoë Sutton, my success story."

She was wasting her time. He'd never understand. "You succeeded at nothing. It's time for your punishment. This is for all the women you hurt."

She opened fire. The blasts within the confines of the car deafened her. The windshield deflected the first two bullets, but the hole they left in the glass made a clear path for the shots that followed. She stopped firing when his body fell still against the hood of the cruiser.

In that moment, Zoë was lost. Her life had been on hold for so long, weighed down by this monster's invisible presence, and now he lay dead. It was over. She was free. It was astounding that the resolution was so simple in its execution. All it had taken to stop the Tally Man were a few gunshots. In her mind, he'd been more than a man, bigger and more powerful, but the bullets had proved he was human, after all. It didn't seem possible that it was over. All she could do was stare at Marshall Beck's dead body—all his contempt and hatred gone with him.

The cruiser's engine fluttered, then caught itself just before stalling. She wasn't going to die here in the blaze. She put the cruiser into reverse and it shuddered back. Marshall Beck, the Tally Man, slid from the hood and into the flames. She turned the car around and drove out of the fire.

CHAPTER THIRTY-TWO

Zoë's dad appeared in the doorway to her bedroom, with her younger brother. "What's next?" he asked.

Zoë finished writing *Bedroom* on the three cartons in front of her. "These boxes here, the mattress, and the box spring."

They started with the box spring. She squeezed past them to help her mom wrap and pack all the crockery in the kitchen. In spite of how little she owned, it seemed to be taking forever.

"I'm so glad you're coming home," her mom said with a smile.

"Just until I get myself back on my feet."

"For as long as you like, sweetie."

It had been a long three weeks since her showdown with Marshall Beck in Burnt Ranch. With Greening and Ogawa chaperoning her, she'd spent two days with the Trinity Sherriff's Department, giving statements and helping to pinpoint the graves of the Tally Man's victims. They'd unearthed them, and DNA testing had confirmed that the grave Marshall Beck had identified as Holli's was correct. Greening and Ogawa brought her back to San Francisco after the Trinity County District Attorney's office confirmed they wouldn't be filing charges against her for killing Marshall Beck.

If she thought she'd be returning to the quiet life, she'd been dead wrong. The media made that impossible. Jarocki put her up at his Napa home until the fervor died down, but even after it had, it was impossible to move back to her home or job. Too many people wanted to talk to the Tally Man's only surviving victim. She quit her job at the mall and gave notice on her apartment. Jarocki offered her his place long term, but suggested that maybe it was time to reunite with her family. It had been a tough call to make, considering how she'd shunned them, but they welcomed her with open arms. It made the guilt of pushing them away sting even more. Now they were here, helping her move. She didn't know how going home was going to be, but she didn't know how anything was going to be from now on. It was all unwritten. "It's all potential," as Jarocki had put it. The specter of the Tally Man no longer bound her. She found that kind of freedom scary.

"Hello?" Greening stood in the doorway. "Is it OK if I come in?"

"Yes, of course. Come in."

He entered the kitchen.

She looked at him in his jeans and T-shirt. "Are you here to help us load up?"

He smiled. "No, there's only so far I'm willing to go as a public servant."

"Should have known. This is my mom, by the way." She introduced him to her mom, then her dad and brother as the two carried her box spring out the door.

"I know you're busy trying to move, but could I talk to you for a minute?" he said.

Zoë turned to her mom.

"I've got this," her mom said. "You talk."

For privacy, Zoë walked Greening outside and halfway down the second floor walk. They watched her brother and dad manhandle the box spring down the stairs and over to the U-Haul.

"How are you doing?" he asked.

It had been a mixed few weeks. Her emotions had been sent on a roller coaster ride, so many lows and highs. The highs of her family's acceptance and finally being free of the Tally Man's grasp. The lows of accepting Holli's death. Killing Marshall Beck should have been a guiltless task, but taking a life, no matter how justified, was hard on the soul.

"OK. Dr. Jarocki is helping me deal with the fallout from all this."

"Good. I'm glad," he said. "Happy to be leaving?"

"Happy to be getting away from the noise."

He nodded. "I can understand that. Where are you going?"

"Home with my parents. San Jose."

"Did you go to Holli's funeral?"

She nodded. Holli's parents had invited her. "It was on Tuesday in Sacramento. It's where she was from."

"I bet that was tough."

It had been, especially when Holli's mother had hugged her after the service and whispered, "Thank you for returning our daughter to us."

"My parents came. It made it a little easier."

"I'm glad to see you've reunited with them."

As hard as it was to do, she was glad too. She'd missed them.

"Any news on the other victims?"

Greening shook his head.

Holli was the only one of the Tally Man's victims the police could identify. The identities of victims *I*, *II*, and *V* were still a mystery. Beck had kept no records, so their identities had died with him. While she knew many of the cops were glad she had put the

Tally Man down, some would have liked him to have been taken alive in order to find out who he'd buried at the Palomino Ranch.

"What happens now?"

"The remains will be kept as evidence for now. We know where Beck lived and worked over the last few years, so we'll cross-reference missing persons in those places with his preferred victim type, and go from there."

"That's a long shot."

"Yes, it is."

"And if you're not successful?"

"The bodies will be released for burial."

"As Jane Does?"

"Yes, as Jane Does."

It was the worst of outcomes. Not only had Beck robbed these three women of their lives but also of their identities, resigning their families to a lifetime of purgatory. Maybe she'd been wrong to kill him. Killing him had given him a victory.

"If that should happen, will you let me know? Someone should be there to mourn these women."

"Sure."

Zoë's mom came out of the apartment with a box marked *Kitchen*. She glanced their way and smiled.

"I need to get back. We want to be on the road by noon."

"Of course, but just one more thing. What's the future hold for Zoë Sutton? Back to grad school? Another mall-cop job?"

She smiled. "I don't think so on the school idea. It's not me anymore. Mall cop, definitely not."

"So, no plan then?"

"Not this minute, but one will appear."

"I know it will." He pulled a folded letter-size envelope from his back pocket and handed it to her. "And it has."

"What's this?" she said, peering inside.

"It's an application to be an SFPD police officer."

She looked at him in surprise.

"You said to me you wanted to make a difference and wanted to protect people from another Tally Man. Here's your chance to do that. Zoë, you can be anything you want, and if you want this, it's the right time to do it."

His conviction and faith astounded her. She had so little in herself that it was hard to accept anyone else's. "Don't you think my misdemeanor convictions will get in the way?"

"No. Not when you consider you'll be the only applicant to say she stopped the Tally Man."

She smiled but shook her head.

There was no smile from him. "There are people backing this if you want it."

"People like you?"

"I'm one, Officer Martinez is another, and so is the SFPD's top brass, but forget me and everyone else." He tapped the envelope with the application inside. "Answer this simple question: Do you want this?"

Her answer was simple—she did.

The end

ACKNOWLEDGMENTS

I would like to thank Jerry Boriskin, PhD, of the Veteran's Administration for all his time and help on the issues of post-traumatic stress disorder. As always, thanks goes to Special Agent George Fong (retired) of the FBI for all the cop-stuff help. And special thanks to Thom Futrell for all the fight lessons. Zoë couldn't have won without you. My undying thanks to Joel Arnold, Bonnie Moebeck, Kristi Thomas, Jeff Hall, Mick Tolley, Brad Ellis, Laurie Hernandez, Rick Sobona, Gregory Solis, Karen Haldane, Judy King, Tom Fisher, Seán Dwyer, Dinah Ortiz, Michaela Shannon-Sank, and Craig Cook, who volunteered their names to be part of this book. Finally, thanks to my wife, Julie, Jenna and "The Girls," and Anh Schluep for their critical eyes, support, and patience throughout this book.

ABOUT THE AUTHOR

 A former racecar driver, licensed pilot, animal rescuer, endurance cyclist, and occasional private investigator, Simon Wood is also an accomplished author with more than 150 published stories and articles under his belt. His mystery fiction, which has appeared in numerous magazines and anthologies, has earned him the prestigious Anthony Award and a CWA Dagger Award nomination. In addition to *The One That Got Away*, his books include *Accidents Waiting to Happen*, *Paying the Piper*, *Terminated*, *Hot Seat*, *We All Fall Down*, and *No Show*. Originally from England, he lives in California with his wife, Julie. Curious people can learn more at www.simonwood.net.